I0522513

What had he gotten himself into this time…

A pair of headlights coming from town swerved off on the logging road. An SUV whipped past Moss's car which he had pulled off in a dry creek bed, and camouflaged with branches. Several more cars arrived, turning on their bright headlight as they reached the tarmac, and in a few minutes, the airstrip was lit with battery operated lanterns as well. Then from a side road through the woods, a stretch limousine crawled beside the landing strip, adding its lights to the others. It was a beautifully organized operation that only professional criminals have the expertise and the hutzpah to pull off.

Moss realized whoever it was behind this had local boots on the ground. At least two cars had come from town, and he would bet anything at least half of those participating in this operation were local boys from some berg nearby. As he and McDermott watched from their hiding place in the bushes, a small twin propeller plane came out of the night, landing expertly on the makeshift runway.

Several men rushed out, got a briefcase each, and went back to their cars. Moss counted seven briefcases total. A chauffeur in uniform carried an envelope back to the pilot, carried on a brief conversation, and wished him a safe trip in a language that sounded to Moss like a cross between Italian and Spanish. The little plane taxied down the runway and took off into the night sky, blending in with the canopy of stars. The whole thing took less than ten minutes.

The lanterns were gone, the cars were gone, the limo took off, all in that brief time. *Commandos couldn't have done it better*, Moss thought.

Grover Moss is bored. A former big-city detective, he misses the mind-numbing parade of bums, drug dealers, prostitutes, murderers, and violence only big cities can provide. He has followed the beautiful but capricious Chantal West to her home town buried deep in the thickets and swamps of South Georgia where he feels buried as well—until he discovers a reclusive wraith of a man who says he's murdered his father and buried his body under the floor of the mill, that is. As the Julia Springs Police Chief, Moss is intrigued enough to follow up on the story. But as he digs for the truth, he gets a bagful of shocks and discovers corruption on a massive scale…

Praise for Trisha O'Keefe

Hanahatchee

A delightful labyrinth of connection and support.

Highly recommended!!!!

Love Sone of the Chinaberry Man

The long-awaited sequel to *Hanahatchee* is finally here…and it does not disappoint.

The story blends classic folklore with an eerie and suspenseful narrative.

Anyone looking for a gripping page-turner with high stakes and plenty of action will find themselves unable to put this book down until the very end.

RECOMMENDED by the US Review

Poseidon's Eye

Loved this thought-provoking book.

Of Unknown Origin

….this book still grips the reader's attention from page one.

The Mama Tree

…so exciting and unpredictable you refuse to move from the couch until you finish.

ACKNOWLEDGMENTS

Black Opal Books, Faith, my editor, and Jack for superior artwork

THE

GATOR

HUNTER

TRISHA O'KEEFE

A Black Opal Books Publication

DEDICATION

*To my editor Faith, all my cousins,
and all my faithful readers.*

CHAPTER 1

D ie, damn you, die!"
With a muffled shout, Grover Moss catapulted upright in his desk chair, fighting off a dream. The dream, as was the way with cowards, took the easy way out. It slipped through the half-open window and joined the mist dancing in the street among the passing cars, leaving its victim feeling like a fool, mopping the sweat running down his face.

"Say what, Chief?" From the other room, Earlene's nasal twang sliced like a knife through the heavy air.

Embarrassed, Moss cleared his throat. "Nothing, Earlene. I was just trying to swat a fly." He knew he wouldn't get away with that excuse. His secretary's hearing was as sharp as her knitting needles.

He pictured Earlene's thin eyebrows rising to her hairline. "Oh, I just thought you was dreaming about killing Mayor Clark, is all. Don't blame you one bit, only you'd have to get in line. There's lots of people ahead of you."

The police radio warbled just then, but Moss didn't get his hopes up. Even Earlene had a defeatist attitude in her running commentary. "That's probably Martha Wilkes again, saying her husband's ghost is up in her attic eating her out of house and home which is what killed him in the first place. Weighed over three hundred pounds when he died. If he's up there, bet that old attic's squeaking up a storm."

Moss shook the shadow of the dream off. Probably what was chasing him had been the specter of boredom which was enough to kill anybody, let alone an inner-city detective. He checked himself—*former* inner-city detective. There hadn't been enough action around this little berg to raise the pulse of a meth head.

Another warble and a voice came over the police radio. "Hello? This is Prescott. Is anybody home? Over."

Moss squirmed and fought the urge to pick up the receiver. "Ears, you gonna get that?"

"I'm on it, Chief."

It would take a four-alarm fire to make Ears lose his online game and actually play dispatcher for the Julia Springs Police Department. Things moved slowly down here in Georgia. He was still getting used to that after five years. An image of thick syrup slowly dripping from a jug formed in Moss's mind as Ears got to the phone.

"Yeah, Sarge, come in."

Even the clouds groaned with boredom, squeezing out drops the size of quarters to plink out a lazy tune on the brown hydrangea leaves. In winter, everything in Georgia got brown and drippy, even his mood. Moss couldn't resist a moment of nostalgia, remembering how the buskers in front of the Memphis train station, sporting bright mufflers and Santa hats, would be competing with the Salvation Army to see who could play the worst Christmas songs. Their instrument cases would be filled with baggies of fake meth, presents for the druggies who shuffled along, hunched against the biting wind off the Mississippi.

Ears's cell phone clattered on the desk beside him, a sure sign either Mrs. Wilkes wasn't wrong or it was really a four alarmer. "Oh, my god, no kidding? Where abouts?"

"Real professional, Ears." Moss gave a big man's sigh and went to the door of his office. "What?" he asked, expecting no more than a cat up a tree or a cow on the road.

The dispatcher turned around in his chair, his eyes round with horror. "They found a body at Howland's Mill, Chief."

Moss was unmoved although this beat swatting flies. "So follow procedure, Marv, take down the address, caller's names, phone num—"

"Yeah, I did all that, but get this, Chief. It's Mr. Howland and he's been missing for nearly fifty years."

"How do you know it's him if they just found the body? Maybe it is, maybe not. People don't look the same after fifty years of being dead." As he strapped on his sidearm, Moss shooed away the thought of the cold beer and Mrs. Wilkes cringing on her porch among the Boston ferns.

"But they always said—"

"Tell Prescott I'm on the way."

"That's the thing, Chief. He hung up."

Marvin Thomas looked around blinking, his long, horsy face squeezed between the headphones. You could tell he was Earlene's nephew. There was a family resemblance.

Moss sighed again. "When will you guys learn to follow police procedures? Hold the fort, Ears. And tell Prescott to meet me at…what's the address again?"

Ears looked up from his game, a weak eye muscle allowing his left eye to slide toward his beaked nose. "Howland's Mill, Chief. You know, out Howland's Mill Road," he said, as if the mill were a building etched in everybody's memory like the Washington Monument or the Alamo.

His quizzical look had "outsider" written all over it.

Thank God for the GPS, Moss thought. *I could end up in Siberia.* "And when Lee comes on at five, will you tell him to take a look in Mrs. Wilkes attic again?"

"Come on, not again, Chief. That's the fourth time to-day!" Earlene was all set to go home, even though it was just four forty-five. Her shopping bag was crammed full of knitting yarn, a pair of knitting needles stuck like crossed swords in the bun at the back of her head. "I'll go by her house on the way home and see what's wrong. She and my mother go to the same church. Poor guy. If that's his ghost, I don't blame one bit for coming back to haunt her, the way she henpecked him."

He avoided getting into a discussion about the existence of ghosts. "Last time I looked, Earlene, you weren't a sworn officer of the law, and if you should get hurt going over there—"

"Aw, don't worry about that. I won't sue or anything. Relax, Chief. It's just a friendly visit, okay? Besides, I've always got my knitting needles, just in case. Just like James Bond, licensed to kill except I'd hesitate at poking a hole in poor old Mr. Wilkes."

"That's exactly what I'm afraid of. Like I said, get Lee to go over to Mrs. Wilkes' place when he comes in." Shutting the station door, he stepped gratefully out into the late afternoon.

It was one of those humid December afternoons in South Central Georgia when not even the fleas on a yellow dog had the energy to move. Even the forecast was nothing to celebrate, promising to be seventy-nine degrees and rain on Christmas Day. However, Grover Moss was always hopeful things were going to change. Julia Springs and Kenya, wife Number Two, had taught him that. Both the town and his wife were survivors who had changed up their game after a rocky start. Both the town and his wife had changed their names and their appearance to suit the demands of others.

However, he was learning hope could be a two-edged sword. Like love, hope could hurt more times than not. Like the times he had gone home at the end of the day thinking he was getting old and fat, and, sure enough, Sheldon had called him old and fat. Of course, Kenya's oldest boy had always had a grudge against him for marrying his mother and not being his real father. Add to that, the times he had to arrest some white, over-privileged dudes with the N-word astride their lips like a night rider, and you had a perfect case of the Memphis Itch: itching to go back to Memphis and give up trying to be a small town Southern cop.

On the way out to Howland's Mill Road, Moss felt a weird chill as the woods grew thick with mist. In the watery world the vine-covered trees appeared to be monstrous shapes, choking out the feeble light of a winter sunset.

He tried to shake it off with a little Bob Marley on the CD player, but the eerie feeling even put an evil twist on the Caribbean beat as he drove deeper into the swamp the locals called The Thicket.

Give me the dirty cement of Memphis any day, he thought. *At least I know who my enemy is and where they're most likely to hide. Out here, everything is hiding.*

Something about the watery world brought back the dream just when he thought reason and daylight had destroyed it. The dream always had an atmosphere of its own, a greenish hue like the light coming from the swamp on either side of him.

Moss felt a choking sensation and a kind of paralysis as something advanced on him. measuring his life in thick bubbles. Suddenly it was there in front of him, rising up out of the primordial slime.

Moss was gripping the steering wheel so hard, he almost missed the sign for Howland's Mill Road, an unbelievably sharp left turn off on a dirt road through the very swamp he had been trying to avoid. The police department's only SUV bounced along the rutted road with mud puddles so deep, they would have swallowed a smaller car. Turkey buzzards bounced away from the road kill they were shredding, only to hop back again as soon as his vehicle had passed. Buzzards were inevitable signs of death in the South and Moss shivered as the chill spread to his gut.

He slowed down and turned on his bright headlights to pick up any more hazards in his path. The only sign of life was the rusted, beat-up old truck down along the creek which trickled through the swamp. There was a new tackle box and cooler in the back that gave him the impression that owner might be gigging frogs, a nightly past-time in these parts.

Still, Moss made a mental note to check and see if the frog-gigger was still there when he left the mill. That was if he ever got to the mill without breaking an axle, he thought as the SUV shuddered through another crater.

He almost passed the mill buildings buried in a grove of trees, but he saw the mill pond with its old spillway forming a rocky bridge across the trickling creek he had passed earlier. The stagnant water was choked with water plants and enough water lilies to satisfy any French impressionist painter.

But underneath the pretty flowers was a breeding ground for mosquitoes and water snakes, copperheads and moccasins. He made a mental note to get Mosquito Control out here when he got back.

As he parked the SUV beside Stu Prescott's patrol car, Moss couldn't suppress a shiver. There was something that looked haunted about it like the scary movies he had seen as a child. Prescott put the feeling into words.

Stu Prescott greeted him with, "Creepy old place, right, Chief? Like a zombie movie or something."

"Got your flashlight and pistol, don't you? You can take on a whole swarm of zombies, Pres. Besides you don't have much brains to eat," Moss added in a lower voice.

Prescott didn't make a move. "Steverino said he's on his way. Better wait for him to back us up, don't you think?"

"I believe you're scared, Pres. Come on, I'll hold your hand. Meanwhile, you can start telling me how it was you found a body way out here in zombie land."

"It wasn't me that found it, Chief. It was some teenagers come running out of the place just as I drove by." They were picking their way through the tangle of woods surrounding the old building, sometimes hacking their way through vines of kudzu wrapped around other thorny vines.

Moss knew better than to ask Prescott what he was doing way out here in the woods when he should be parked somewhere strategic so he could some speeder a ticket. "You mean you haven't seen the body yourself?" In spite of the threat of copperheads and other snakes that hung around water, Moss stopped and looked back at Prescott, the only full-time cop in the Julia Springs Police Department beside himself. "Did you even get their names, Sergeant?"

"No, but I'd know them if I saw them around, Chief. I think one of 'em is old man Bradley's youngest."

"You think." Moss moved gingerly on through the knee-high brush. Give him a city sidewalk littered with cigarettes and condoms any day. "Did these boys say what they were doing messing around out here in the first place?"

"That's it," Prescott said. "Just messing around, I guess. Like they were bored. Not a lot to do around The Springs for kids."

Finally, the two officers emerged on what looked like a stone patio.

"I guess this was their loading platform." Moss looked up at the two-story building, its roof partially collapsed. "If this is a prank call, I'm going to put you and Marv in a cell for a night." Shining his flashlight on the floor, he said, "Look, there're footprints in the dust. Sneakers. So the kids were in here."

"Maybe a meth dealer wanting to throw us off the trail." Prescott always sounded like a marshal in the western re-runs which Pres watched religiously. "The kids were pretty scared."

"Don't suppose they said where this body was at, did they?" Although the faint five o'clock sun was at their backs, Moss stepped through the gaping doorway, shining the flashlight around to make sure he wouldn't go crashing through the rotten floor. The old mill wheel was still attached to the building, although covered with vines which snaked up from the water.

"Hello, Julia Springs Police coming in." Moss's booming voice dislodged a few birds and two mice nesting in the rafters. "Anybody here? Better show yourself if you are. Check that room over there, Pres. Looks like an old office."

Prescott was headed for an adjacent room, gun drawn, when the door opened just a crack. The creaking sound froze him in mid-step. He looked like a bird dog on point, pistol outstretched, poised on his front foot." Show yourself or I'll shoot!"

"Pres, put the gun down. Probably just—" Moss started to say an uneven floor, but the words froze on his tongue. The door opened a little wider to reveal a ghostly face surrounded with long strands of white hair.

A feeble voice implored, "Don't shoot me. Ain't got any money." The door opened wider, allowing a glimpse of a pale, frightened eye. Prescott backed up a step closer to Moss.

"Didn't I tell you there were zombies around here?" he muttered.

"Zombies don't smell like shit, Prescott, because zombies don't have to shit." Moss's voice grew megaphone loud. "We're police officers, sir. Are you okay? That's all we want to know."

The door creaked open wider and in the doorway stood a barefoot wraith, clothed in rags. The only thing alive in his countenance were his eyes, peeking out through a cascade of white hair.

They were opaque, the color of old blue jeans but they fearfully raked over the two officers with the intensity of laser beams.

At last the wraith spoke in a tremulous voice. "You fellas lookin' for a job?"

Carefully as though in slow motion, Moss put his pistol away in its holster. In a low voice, he told Prescott to do the same. "Squatter, Pres. Put your gun down slowly." Raising his voice again, he said," It's okay, sir. We're just looking around." He had seen too many homeless people on the streets of Memphis not to recognize one holed up in the only vacant shelter he could find. This being an old mill, he had probably found some sacks of flour and corn meal to survive on by the pasty looks of him.

"We got a call about a body around here. Nothing to worry about, though. Probably just somebody pulling a joke." Moss sniffed the air. No smell of decay, nothing except an old derelict needing a bath and clean clothes.

The squatter was full of surprises, "No, it's true. There

is a body here." The old man looked from one officer to the other. "You got to believe me."

"We know. But it's up walking around," said Prescott, rolling his eye at Moss. "Right, Chief?"

Moss pulled out his phone and the wraith started to close the door again. "Don't shoot me. I'll go quietly."

Seeing his apprehension, Moss slid the phone back in its holder. "Okay, sir, you say there's a body around here? Could you show me, please?"

The door opened and the old man shuffled out, his bare feet immune to the splintered floor. Moss realized he was nearly blind. "It's under here." The old man pointed to a space in the corner covered by an old chest. The chest was covered with cobwebs and dust, but there was a square in the dust where it had been moved recently. A few floor boards had been pried up, probably by the kids Prescott had seen running away.

"Have you actually seen it yourself, sir? I mean recently?" Thinking it was some kind of hallucination, Moss concentrated on getting this old man some help. Maybe social services would find a place to put him. "Pres, go outside and give Doreen a call. Tell her we've got a ten-seventy-two. See what she can do, pronto."

He almost missed the old vagrant saying, "I know because I put him there. Me and Mama."

Pres stopped and turned around. "So you know who it is? Who is it?"

Moss was about to reprimand his sergeant for jumping in like that when the old man surprised them both. "It's Daddy," he said, nodding his shaggy head. "I know because I killed him. Mama said I did."

"You killed your own daddy and then buried him under the floor?" Prescott looked from the old man to Moss who just winked. "You want me to look, Chief?"

"Hold on, Pres. So, sir, how'd you do it? I mean

what'd you use—a knife, or a gun?"

The old man looked puzzled. "I don't understand. Do what?"

Moss humored the old vagrant. "Well, sir, you said you killed somebody—"

"My daddy, yes, sir. But that was a long time ago. At least a couple of years. No, more like ten."

Moss sighed, a mental picture of that glistening beer sprouting wings and taking off into the sunset. "Well, sir, you'd have had to use a weapon—like a knife or a gun to kill somebody."

"Or a rope," added Prescott. "Maybe you strangled him with your bare hands, even." His sideways glance told Moss to join in the fun.

"Sergeant, I gave you an order." Moss hoped the tone in his voice would give Prescott a hint before he had to use a sledgehammer.

"Yeah, Chief, but I'm not leaving you alone with this…man."

Moss got the sledgehammer ready.

"Oh, no." The old man seemed to be carrying on a conversation with an invisible companion. "Mama would never allow guns in the house. Or knives. Or anything like that."

"So you lived here, then? How long ago was that?"

The vacant blue eyes turned to Moss. "Why, all my life. I've lived here all my life. I'm John Howland, Junior and this is my home."

CHAPTER 2

Middle Georgia Regional Psychiatric Hospital took Howland away in an ambulance. Social worker Doreen Murphy rode with the old man all the way, holding his hand. "He kept calling me Mama," she said on the phone the next morning when Moss called to see how the old man was holding up. "You know he's almost totally blind. Cataracts."

"Good thing he is. Mistaking you for his mama, he'd have to be." Moss chuckled. Doreen was about thirty-something, a cute redhead. "Man has got to be eighty if he's a day."

"Thanks, I think it's the hair thing. Maybe his mother had red hair. Anyway, they're evaluating him now. He's so emaciated they're giving him an IV for nutrition and hydration first, though. Poor thing, he doesn't look as though he's eaten a meal for ages."

"I don't know. Prescott says he's probably a zombie that eats brains."

Doreen laughed, a bright sound on a gray morning. "Pres is a trip! Tell him not to watch those horror movies and get a life!"

"I've tried, but I think he's one of them. Anyway, call me when I can come over and see Howland, okay?"

He hung up and leaned back in his squeaky swivel chair. They were going back to Howland's Mill at eight-thirty that morning to look for the body John Howland said he put under the floor lord only knew how many years ago. The body of his father he said he killed.

Two of his deputies Steve Owens, Cal Hall, and full-timer Prescott were all going. Steve was bringing his drug dog, Molly, a black lab mix to see if the mill was a hiding place for crystal meth storage, or any other drugs. It was only a routine, but those kids must have after something.

Marv was tracing the tipster's call, figuring it was local. And Kenya was away which made everything in Moss's life hold its breath until she returned. Moss looked out the station window at the oyster shell clouds which threatened rain around lunch time. He thought he could smell the scent of her perfume. God, he loved that woman! She ruled his world.

"Let's go," he said to Prescott who was eating a cinnamon bun from Saranjii's across the street. "And wipe your hands, will you? I hate sticky steering wheels."

They got to the mill and went straight to the place Howland said he had put the father's body under the floorboards. Steve's dog, though not cadaver-trained, showed great interest there, scratching the torn up floor and wagging her tail as she looked up at Steve.

The deputies removed the steamer chest which turned out to full of harnesses and yokes. Those were for the mules that used to turn the stone grinder when the stream was low, Cal Hall told them. Aware of the strange looks turned in his direction, he hastily explained, "My grand-dad used to keep a team."

Steve had to keep Molly from jumping down to the earth below. The odor of dampness and mold drove them all back a step. The deputies put on their environmental masks, looking like surgeons about to perform an operation. Molly, wearing a bright red bandana, kept wagging her tail, looking pleased with herself.

They didn't have to dig far down in the loamy soil below the floor. Steve hit something with his shovel and held up his hand for the others to stop digging.

He proceeded to scoop the dirt carefully until he had uncovered a skeletal foot. He looked up at Moss peering down from the mill floor. "Better call County. There's definitely somebody down here."

"By God," Prescott whispered. "That old man done in his daddy."

The county's CSI team came and roped off the mill in yellow tape. "Perfect place for a murder," one tech muttered. "You probably never give two glances at this old wreck of a place. Rumors go a long way back about this old mill. Now, I see why."

"Why? What did you hear?" Again, Moss knew it marked him as an outsider not to know the local scuttlebutt. But this was shaping up into a murder investigation. It was time to quit acting like he had grown up around here.

"We kids used to come here at Halloween just to see a ghost," said another technician. "Rumor was, it was haunted."

"Must've been the old guy we found yesterday." Prescott said. "He looked like a spook." There was a lengthy silence. Then Prescott looked at Moss. "Sorry, Chief. I didn't mean…" Moss didn't get the Jim Crow term for black, being a child of the twentieth century and not from these parts.

"I thought you said he looked like a zombie, Pres." That was followed by relieved laughter which told Moss knew he had missed something. He wished Quade Walker was here. Quade would have played straight with him. A wave of sadness came over him which made him miss the cool Memphis bars more than ever. This definitely wasn't his scene, tramping around swamps instead of dirty streets.

When Sheriff McKenzie arrived, he got down to business without the usual preliminaries—inquiring into your family's health, your latest ailments, or your take on the most recent Georgia ball game.

"Hey, Moss, what's going on here?" He took a look around the office storeroom. "I hear you had a tipster. Any luck tracing the bastard?"

They shook hands, Moss towering over the short, bushy-browed McKenzie by at least a head-and-a-half. Moss was aware of his position as one of a handful of black law enforcement officers of rank in the counties below the Fall Line which began at Columbus. He knew he had a lot to measure up to, having replaced Quade Walker when Walker died foiling a plot to blow up a jet. But he was building a reputation for keeping his cool when faced with prejudice.

McKenzie appreciated that and matched it, man-to-man.

"None, unfortunately. It was made from one of those pay-as-you-go phones But Ears is on it, for what that's worth."

"Still into those damned games, is he? You ought to fire that useless bastard and get you a real human being. I see they've found the body." They glanced over at the CSI techs who were raising up a body bag. "The techs will have to make a body cast in the dirt before water gets in there and screws things up. The place gives me the creeps, you know? Besides, the mosquitoes are as big as horses around here."

"We found an old man living here who says that's his daddy in the body bag. Says he killed him. Same name except for the junior. Says he's John Howland, Junior."

Moss swatted a mosquito on his arm, a big one that squirted blood.

McKenzie's bushy eyebrows moved upward. "You mean, he killed his own father?"

Moss nodded. "He admitted it outright. We'll see what the shrinks say. Personally, I don't think he did, though. He's not playing with a full deck."

"Why? Why do you think he didn't do it when he said he did?"

"For one thing he couldn't say how he did it. Just kept saying he did it. You can look around here. Would any sane person live like this?"

The sheriff glanced at the cob-web covered office. "Uh huh, see what you mean. Where is he, this John Howland, Junior?"

"Middle Georgia Regional. Doreen's got him."

McKenzie chuckled. "That should cheer him up quite a bit. I know it would me."

"I don't know. Kept calling her Mama, she said."

Mackenzie's moustache crawled out into a smile. "Bet she loved that."

The medical examiner confirmed that the skeletal remains were over fifty years old. According to dental records, the man was John Howland, owner of the mill. The son had confessed to killing him approximately fifty years previously. Open-shut case.

But Moss wasn't so sure. Something kept nagging him as he sat nursing a cold beer, watching Alabama romp all over their opponent in the SEC playoffs. His five year old son, Wilson, was playing with their robots on the hardwood floor with his brother Sheldon and seven-year-old cousin. Zeb.

The game consisted of seeing which robot could out-body-slam the other. Since the robots were made out of old vacuum motors with recycled body parts, the noise was deafening, especially when the body parts clattered to the floor.

Suspecting Sheldon was trying to drive him away from the TV so he could use it for his virtual games, Moss attempted to put his foot down. "Hey, guys, take it somewhere else far away, will you? I'm having trouble listening to the game."

Wilson and Zeb got up to go, but Sheldon simply pretended not to hear. "Sheldon, that means you, too." Sheldon had that look on his face, the one that says you can't boss me around because you're not my daddy. Moss knew the look well. If he got tough, Sheldon would go whining to Kenya about Moss being mean.

But Kenya was away on tour with her trio, West Times Three, promoting their latest CD, and her sister Ashlee was in Atlanta, handling the bookings. "Look, man, it's just us guys until Mom gets back. We got to stick together. I want to watch the game and you want to do the linebacker thing with Piglet. Let's give each other some space, okay, son?"

Wrong move. Sheldon stood up, his face darkening with anger. He was itching for a fight. "I'm not your son and don't want to be either."

Moss took a deep breath. "That's not what I asked you. Take Piglet out of the porch or up to your room or wherever. Now, like I asked you."

Sheldon stood his ground. "Or?"

"I'll have to take your cell phone away. Or your X-Box. Or Piglet. Or all three if you keep on giving me a hard time. Your choice." Moss missed a crucial play just then. Alabama fumbled and their opponents fell on the loose ball. "Damn!"

"Ha, ha, Alabama is losing. They're losers like you." Sheldon got ready to run, but Moss just held up his cell phone without taking his eyes off the TV.

"Want to talk to your mother? She's heard everything you said. Go ahead, because this will be your last conversation for a while." Touchdown. Only for the other side.

When Sheldon had stomped off to his room, leaving Piglet on the family room floor, Moss remembered something. Something the old man had said when he and Prescott first discovered him. Something about his mother telling him he murdered his father. John Jr. must have been a child then. Why didn't he remember a heinous act like killing his own father? Why'd she have to tell him that he did it? Unless he was innocent. Or crazy. Or both.

And who was the mysterious tipster?

Moss was on the phone again, this time to the County Clerks' office. Closed. He called his secretary slash dispatcher, Earlene Thomas. She was a local and knew everybody. If not, her mother did. Earlene answered, "Julia Springs Police Department." The twang in her voice sounded like a tired banjo.

"Anything happening?"

"Not unless you count Mrs. Wilkes' ghost in the attic and the Gibson's cat." Sound of Earlene chewing with the TV in the background. Moss recognized the Alabama game at half-time.

"Alabama's rolling again. What's wrong with the cat?"

"Got run over by the grocery truck. I sent Pres out to console the kids and the delivery guy. He's a mess."

Good use of taxpayers' dollars, Earlene. "Say, Earlene, do you know anything about John Howland's family? I mean, his mom and dad?"

"No, but my mom would. I'll get the lowdown and get back to you, okay, Chief? That's Mrs. Wilkes again, gotta go."

"Mrs. Wilkes can wait." But Earlene cut him off.

Seething with frustration, Moss called Prescott who

was in the middle of consoling both grocery delivery man and the family of the deceased cat. "Pres, who was the Bradley kid you saw running away from the mill? Can you locate him?"

"Who? I can't hear you for all the screaming, Chief."

Moss repeated the question.

"You mean Danny Bradley? You want to bring him in? On what charge? Trespassing?"

Moss felt his patience running out. "Just bring him in, Prescott. Just for questioning,"

When he hung up, he remembered he had forgotten to check on the frog gigger on the way back from the mill last night. Rather than call Prescott back, he made a mental note to ask him, that is when the sergeant wasn't busy playing therapist.

∽∽∽

Dan Bradley was a skinny, nervous boy who slumped down in his chair, displaying boney knees through fashionably-torn jeans. His scraggly brown hair escaped from a pony tail to brush his bristling jaw." I haven't done nothing," he muttered. "You can't hold me. My dad said."

Moss explained he just wanted to ask a few questions about the body at the mill. "First of all, why were you there at all? At the old mill, I mean."

Danny shrugged, nervously twisting small gold earrings in one ear with tobacco-stained fingers. "Just kicking it, I guess. Just like looking around. Nothing else to do."

"So you pull up a few floorboards just for something to do or were you looking for something. Meth, maybe?"

The boy squirmed in his chair and looked around at Prescott. "Do I have to answer that, Pres?"

Pres nodded. "If you were just looking around, why did you pull up the floorboards in that particular spot? Or were you looking for something in particular? Drugs? Money, whatever."

Danny slouched further down in his chair and set his unshaven jaw. "I want a lawyer."

"Look, just tell me what you know and you won't have to have one. It was you who called us, right?" Moss waited. "Do your parents know you use meth?"

"I don't use meth."

"What's that all over your fingers, then?" Settling back in his chair, Moss figured this kid was hiding something. "What were you looking for then? Weed?"

Danny's copper-colored eyes slid sideways. "If I say yes, what you're going to do to me?"

"We didn't catch you with anything on you, so just tell us why you what you were looking for, and we'll forget the trespassing charge, okay? That okay with you, Sergeant Prescott?"

Prescott looked as if he'd hit with a brick. "But I thought you said—"

"Never mind what I said a little while ago. This young man has impressed me as a clean, honest citizen who knows right from wrong and respects other people's property. He found something suspicious and reported it like any good citizen should so we should commend him, not punish him. So if you have anything else to tell us, we'd be grateful. In your own good time, that is." Moss kept his eyes on Bradley, knowing that Prescott was looking at him as if he had grown two heads. "You know where to find us, Danny. You're free to go. Sergeant Prescott, give the boy a ride home, will you?"

Nobody moved. Moss busied himself with papers on his desk. When he looked up the kid was staring at him. "What's wrong? I said you can go. Pres, take him out."

Danny cleared his throat. "Uh, I got something else to tell you."

Prescott echoed, "He's got something else to tell us."

"Fire away, then. You won't mind if I do some paper-work. I don't like things to pile up, you know." Playing the part of the pencil-pushing cop, Moss went one by one through the papers he had already signed.

The leader of the pack was insulted by Moss's show of disinterest as Moss knew he would be. "Oh, I get it. You think I'm not serious, like I'm just a punk that hangs out with losers like myself, is that it? I can see why you got appointed police chief. You're like the rest of them fat ass pencil-pushers that sit around all day and do nothing and get the taxpayers to pay them for it."

Pres started to object but Moss stopped him. He looked across his desk at the kid in the chair. "That what your dad says?"

"Yeah and the rest of us too."

"And I bet they call me that nigger police chief, right?"

The answer was a snarling "yeah" that meant what're-you-going-to-do-about-it.

With the air of a man who had heard that all before, Moss put his pen down and leaned back in his chair. "Well, Danny, to each his own opinion. I'm trying to do my job, but if upstanding citizens like yourself don't help, you're right, I'm just spinning my wheels. Look, it's about time for my dinner. I'm on duty tonight so I've got to take off." He pushed his chair away from his desk and gathered up a few papers.

"We were looking for anything they left behind, okay?" Danny looked around as if someone might have heard him. "Shut the door, Pres, will ya?"

Prescott took two steps toward the door, saw Earlene was recording the interview, and moved back toward the

Bradley kid. "Who left what behind?"

"Those guys that do the drug drop every couple of weeks. Some other guys in SUVs and kick-ass trucks don't leave much behind when they haul it off. But every so now and then, we find bags of stuff they dropped. They're in some helluva hurry to get out of there, I'm telling you, man."

Slowly, Moss began to piece together the story of some kids messing around Howland's Mill one Halloween night, had witnessed several trucks already there unloading boxes of what turned out to be drugs—cocaine, heroin, and marijuana. No sooner than the trucks had arrived, other vehicles arrived to take the boxes away. The action only took a few minutes, so perfectly orchestrated was it. In under five minutes, everyone had vanished into the night.

"What do you do with the stuff you find?"

The kid in front of him shrugged and tossed his mane of long hair. "It sells for big money up in Macon or Atlanta. We may keep a bag of weed now and then for recreational use, but hell, we can grow weed back in the woods so we sell it and divvy up the money. We know it's hot or they wouldn't distribute it at night like that. Maybe it's like stolen or something. They all talk Mexican or some kind of gibberish except the black guys who talk like big-city gang-bangers. Anyways, if they saw us watching, they would kill us for sure. That's too big an operation not to be blood money, know what I mean?"

Moss nodded. It all made sense now. That's why the road leading to the mill was so rutted and poor old John Howland was so afraid to come out of hiding.

The men must not have gone into the mill, but if they were there and gone inside five minutes, they wouldn't have time. It all made sense now except for the body the kids found under the floor. Probably some poor sap who was in the wrong place at the wrong time.

With a warning to stay away from the mill, that it was now a crime scene, he let Prescott take the boy home. With no license plate numbers, and the rain washing the tire tracks away, there was really nothing but the kid's word to go on. Unless the old man had seen something that might give a clue to who and where these men were coming from. Whoever was behind it though really had their routine down to the split second, that was for sure. No amateur operation, but professionals to the max. That could only mean big money, the kind only organized crime can afford.

On the way home, Moss called Prescott again. When Pres answered, there was shouting in the background so that the sergeant had to shout into the phone. "What's going on now? Did the grocery guy hit another cat? Who's doing the yelling?"

"Old man Bradley is who. He's been giving me a piece of his mind for the last ten minutes, like how I should be police chief and not you, how he's sick of the law interfering with decent citizens like him, and yada, yada, yada."

"Don't smart talk me, Presley!" a disembodied voice yelled. "I got a right to my opinion, too!"

Moss visualized the scene in his mind. "I get the drift. Bet he has a couple of pit bulls on chains in the yard that he threatens to let loose on you, am I right?"

Prescott's voice wobbled. "Right, Chief."

"Tell him to chill out unless he wants to spend a night in jail for disturbing the peace and threatening an officer of the law, okay? If he doesn't take the hint, you're calling Deputy Reed for backup."

Pres said that was okay.

"Let me hear what he says."

Pres pointed the phone at Bradley while he told him

what Moss had said. Bradley answered something about where he could stick the law but quieted down after that.

Prescott was back. "Whew, that was getting hairy. Thanks, Chief."

"Listen, I saw an old beat-up truck parked down in the swamp last night. You know who that truck belongs to?"

"Sure, that's ol' Gator Joe's truck. He's out there most nights hunting gators."

"Now, I've heard everything. What does he do with alligators? Forget I even asked. Don't want to know. Listen, ask old Gator if he's ever seen a lot of trucks come to the mill at night, will you? See if Danny's story holds water or not."

"Right, Chief, but…"

"But what?"

"See, Gator Joe is kind of mysterious. Nobody knows where he lives at or anything. He's a swamper, see."

"Sergeant, in case I forget, remind me what you were doing on Howland Mill Road last night when your post is at Saint Michael's Rd. and County Highway Two-Forty-Nine. Herding buzzards, maybe?"

"I was going to explain, Chief. See, my aunt lives out there. Her backyard backs up on the swamp."

"In that case, I bet she knows ol' Gator Joe. Ask her, Pres. Do a little detective work. I'm heading home right now but I pulled duty until midnight so I'll be at the station if you call in, okay?"

Mrs. Marshall was in the kitchen making dinner when he got home. He told her he was on duty tonight but he had arranged for a babysitter to come over. 'I'll watch the boys until she comes," she said. "Being a policeman must be so interesting."

"I wish," Moss said under his breath. "But Christmas is coming and Santa might just stir up some excitement."

ഗഗഗ

Rhonda Wilkes had moved to town after her husband died. As a rule, she didn't venture past yard of the small frame house beside the main road through the town. But when she saw Moss's SUV, she ventured as far as the porch.

Seeing who it was, she went back inside and slammed the front door so hard, its Christmas wreath of candy fell off.

Moss knew why. People in the town which was predominately white, still couldn't get used to a black police chief. There were even rumors that Moss had even killed the former chief, Quade Walker, a local boy and football hero, wounded war hero aside. Or he had married a local girl, Kenya Jones, with a scandalous past, who now was so rich she had bought him the job.

Ashlee, Kenya's youngest sister, had told him that one, just before she left for Atlanta. "That's why I don't stay here," she had said. "Because you never shake off the past. People still judge you by the mistakes your parents made or the color of your skin. In a city like Atlanta, nobody knows anything about you but what they see."

"In that case, I'd still be scary-looking," he remembered saying. Now, he tapped as lightly on Mrs. Wilkes closed door while she peeked out the lace curtains.

"Mrs. Wilkes, Chief Moss here. Just checking on you."

The door opened a crack big enough to let a roach through. "I didn't call you. Besides Mr. Prescott usually comes by. He brings me my medication from the drug store."

Now we've got a delivery service going in addition to cat cleanup and grief counseling. Next, we'll be doing take-out.

"Sergeant Prescott's eating dinner right now. Mind if I check your attic, ma'am."

The

The door opened just an inch. Suspicious eyes stared through coke bottle lenses. "I'd rather wait for Mr—"

"I promise I'll tell him." *No lectures on making false calls to police*, he told himself.

"Well, just the attic. The stairs are straight ahead."

"I promise that's all."

He mounted the squeaky stairs to the attic door. No cobwebs. Someone, probably Pres, the delivery boy, had been taking a look around. Mrs. Wilkes was watching him from the hall as he went in with a flashlight. Nothing, just junk, old curtains, dressmaker forms of all sizes, mirrors. Dust bunnies all over the place. Moss walked in cautiously. The floorboards were loose in places. Remembering falling through the ceiling at Magnolia Alley, he played the flashlight over the floor. Visions of John Howland Sr.'s body under the floor at Howland's Mill flashed through his mind.

He went out and closed the door. "You ought to get a bolt put on the door, just in case," he said to the woman watching him from the bottom of the stairs. "That way, only you can get in. Do you mind if I take a look around the rest of the house?"

It was neat but dusty as he went from room to room. A cat followed him, bumping his leg whenever he stopped. Moss hated cats. They made him sneeze. With long strides, he made it to the kitchen ahead of the cat and Mrs. Wilkes who had been shuffling after the cat. They all ended in the spacious kitchen together. The cat purring and rubbing his leg like it was glued on.

Moss had to escape somewhere. He looked around in desperation. "Where does this door lead?"

"Oh, that's just the old root cellar. Would you like a

cup of coffee?" The cat leaped up on the sink as if it were a part of everything his mistress did. "I've got some real good Lane cake, too. Best I've ever made." Mrs. Wilkes turned to him. "You're the first colored man I've ever invited to have Lane cake and coffee. I guess the way the world is going, you have to move with the times."

"I'm honored to be the first." Keeping the kitchen table between him and the cat, he looked at his watch. The second half of the Alabama game was on. Every male under seventy would probably be watching with a beer in hand. Moss stifled a sigh with a sneeze. He could always watch replays. "That would be nice. Thank you, ma'am. Do you mind if I go downstairs, to take a look? You don't have anybody else staying here, that right?"

Mrs. Wilkes busied herself with the coffee cups. "No, except when my daughter comes with the grandkids."

"When is that?"

"Last Christmas. She said she was taking them to the beach this Christmas though." It was hard to miss the note of wistfulness in her voice. "Said she'd stop by on her way and leave my presents."

"Why not go with them? The beach is nice this time of year. No tourists."

The cat looked as if he was deciding whether to leap on Moss's shoulder or lick the creamer on the sink.

Mrs. Wilkes put an end to that suggestion. "I can tell you the last time I went to the beach with my husband, I got the most awful sunburn…"

The cat gathered its haunches for a leap. "They've got sunblock now. I'll just check the cellar and be right back.

He clambered down the narrow stairs, checking every corner with his flashlight. There were a swirl of footprints in the soft red earth floor and the stairs were swept off neatly. There were a few cobwebs in the corners of the stone foundation where stacks of dusty canning jars towered almost to the ceiling and stacks of sweet potatoes sat neatly sprouting for spring planting. The lines in the dirt could only have been made by a broom, Moss figured. Mrs. Wilkes had been tidying up the root cellar. The cat kept him company until it caught the scent of something that sent him scurrying back upstairs. Probably the piece of Mrs. Wilkes' Lane cake lying in his dish, Moss thought.

Mrs. Wilkes leaned into the doorway above the stairs. "Yoo hoo, Chief. Coffee's ready."

"Pretty good supply of canned tomatoes you've got down there, Mrs. Wilkes. You put those up yourself?" They were having their coffee at the kitchen table and he had to admit the Lane cake was delicious. He polished off a slice three fingers deep and she cut him another one just as big.

"I had a bumper crop last year and enough squash and peppers to feed an army. I eat all year on things I grow myself that way."

The cat was loving his leg again. He could feel something wet on his shoe. Moss tried kicking it away. "I noticed you keep it real tidy, too. I used to be scared to go down to my uncle's cellar even to get a jar of pickles I loved."

"I try to keep the cobwebs down. Lucifer here does a good job of catching mice so I don't have to worry about that. Can I wrap up a slice a cake to send home with you?"

Lucifer was a good name for this cat, he thought. "You ought to sell your cakes. They're better than store-bought. I'm trying to get a little farmer's market together in The Springs, up on the square. You could retire all over again on what you'd make selling those cakes."

When they were on their way to the door, he brought up the subject he had been preoccupied with all day.

"You didn't know John Howland, by chance?"

"Johnny? Certainly do. I went to school with him. He really had a crush on me." Mrs. Wilkes coyly preened her straggling grey hair that escaped from her bun.

"What about his parents? Ever meet them?"

Rhonda Wilkes picked a dead leaf off a house plant by the door. "We belonged to the same church, the Howlands and my family. His mama was a real dragon, I remember. A real fire-breathing dragon. Real hoity-toity, too. Thought she was better than anybody else just because her husband ran a mill and she came from a wealthy family."

"Do you recall her name?"

"Certainly do. Arqueta. She was a Talley from down in Savannah. There was some scandal about her, though. I can't recall it right now, but I remember everybody whispering when she was around."

Moss made a note on his phone. "Thank you for the tea. I'll send Sergeant Prescott over tomorrow to check out your cellar."

"That would be nice. I don't get much company. So many friends are dead."

He spent most of the next two hours online, scrolling through the archives of Savannah history. Lots of Talleys from colonial times on up to the present, but no mention of Arqueta except as a daughter of one Morgan Talley, president of Global Finance and Trust. When it went through bankruptcy, it was renamed Howland—Spencer Corporation.

Toward midnight, Moss thought he heard something in the alley out back of the station. A pack of stray dogs had been running around, knocking over garbage cans lately. He had called Animal Control but they said the county shelters were full.

People were dumping dogs at a record rate this year as

they did when jobs were scarce and evictions plentiful.

But the garbage cans were intact and Moss was just about to close the door when a voice beside him said, "I hear you been looking for me."

Is spite of himself, Moss jumped nervously. Then he saw the rusted pickup parked at the end of the alley. It was Gator Joe. "Come in, Gator. Want some coffee?"

"Got anything stronger?"

"Jack Daniels do?"

"Do me just fine." Gator shuffled into the light, squinting as though the dim light from the front room hurt his eyes.

Moss took the hint and pulled out a new bottle from under the counter where he stashed it away from the cleaning lady's sharp eyes. He poured at least two fingers of whiskey in each glass and handed one to Gator. It was gone in one swallow. Gator held the glass out for another one and Moss poured. "Thanks for coming in. Can I call you Joe?"

"Call me anything you want…swamper scum, gator-getter. I go by most anything. Joe's all right, too."

Working for twenty years on the Mississippi water-front in Memphis, Moss had run into some strange-looking people, but he had to chalk Gator Joe as number one. He gave the impression of being half-plant, half-human, with a little reptile thrown in. A kind of organic man. Joe's long hair, partially braided in graying dread-locks with an eerie green tinge, spilled down his back and shoulders like kudzu vines. From that curtain of greenish hair, he squinted out at the world uncomfortably with eyes the color of swamp water. His clothes were equally organic—moldy green, ragged as if his occupation de-manded camouflage.

"Sit?" Moss indicated a chair in the little kitchen.

The hair moved back and forth in a gesture of denial.

"Got to go. Got to get to work hunting them gators and frogs. Restaurant want gator steaks. Pay good money. Keep Joe in whiskey." Gator grinned, showing a set of gleaming choppers. "Seen a thirteen-footer in the mill pond the other night. Bet she's pregnant, too," he said, running a coated tongue over his front teeth.

Seeing his chance, Moss plunged ahead. "The mill pond? When you were out there, maybe you've seen something funny going on at the mill?"

Gator Joe regarded him with a reptilian look. He slid his glass across the table at Moss once again. "Like?"

Moss poured him another shot. "Like a bunch of SUV's and trucks around there for a short time, say five minutes and then pulling out of there fast."

"When?" The green eyes watched him through the curtain of hair.

"That's the trouble. I don't know exactly when but I do know it would be at night. Late at night."

"Gator moving then. Busy time. Joe got to go now, Chief. Talk later, okay?" Gator Joe headed back out the door, leaving a stink of sour clothes behind him. Moss fought the feeling he had just been conned out half a quart of Jack Daniels.

"So you'll tell me if you see something, right?"

"Maybe. Depends." Gator Joe paused without turning around.

"On what?"

"On how much whiskey you can come up with." Again, the audacious smile that was not meant to be reassuring.

When Gator was out in the alley again, Moss went to the kitchen and washed up the glasses. That goldmine of information had cost half a bottle of Jack Daniels. Unless John Howland, Jr. recovered his wits, he was stuck with the word of a kid whose brains were fried on drugs and whose father who had such contempt for the law, he threatened to turn the dogs loose on any representative of law enforcement.

The next day his search took him to the County Clerk's archives. He found Arqueta Talley had married John Howland in 1943. In the middle of World War II, Moss thought. They had one son John Jr. born in 1943. Married in March, baby born in November. Typical war-time shotgun wedding, he thought. Neither had a date listed for death.

The local newspaper archives of March, 1943 turned up one more bit of information although Moss had to squint through microfiche to read it. Arqueta also had one son by her first husband, Lieutenant Julian Spencer who was killed in 1942 in France. Her bridal photo of her marriage to Howland revealed an attractive blonde with a mouth full of white teeth any predator would have killed for. In fact, there was something hawkish about Arqueta, as if she were about to pounce on unsuspecting prey. Moss had a feeling that prey was John Howland.

He paid the librarian for the printout which was even blurrier than the original and, on the way back to the office, did the math. That would mean Arqueta Talley Howland would be somewhere in her upper eighties or nineties by now. He wondered if the staff at Regional had got anywhere with getting information out of Howland, Jr. so he gave Doreen a call.

"What's up, Moss?" Typical Doreen. She was the type caller ID was invented for.

He filled her in on what he had dug up in the archives and she kind of gave a ladylike snort. "No surprises there. The last poor old John heard, she was in some nursing home over in Dublin. Georgia, Moss, not the other place. That was when he was living in the woods, afraid she'd come back."

"*Huh?*"

The social worker's voice sizzled with outrage. "You heard me right. She had long ago kicked him out of the house after she said he killed his father."

"But he couldn't have been more than a kid when he did the deed—if he did it at all."

The comeback was fast and smart. "You got that right."

"So what did he do, where did he go?"

"Moss, you credit me with more miracles than Mother Teresa if you think I or anybody else around here is going to get too much sense out that poor old thing. He's been starved, beaten, whatever—" Doreen's voice trailed off in frustration.

"Whoa! Who beat him up?"

"He won't say…in fact, he looks around and asks 'Are they here yet?' all the time, like he's expecting a bunch of thugs back any minute. I don't think he's imagining it, either. Because the doctors found evidence of old broken ribs on his X-rays."

"No wonder he's crazy," Moss grunted in sympathy. "I'd like some time with whoever did it. If you find out, give me a call."

A sigh and a little laugh came over the phone. "Moss, you know you're on Speed-dial."

Kenya came home and Moss was so distracted by his wife's presence, he forgot about the Howland case until Bernie Segal called him. Segal was owner, editor, and sole reporter for the local newspaper/ TV channel. The newspaper was teetering on the edge of extinction to be followed shortly by the station and Segal would give anything for a transfusion of life-giving news, like a good murder. Moss was about to fob Segal off with the usual "can't comment about an ongoing case" when Kenya picked up the extension.

In her chocolate-covered tones, she said, "Hello, Bernie honey. I'm back and I've got lots to tell you, honey. How about an interview, say tomorrow morning at ten? Fine, can't wait. At the station? Really? I'm gonna be on TV? I'll wear something sexy. See you then, honey." She got off the phone and said from the doorway, "That ought to give him something to chew on."

"To say nothing about you getting some more publicity. And what's this 'Bernie honey'?"

But it was a shot that missed its mark because the target moved into his arms and snuggled up to his chin. He lived and breathed this woman. She was the blood running through his veins, the beat of his heart. Moss ran his hands over her lush body and got lost in her mouth.

Presently he smelled something beside her perfume. "Is something burning?"

"Oh, my Lord!" She ripped away from him and ran to the kitchen.

The stove looked like it was on fire, flames shooting upward. Fire alarms were going off all over the house. He threw a bag of flour on the fire and the kitchen filled with smoke. The fire was out but the damage was done. Kenya turned to him, half-laughing, half crying. "I thought we were hot together, but I didn't think we'd set the house on fire, baby!"

It was a sweet homecoming. Kenya vowed she'd stay until after Christmas, but she was gone again in two weeks. "Honey, it's just up to Atlanta. I'm doing a couple of shows at the Piedmont and then I'll be back by Christmas. Ashlee's going to stay here to look after you and the boys."

"Lucky Ashlee. I can imagine a more relaxing holiday for her like two weeks of mud-wrestling camp."

"Honey, you'll keep them in line."

The story about the body at Howland's Mill was relegated to the local news on the back page of the newspaper and, on the local TV channel, it became merely an aside, sandwiched between the local football team chances in the Regional play-offs and Kenya's razzle-dazzle appearance on the local talk show. Moss congratulated himself for being off Segal's radar although he suspected his glamorous wife had something to do with it. He didn't even bother to read Segal's slathering account of her life in the newspaper—he knew it by heart.

Along with her grandmother Kahalia, called Root Woman by the locals, they lived in the swamp bordering the town. At age fifteen, Kenya joined a touring gospel choir led by the Revivalist preacher, Jeremiah Jackson. She snagged the attention of a record producer, and Chantal West was created. What Kenya left out was a sexual predator step-father, the miscarriages at 14 and 21, survivor of the foster system, the empty affairs, and the glassy-eyed audiences in the clubs and bars she played during dry spells. That was the marvel of Kenya Jones, tiger-woman, borrowed mother of Sheldon and Zebulon, birth mother of Wilson. Sister of Ashlee, AKA Baby Pearl, and Toya, erstwhile mother of Zeb.

A few days before Christmas, he was about to leave for Savannah to follow up the lead on Arqueta Howland, when he got a call from Segal. "I hear you're going to sponsor a junior sports team, Chief Moss. When are the tryouts?"

"What? Where did you hear that?"

"Didn't you watch the interview with your wife?"

"I was out of the office, Bernie. Working on a case."

"Oh, yeah, how's that new thing coming? That body found out in some old mill, right? Rumor has it that it's John Howland, Sr. and that Johnny Jr. killed him, that right?"

Rumor has it, my ass. Nice segue, Segal, only I'm on

to you news buzzards. "Same as the other day. Can't comment on an ongoing case."

The other outsider in town persisted, and Moss fought the kinship. "Oh, come on, Chief, I got to sell some news here. What I need is one tantalizing tidbit. You know, something to keep the readers waiting for the other shoe to drop."

Moss sighed. "Okay, you can write this. We have a suspect in custody, we're waiting on the coroner's inquest, but it looks like the motive was robbery."

"Can I ask who the suspect is?"

"Now, Bernie, you know I can't give his name until we charge him. Now, if you're finished grilling me, I got to get going."

"Later, Chief. But I warn you, you'll be seeing a lot of me in future." Not if I can help it, Moss added silently. Then the bomb dropped. "Didn't that beautiful wife of yours tell you? We've got a book deal going, an autobiography of Chantal West as told to Bernard Segal."

He knew it was useless to talk Kenya out of something when she had made a public announcement. She was just doing what every other entertainer did, just keeping her image alive.

Still Moss gave it his best shot that evening when he got home. This sport thing involved his image, not hers. One by one he trotted out the facts, knowing his wife would dismiss them when publicity was at stake. "For one thing, I did play for Alabama, but that was twenty-plus years ago, baby. I'm so out of shape, my beer belly would make the touchdown before my feet."

She glided up to him, rubbed the entire front of him like he was a roast going in the oven, and purred. "All the more reason for you to get buffed up, baby."

"Kenya," he whimpered. "I'm black, and I'm an outsider. Nobody'll show up except maybe the Klan."

She licked his ear. "All the more reason you should do it. Reach out to the community. Show 'em you can contribute. Besides, you've got Prescott and two other deputies to help you."

"How do you know?" The awful truth was indelibly written in her topaz eyes. "You didn't ask them already, did you?"

That irresistible naughty smile. "Oh, yes, I did. Called them myself."

He read somewhere the French call it a 'fait accompli'. Something already done. He was more than done. He was toast. No more beers after work. No more couch surfing after work. No more quiet runs in the park. He's be followed everywhere by a pack of Sheldons yipping at his heels.

The one consolation was the drive to Savannah after giving Bernie Segal a story that rocked the village of Julia Springs. Tryouts Starting For Junior Sports League. Not football league, not Toss and Kick League, but all four sports, all four seasons. He felt like he had joined John Howland in the psychiatric ward.

CHAPTER 3

There were Talleys all over Savannah, but only one lived on the tree-lined squares frequented by the historic tours. His name was Morgan Talley. A uniformed maid ushered him into the study, as she referred to the oak-paneled room. Morgan Talley graciously introduced himself as Arqueta's nephew. An urbane, old-money type, Talley had Moss watching his diction, pronouncing his Rs and sitting straighter than usual in the leather armchair. Did people really live like this?

"Arqueta." It came out as a sigh with a shake of Talley's elegant, grey head. "Now that's a name I haven't heard in years."

Moss plunged into deep water. "We found a body under the floor in the old mill she owned with her husband, John Howland. Also, his son, John Junior, was wandering around in some kind of delusionary state. He's in Georgia Regional undergoing tests right now. Can you tell me about his mother, sir? I gather you were out of touch?"

Talley took the news like an aristocrat—no frown, no exclamation of horror, just raised eyebrows and a look of polite interest. "How about that?" he said after a period of silence while he was probably thinking of which lawyer to call. "You see, Detective—"

"Excuse me, that's Chief Moss. Go on, please."

Talley took the correction in stride. "I was just going to say Aunt Arqueta was disowned by her father after she had a child out of wedlock and the man was killed in the war. Julian Haughton Spencer was his name. The Spencers were a very prominent family here and close friends of my grandparents. Julian and Arqueta were high school sweethearts and she gave birth to a son after he was killed. Because of her father's disapproval, she went to live with Spencer's family for a time and when she married Howland, my family used to call her from time to time to see how she was getting on, but she always hung up on them.

"I remember them saying she was always headstrong and mean. Frankly, that's about all I know about Aunt Arqueta. Oh, one other thing. I believe she did come back here to Savannah once. I remember the shock when she showed up at my grandfather's funeral. He was in banking and was a pillar in the community, that sort of thing.

"Anyway, right when the vicar was speaking at the graveside service, Arqueta marched up and spat on the coffin. Then she emptied a bag of excrement—I presume it was hers—wouldn't want it to be anybody else's—and dropped it on the coffin lid. Then she marched away. I thought it was the most hilarious thing I'd ever seen but then I was only about twelve at the time."

"Wow, must've have caused quite a ripple."

"I'll say." Talley's face said it didn't. "Can I get you anything, Chief?"

That was his invitation to leave, his mother had told him. "No, thanks, but if you think of anything else, here's my card. I'd like to stretch my legs first. Long drive and all. By the way, you don't know what happened to her son, the one she had by Spencer?"

Again, the polite look which concealed a whole agenda of who to call first. "Cousin Julian? I hear he's a big business man somewhere in Atlanta."

"Anything to do with Global Finance and Trust?"

"I see you've done your homework, Chief. Impressive. No, I'm afraid that's my baby. You see, I inherited my father's position with Global after he stepped down— retired and since my uncle had made some bad invest- ments. He signed over his shares in the company to my father."

"So now you're the head honcho?"

Talley's smile was cold. "How aptly put. About Cousin Julian. The Spencers took him under their wing when he ran away after John Howland disappeared. You know the South, at least in those times. His mother was a fallen woman. Pity the child, but stone the woman. Any- thing else you want to know, just give me a call."

"They never married then? Julian Sr. and Arqueta?"

The question seemed to annoy Morgan Talley as if he had made a social blunder. "I already told you that, Chief Moss."

"Just wanted to make sure, that's all." He thought of showing Talley the article from the Julia Springs paper that told readers this was Arqueta's second marriage, but thought better of it.

As Moss turned to go, he found himself facing the open jaws of a crocodile. Next to that was the head of a tiger with a snarl that said he didn't die easily. In a knee- jerk reaction, Moss put his hand on his service revolver. "Who's the big game hunter?"

"I keep my hand in occasionally." Behind him, Talley chuckled. "That wall always gets a reaction from people, having the animals at their backs. Strange how people don't notice them until they get ready to leave."

Moss didn't share the joke. "I'll bet. They all look pretty fierce." He moved closer to the wall. There was an

American mountain lion and an elk among the more exotic beasts like the white rhino and the lion.

Talley was behind him, making sure he chose the right door. "Do you hunt, Chief?'

"Deer, mostly. My wife doesn't like the smell or the taste of venison though so I have to give the meat away."

"Come down sometime during deer season. I've got a hunting preserve of one hundred and fifty acres just off the coast. I'll treat you to as much meat as you can ship home—wild turkey, duck, and the occasional alligator steak. You said Julia Springs? That's near Macon, isn't it? In fact, tell you what. I go up there on business often so I'll pick you up sometime."

Moss knew they were just being polite, he and Talley. He hesitated by the door. "One other thing, do you remember why he ran away? Cousin Julian, I mean."

Talley shrugged. "Wouldn't you with a mother like that?"

The motel was Spartan-free cable, ice, coffee, a decent bathroom and king-sized bed for tired truckers and cops. He was stretched out with a beer when Kenya called. The sound of her voice made him ache.

"How's it going?"

"I always thought black woman always had it bad. I learned today that back in the day, it was women, period."

"Halee's come down from Atlanta. And Ashlee and would you believe Faun?"

"I knew Halee was coming. I just forgot, in all the flap about you signing up every nine through twelve-year-old in the county so Uncle Grover could babysit them." Halee was his daughter from his first disastrous marriage made even more disastrous by his two tours in Afghanistan. Her mother had remarried three times but Halee was a millennial, looking for anything that was real and instant.

She had gravitated back to Moss and found it.

"You'll get over it, honey." Silently he added, *you always do*. This was no time to get snarky. "See you tomorrow?"

"About five." Her husky voice was ever full of promises oozed over the phone, creating an earworm that reverberated to his nether parts.

༺༻

At the motel Moss decided spartaness didn't extend to warm beer so he grabbed the cardboard ice bucket and went out to the ice machine. He was filling the bucket when he was struck from behind.

He woke up in his own hotel room stretched out on the bed. A large, dark figure stood next to the bed, his dark eyes glittering through the holes. Moss could feel a gun pressing at his left temple.

Moss's first coherent thought was the man was strung out on cocaine. He'd seen enough addicts to know the look.

"You a cop." It was a statement, not a question. "What you want to know about Julian Talley for?"

"Get the gun away and I'll tell you."

"How 'bout you tell me now or I'll blow your brains out," replied the ski mask, pressing the barrel harder against Moss's head.

"Then you won't learn anything, moron. Take it away, I said."

"I'll give the orders, bitch," said his captor.

Out of the periphery of his vision, Moss could see two more dark shapes in the room, going through his suitcase. Hood Number 2 handed Hood Number 1 his wallet. Another had his car keys.

"Sssssst, somebody's coming!"

Everybody froze, except Moss. Taking advantage of the split-second distraction, he used his long legs to batter the man holding the gun in the gut and send him staggering backward. Then he rolled off the bed into a head-butt the Crimson Tide would have been proud of. As Hood Number 1 went down like a fallen tree, his head hit the night stand with a loud, satisfying crack.

The gun went off harmlessly, sending a bullet through the ceiling. Moss recovered the pistol, fired at the other two scrambling out the door. Getting to his feet, an electric pain shot through his abdomen and Moss straightened up with difficulty, ready to pursue the other two hoodlums. The man on the floor wasn't going anywhere for a while.

Just then he heard a scream, then a shout, tires squealing in the parking lot. The sound of a siren followed.

"Seems like your homies ran out on you." He jerked the ski mask off the man's head. There was something vaguely familiar about the man's face. A security guard burst in the doorway.

"I heard shots. My god, what happened?" The dude wouldn't have lasted two seconds in Afghanistan, coming in a door like that.

Moss just shook his head. "Everything is under control, and as long as this guy is cold-cocked, I'll put some cuffs on him if you hand me the pair you've got on your belt, and then you call the cops, okay, sir?"

"But—"

"I said call the damn cops, sir. That's an order!"

That's when he realized the hoods had worked him over pretty good. He recognized the electric pain was a cracked rib or two. But the woofer in his head took precedence over everything. That head-butt on top of the pistol whipping was still exploding in his brain.

After cuffing the man on the floor, Moss sat back down on the bed, so heavily the frame squeaked.

CHAPTER 4

When summed up, his injuries didn't amount to him getting out of coaching the Junior Sports League. His deputies were all too willing to step in for him. Even the part-timers volunteered two afternoons a week though they were working other jobs as well as farming. Moss watched from the sidelines, while nine to twelve year olds did everything to a ball except kick it or pass it. He figured the whole thing would collapse in a couple of months like an elephant falling over from its own weight.

Meanwhile, he looked Wynnton Spencer up online. It turned out there were eleven men by the same name in greater Atlanta alone. Although some of the names were on file for DUIs, none of them appeared to be the type to hire goons to do their dirty work.

The mug shots of the three men who had jumped him in the motel appeared in the Savannah paper and Moss figured out why the man with the split skull had looked familiar. When he happened to leave the paper lying on the dining table at breakfast, his sister-in-law Ashlee snatched it up. "Oh, no!" she shrieked and then clapped her hand over her mouth.

"What?" Kenya was getting coffee at the counter.

Ashlee shoved the paper toward her sister, still rolling her eyes from side to side, first to Moss and then to Kenya. "Oh, sweet Jesus! It's him all right." She passed the paper to Halee who looked at the photo of her father's attacker with venom.

"Scum," was her only comment.

Meanwhile Moss looked on helplessly as the paper was slowly passed among the women. "Will somebody please clue me in on what's going on?"

"Don't you recognize Toya's boyfriend? Zeb's daddy? You had to throw him out of this house, as I recall." Kenya came back to the table and sat down

"I thought there was something familiar about the guy, but it wasn't exactly a social visit. He had a pistol to my head."

The thug's name was Cory Williams, Zeb's father, or one of them. Moss was prevented from interviewing him because the DA had already charged him with armed robbery and assault. So as a professional favor, he called the detective on the case and asked him to find out the name of the man they worked for, saying it was related to another case.

"He already gave me a name," the detective said. "For what it's worth, it's some honky called Howland. Sounds like a white dude, right? But the only Howlands I can find are dead. What do you expect from a liar, Moss? The truth?"

Moss put down the phone and sat back in his squeaky chair with a sigh. Williams was giving the detective the names of dead people. The only live one was in the psychiatric ward at Georgia Regional. Either way, he was back to square one.

His daughter Halee signed on as the basketball coach. As a six-one college All Star forward, she certainly qualified. "And it's something I can give back," she said, giving his stubbled cheek a kiss. He couldn't figure it out. He was suddenly on the short list of everybody's favorite charity. Even Kenya donated the proceeds from two shows in Atlanta to buy the League uniforms. Bernie Segal had all the stories he could use.

Instead dodging all the attention, Moss took the easy way out. He assumed the role of wounded warrior, sucking up the spotlight like a dry sponge. He was getting used to it when he got a break in the Howland case. It came from, of all sources, Earlene's mother.

It was two weeks before Christmas when Earlene parted with the information. "Oh, yeah, by the way, boss. I forgot to tell you. I asked Mom about Arqueta Howland. She said last she heard she was over in a nursing home in Macon. Might still be, for all she knows. Mean as a snake, she said. Said Arqueta would pour water on a drowning man. And she asked that you not mention a word about who told you. She said she was afraid Arqueta might come after her. Arqueta always had a knack for revenge."

There were over ten nursing homes in Macon. He split the list with Earlene and Deputy Reed and started calling. On the third try, he hit the jackpot. They had, at one time, a patient named Howland, Arqueta, born in 1918, but unfortunately, she passed, God rest her soul.

About that time both Earlene and Reed let out a shout. You would have thought they had just won the lottery, he said later. Seems Arqueta had made a tour of the nursing homes in Macon and been thrown out of one after the other.

Starting with the most recent one that had listed Arqueta Howland as a resident on his bulletin board, Moss drove the fifty miles to the one story, modern facility near the Ocmulgee River. He asked the director, a steely woman with the unctuous smile of a funeral director, if

Arqueta had any regular visitors while she was there.

"None that I can recall. May I ask why you're inquiring? You're not family, I take it."

"I'm Chief of the Julia Springs Police Force. It has to do with a case I'm working on." He briefly outlined the situation—old John in Georgia Regional, the body of his father under the floor at the old mill. "He says his mother told him to kill his father. But he must have been only a child at the time."

Ordinarily, people looked shocked when they heard the story. But the director didn't alter her pasted-on smile. "That sounds like something Arqueta would do." Still wearing her smiling mask, the director made an intercom call. "Unfortunately, Chief Moss, I cannot reveal any information about a client without a records release. You understand. Privacy regulations and all that."

"I can get one. I have one for Georgia Regional. It'll just take time and…"

She cut through the excuses. "But I have someone you can talk to who took care of Mrs. Howland while she was here. Informally, that is. Off the record. Not from this office, just gossip among the staff."

"I understand."

"You see, we had accepted Mrs. Howland on a temporary basis. She simply had no other place to go, and we had a bed open in our psychiatric facility. And, well, she ended up here, is what I'm saying." Something began to tear at the director's mask.

"Could I ask why she was shuffled around like that? She must've done something bad to be kicked out of a nursing home."

"Off the record, Chief Moss?"

He nodded. "Off the record."

"Arqueta had tried to kill everyone—a roommate, one of the staff, even a doctor, at every facility she was a patient in." The mask finally crumbled. "In fact, that's how she died, trying to kill her doctor, but instead she fell and hit her head on the bed rail—"

A nurse knocked on the doorframe, hesitating when she saw Moss in his police uniform. She was twenty-something, pretty and curvaceous in her blue uniform.

"But here's Damaria now," the director continued. "Damaria, Chief Moss here would like to talk to you concerning Mrs. Howland. You took care of her until she passed, didn't you?"

"Yes, ma'am." There was a question evident in the nurse's eyes.

"It's all right. You can chat out in the commons. Nice meeting you, Chief Moss. Sorry I couldn't be of more help." The director assumed her mask again, indicating that the visit was over.

He and the nurse sat in the big open room as impersonal as bus station and looked at each other. "I wouldn't put my dog in one of these places, even if I had a dog."

Damaria laughed, showing fine white teeth all the whiter against her dark face. "Want to know something, I wouldn't either."

"So tell me about old Arqueta. She was mean as a cornered bobcat, I take it."

"Meaner. I swear that was the meanest woman who ever lived beside my grandma. Why, she died trying to stab the doctor with a knife she had hid in her diapers. Fortunately for everybody, she had a massive stroke doing it and died on the spot."

"The doc get hurt?"

"Not cut bad, but he quit the next day." Damaria shook her head. "Damned if I didn't think about it but I can earn class credit toward my RN by working here."

He asked if Arqueta, between plots to kill people, had ever mentioned having a son named Julian.

"Oh, sure, she talked about him all the time. Julian this and Julian that, but he never came to see her, though. Never once in the year she was here, In fact, now that I think back, Arqueta never had any visitors."

Moss grunted affirmatively. "Probably killed 'em all off."

Damaria flashed a smile at the thought. "But I know one thing. Somebody paid for her to be here. A private room even. That don't come cheap. Not in this place."

"Any idea who?"

The nurse shrugged. "Maybe this Julian. When I asked where he lived, she said 'all over.' Oh, yeah, and someone always sent her flowers on her birthday. No card, though."

"She ever mention a son called John?"

The nurse's eyes went wide. "Never. I didn't know she had any other children. She was very weird, Miss Arqueta was. I know they get weird at that age, but she was weirder than most. Evil was more like it. You know, she tried to drown our cat? Tried to flush the poor thing down the toilet, but I just happened to stop by her room about the time the poor kitty was going down for the third time." Damaria paused to giggle. "And we couldn't keep fish in the fish tank. She would stick her hand down there and, next thing we knew, we'd find fish guts floating all over the water. I tell you the poor custodians got tired of changing that water."

Moss left with a couple of key bits of information. That was all they were, bits of leads. On the way out of town, he stopped in at the florist shop nearby the nursing home. No, they hadn't delivered any flowers to an Arqueta Howland. He might try the bigger florist on College Street. They did telephone orders.

There he struck pay dirt. Yes, a couple of years ago, someone from Atlanta had placed a standing order for flowers to be delivered to Arqueta Howland. It was current, to be delivered to The Heavenly Gates Cemetery every year on her birthday. He got the billing address: Howland Corporation, 4710 Orchard, Atlanta, Georgia.

High on caffeine, feeling like his detective skills weren't all in the advanced stages of rigor mortis, Moss was boogieing down the highway home, seat-dancing in his SUV, when the police radio suddenly squawked something about a shooting. He had turned up the hip-hop and hurriedly turned it down to listen.

It was Prescott. "Ten-seventy-eight, ten-seventy-eight."

Moss pushed speaker button. "This is Moss. Speak English, Prescott. Location?"

Pres was obviously looking up the codes on his sun visor. "I got a one-oh-nine-C, Chief. Get that? A one-oh-nine-C."

"Ten-four. Where?"

Pres was now teetering on the verge of hysterics. "At the newspaper office. It's Bernie Segal, Chief. He's been shot bad. Ambulance is on its way. Blood all over the place."

"Ten-four. En route to the scene." Moss turned on the blue light, the siren warned everybody to get out of his way, and the traffic cleared in front of him.

CHAPTER 5

Who would want to shoot Bernie Segal? On the way back to Julia Springs, Moss ticked off all the possibilities. Maybe in his zeal for the headline that would keep him in business, Segal had rattled the skeletons in somebody's closet. Mayor Clark didn't like him coming to town council meetings and reporting a bunch of good old boys swapping golfing stories while ignoring complaints about cows trampling down fences or septic tanks overflowing.

The school board, made up of approximately the same people, hated the way Segal had pointed out to the literate public that the county schools had the worst graduation rate in the state and was on a par with Alaska.

The Historical Society, made up of the wives of the same people on the School Board and the town council, hated him because Segal had pointed out in a series of articles that said the most powerful people in the county were the descendants of former slave-holding families and that there were few if any people of color on any of the representative boards.

"What right has that little Jew got to come down here and criticize us, I want to know?" Mayor Ashton Clark was overheard talking to one of his golfing buddies in

Pop's Place, a hangout for the landowners around The Springs. The remark went around the circuit until it got back to Grover Moss.

Ashton was the heir of the powerful Clark family who had foreclosed on every cropper around Julia Springs to acquire land for the railroad a century ago. It made them rich as Croesus since they were influential in putting a line through town which Julia Springs the hub for the whole region. For a while, that is. After World War II, railroad died as trucking became king.

He would be the first to admit Segal could be annoying, but Moss could think of at least half a dozen locals who were downright obnoxious. The difference was, they were native to Julia Springs. Like him, Segal was an outsider, down from Atlanta. Big city written all over him. Probably a transplant from the North.

His secretary Earlene, that source of all gossip, gave him two more reasons. "You know he was gay. And a Jew, on top of that."

"Is, Earlene," Moss corrected. "He's not gone yet. He might pull through yet. Then we'll see what happened. In the meantime, I don't want you talking about the case, understand? Not even to your mama." He stopped short of saying that would be like announcing details of the case over the P.A. system at the Friday football game.

"Yes, sir, Chief." But he didn't believe for a New York second she meant it.

Segal was at Mercy Hospital in Macon where doctors had performed emergency surgery to remove bullets from his shoulder and his back, both the same caliber, but fired from different directions.

County CSI was all over the place like white on rice and left just as fast. Motive as far as they could tell was robbery. Safe opened, scattered tens and ones on the floor.

"They just wanted the big stuff," one tech commented as he was leaving.

Candlelight vigils were held at the tiny newspaper office and TV station while Bernie and the seedling media empire he had founded fought to stay alive.

Two days after Bernie was shot, a young man in a Jeep showed up, unlocked the door of the newspaper office, and turned to the people gathered outside.

As if he were announcing his candidacy for public office, he said, "I'm Bernie's nephew, Rey, and I'm going be interim editor of the Post. It'll be a little late, but you'll have an edition on your porch by two o'clock tomorrow." The door closed and Reynolds Chapman got to work.

As the interim manager of the fledgling TV station, Reynolds Chapman carried on with the erratic zeal of an Italian film director. He posted the beleaguered camera crew at every practice scrimmage of any team within twenty miles, at re-enactments of famous local Indian battles, and at the Chili Cook Off in the park sponsored by the volunteer firemen.

There was no peace for Moss. He couldn't even drop in for a beer without someone hammering him for the latest on Bernie Segal's condition. Reynolds Chapman called him for an interview so persistently that Moss told Earlene to say he was out. Nevertheless, a cameraman stuck a zoom lens in his face every time he stepped out of the building. No wonder famous celebrities hid and people in their orbit exulted in their reflected light—like his wife, Moss thought. Then he felt guilty. His wife had earned her fame.

When he went up to Macon to check on Segal, he left town by a circuitous route to throw off the cameraman. By day four and three surgeries later, he got the green light to interview the editor and approached the patient with caution. Bernie looked so much like a mummy, Moss half expected for him to be embalmed. His nephew Reynolds was sitting in a chair by the widow, typing on his laptop.

"Who did this to you, Bernie?"

"Do you think I saw the bastards?" croaked the mummy. "No idea, Chief. Sneaked up on me. Got no idea who they were."

"Well, I have an idea." Chapman looked accusingly at Moss. "Since when have Jews ever been welcome in the South especially in small towns like this one? And Uncle Bernie's gay. Isn't that enough to call it what it is? A hate crime." The young man stared at Moss, dark blue eyes blazing in his handsome tan face. "You can't tell me being a black policeman in a small Southern town has been easy. Haven't you run into the same thing, Chief Moss? Remarks about the color of your skin? That you're not doing a good job?"

Moss answered slowly, measuring each word as though they were breadcrumbs through a forest guiding his way back to his starting point. "You can call it whatever you want, son. But you got to back it up with evidence, and there's no evidence to call it a hate crime just because your uncle here is Jewish or even gay. No hateful words scrawled on the walls, no swastikas, no burning crosses. Some people around here are kind of backward, I admit. They believe what they were raised to believe, but they wouldn't kill somebody for believing differently. You know, being from someplace else like you, I learned something about this town watching some of those shows your TV station is putting on. About all the battles that happened around here back in the day when it was still an English colony. The settlers fighting Indians. Then the British came. Some of them were Jewish and even black. I'll bet some of them were even gay, being as no woman in her right mind would want to live out here in the boonies."

A little smile played on Chapman's lips. "Is that off the record, Chief?"

"Strictly." Chapman lowered the papers he had in his hand, revealing his cell phone.

Moss groaned and rolled his eyes. "Oh, no, you didn't have your recorder on all that time, did you?"

Chapman grinned. "Don't worry, Chief, I'll edit out the part about people around here being backward."

"He's sharp," said the mummy on the bed. "Damn, my nephew is sharp as a tack."

Moss got up to leave. "More like a trap, I'd say."

Reynolds Chapman printed Moss's quote saying he didn't think the shooting was a hate crime. True to his word, he left the part about people around here being backward. After all, the county had written it off as a simple robbery which Bernie had interrupted. Two black guys with Glocks wearing ski masks. Open and shut. The District attorney's message to Moss was just to butt out.

After that, Moss spent a lot of time holed up in his office just thinking. As a former inner-city cop, he knew it wasn't a hate crime, or an interrupted robbery either. Whoever the guys were, they meant to kill Segal.

So what exactly was the shooting of Bernie Segal about? True, the newspaper man had stepped on the toes of a lot of big players in this town. But this wasn't exactly Memphis or Atlanta.

At the end of the next week, he paid a visit to Reynolds Chapman's cluttered office above Dr. Morrison's clinic. Moss began by skirting the question. "How's Bernie getting along?"

"Doc said he'd be home by Christmas. He's one tough old bird."

"That's great news, man. Great."

Chapman leaned back away from his computer, rubbing his eyes. "Not so great. I'm afraid the bastards will try again. And next time, they'll kill him." He swept away a pile of papers so Moss could sit down on the chair next to him.

"So you don't believe the DA's verdict either. Got any ideas about the motive?" Moss sat down gingerly, not sure if the chair would hold his weight.

"I've got nothing but ideas, that's the trouble. No evidence, nothing."

"So you don't think it was a hate crime. As I recall, you were pretty adamant about that back at the hospital."

Chapman's good-looking face reminded Moss of Wilson when the three-year-old had done something wrong. "That's my trouble. My mother is Jewish, my stepdad is an atheist. How's that for a dysfunctional family? I think like a Jew. Paranoid. 'Everybody's out to get us' sort of thing."

"I know what you mean. Mama always told me the list of people out to get us included the Klan and the Devil and all the white people in between."

"But didn't you think the same thing at first? You know how pushy my uncle is. What I'm saying is, maybe the robbery was just a cover-up for something bigger."

"Any ideas what that would be?" He didn't want to admit this white boy was echoing his very thoughts. Chapman could just be fishing for hints.

But the young man surprised him. Grabbing a piece of paper from the pile on the chair, he handed it to Moss. It was covered with what looked like a crossword puzzle in hieroglyphics.

"I didn't know your uncle was into ancient languages," he said, handing it back to Chapman.

"I can't read it except the name Howland keeps popping up." Holding the paper so Moss could see it, Chapman pointed to each letter with his pen." See, here and here and here again."

"Could've fooled me." Moss sat back against the creaking chair, suspecting a trap again. These journalists would stop at nothing to get a story.

"Does the name Arqueta Howland mean anything to you? Or Julian somebody?" The expression on the young man's face was hard to read.

Did the newspaper guys have his office bugged, he wondered? "Your uncle knew about the possible murder case I'm currently investigated. In fact, he put an article about it in the newspaper a few weeks ago."

Running his hands through his short, black hair, Chapman sighed wearily. "I haven't had time to get into back issues what with running to the hospital, and keeping the TV station afloat. By the way, your daughter Halee has been a fantastic help. She's been running the morning show like a pro. I haven't been much help at all. How does Bernie do it all? One thing for sure, I wouldn't be doing it for the pittance he gets in return."

"What do you usually do? I mean job-wise." Anything to get the subject off the Howland case.

Chapman looked like he was itching to get back to work. A good sign, Moss thought.

"I'm a script writer for a production company out in Hollywood," Chapman said. "So I can work on my own time basically. I get called out to the coast when the shows are in production but that's even going to Skype now. They're opening a studio in Atlanta sometime this year so I have to get back to the city as soon as Bernie is back on the job."

Ah, the Millennials, Moss thought. Always on the move. Anyway, Chapman was no threat. He was doing his uncle a favor for pennies.

"Sounds more exciting than police work in a small

town, I'll say that." Moss said he had to go. "I'll let you get back to work."

Chapman didn't stop him. "So I'll ask my uncle what he was working on. We can start from there."

Moss froze at the word "We?"

"I know Uncle Bernie always had a little notebook he carried around. Scribbled notes in it all the time. I can't find it anywhere. This was on the chair under a pile of stuff," Chapman said, holding up the crossword puzzle highlighting the name Howland.

Even before Moss got out of his chair, Chapman was on the phone to his uncle. He had a hurried conversation as he walked toward Bernie's' cluttered office. "It's where? What left hand drawer, top or bottom? Okay, I'm looking in the—that's funny. Drawer's a little ajar and it's not here. There's nothing in here but keys and paper clips."

Moss followed him to the door of Bernie Segal's cluttered office and looked over Reynolds's shoulder. The young man turned around and put the phone down. "It's gone. His notebook is gone."

In two strides, Moss grabbed the phone. "Bernie, this is Chief Moss. Listen, can you remember what the last thing…the big thing you were working on that you put in the notebook?" He listened while Bernie muttered a litany of church meetings, weddings, and football games. Then Moss heard him say Wynnton Spencer. "Hold it right there. What about Spencer? Yeah, I know he lives in Atlanta and he has a company called Howland-Spencer. What about him?"

Bernie's reply was faint but audible. "But did you know I know the guy? Lives two doors down from my mother."

"I'm no fool, Bernie. I know you've been snooping around asking questions."

"Okay, so I've met the guy. And I found out he owns a lot of property around Julia Springs. Lots." Bernie's voice was almost inaudible now.

"What? Where?"

Reynolds picked up an extension. "You promise to give me the story when it breaks?"

Moss put his hand over the receiver. "What story? Bernie, this is a police investigation, no media involved. Come on, was that all in your notebook?"

There was a sigh at the other end. "Yeah, the whole enchilada. Names. Numbers. Lot coordinates and sizes. Moss, there's got to be about thirty land holdings between here and Savannah. I bet there's airstrips on a lot of those. Private jobs, not for the public. He's a developer. I'll bet he's waiting for something, something big. He's rich as Croesus. Lives in a mansion on Paces Ferry Road. At least he did. He must be in his late eighties now."

"I'm not going to ask you how you know."

"Easy, Moss. I have my ways. My mother, for one. She knows all the neighborhood gossip. Keeps tabs on everybody."

A nurse came in the room and commandeered the phone. "Mr. Segal will have to rest now. He's getting prepped for surgery."

In the background, Bernie muttered something but it was lost in the gargle coming from the TV.

"Now, now, got to be brave boy." That was the nurse putting the phone down.

Moss went straight from the newspaper office to the County Clerk's office and got the surveyor's map listing the property owners and what they owned. Bernie was right. Spencer Howland Enterprises owned a large number of parcels in counties right down to Savannah and including some coastal lands outside the city. Armed with the addresses of the lots owned by Howland Enterprises, Moss was surprised to see they were all private farms. He found at least one person home on each and asked the same question—did they have an airstrip anywhere on the property? They all said no, there was no airstrip. To a one, they all looked indignant as if he were asking if they were drug smugglers.

One old-timer called him out. "If we did, we wouldn't be living in this godforsaken place. We'd be down in Miami with the rich folks."

As usual that down-home wisdom made him chuckle. They were all just leasing the land they farmed. When he asked the old farmer who he paid rent to, the man eyed him like a curious blackbird, head cocked, one eye sliding over him, taking stock. "What d'you want to know for? Why is a city cop comin' around asking if we got an airstrip for? There something going on we don't know about?"

"That's what I'm trying to find out. You're not under investigation, if that's what you're worried about." Moss blotted the perspiration from his bald spot and got ready to go. "Thanks, anyway."

"Now, don't get in a huff. All I'm saying is be careful about asking folks around here a lot of questions about who they rent from, and if they got an airstrip on their land. Stuff like that."

"Why is that?" Moss paused on the stepping stones leading back to the gate.

"I ain't saying this to hurt your feelings or nothing. Just be careful. Look behind you from time to time. That's all." The farmer grabbed his bucket of lay mash to feed his chickens and Moss went back to his patrol car followed by a flock of dogs that, one by one, peed on his tires.

"Howland Corporation up in Atlanta," the old timer

called. "That's who the wife pays our rent to. And I never hear the end of it. I'm telling you when the man comes around to collect it I never hear the end of it, no, sir." He wandered off muttering followed by a mob of squawking chickens.

Just then a youngish brown girl came out of the farmhouse, carrying a basket over her arm. She was wearing knee-length khaki shorts and a tee-shirt with a strange design on it.

He nodded, assuming she must work there, but she called, "Wait, Chief Moss!"

As she hurried across the neat yard with rose bushes starting to bloom, Moss tried to place her. Not young enough to hang out in front of Saranjii's in a giggling herd, and certainly not old enough to be one of the church crowd, he decided. She must not get to town often.

"Hello, I'm Kedzia," she said, holding out her hand even before she got to him. "The priest of The Glory Road Church. I took Kahalia's place after she passed." He looked so puzzled that she went on. "Your wife's grandmother, I believe. How is Kenya doing?"

When he clasped her outstretched hand, Moss was stunned by a sudden surge of electricity that shot through his fingers. It was almost as though this well-spoken woman had a buzzer in her palm like they sold in novelty shops in Memphis when he was a kid. He stumbled over the words, "Nice to meet you. Kenya's fine, just fine."

She looked at him or through him, he thought, with the curiosity of wild things. Almost as if she was interpreting his instincts as one animal sizes up another. "We miss seeing her at church. Miss her beautiful voice. You've heard about me, haven't you?" It was more a statement than a question.

He took his time answering. "Well, let's just say the people from the Public Health Department have been sniffing around lately. Asking a lot of questions, that sort of thing."

They both knew it was more than that, but he didn't want to tell her until somebody filed a complaint and nobody had yet. Doctor Morrissey who split his time between here and Macon, just shrugged off the state snoops saying people had been practicing alternative medicine since the days of slavery when that's all there was available to black folk.

Kedzia lowered her clipped head and sighed. "It's just a matter of time, though, isn't it? Before they issue a cease and desist order. I'll have to get a lawyer then. Don't know if I can afford one, to be honest."

Moss didn't want to get involved in a public health dispute. This woman could be selling snake oil for all he knew. But a lot of people believed in healers—his wife for one, and herbal medicine. Even his own mother did. "I'm going back to town. Can I give you a lift?"

Kedzia shook her head. "I'll walk, thanks. Motors interfere with my biorhythms."

"You sure? It's a long way."

"Walking is good for the soul and the body, Chief. Oh, and about Howland Corporation. There's an airstrip about two miles down the road from here due East as the crows flies. But you'll find a road like a logging track about a mile down this road. Take that and you'll see it. But as Mr. McDermott says, better watch your back. Those people are dangerous. They squeeze every drop of money from this region they possibly can and put nothing back. And they threaten everyone who complains."

"Who's threatening these people? With what? How?"

The young priestess gestured at infinity. "You name it! Foreclosures. Repossessions. They even resort to sabotage like setting fire to fields and barns, killing livestock. Destroying the harvest. I've seen at least fifteen farmers thrown out on the road, furniture and all with nowhere to go beside the homeless shelters."

"It's Howland Corporation you're talking about, right? Nobody has reported it. My hands are tied unless I have a complaint."

Shaking her head so the threads of gray showed, Kedzia said, "That's just it. Everybody's too afraid to complain."

"Tell you what. You say you personally know of farmers who have gone belly up because of Howland Corporation's harassment. You find me somebody who's willing to talk to me, and I'll investigate, okay?"

His words produced a brilliant smile from the priest-ess. "Thanks, Chief. I'll find you somebody." She turned to go. "And, by the way. Your friend says to tell you he's got your back."

The words sounded so much like Quade Walker, they gave Moss a physical jolt. "What friend is that?"

The mysterious Kedzia just smiled. "He said you'd know. Bye, Chief Moss. Give my love to Kenya."

As he drove away from the McDermott farm, Moss looked in the rearview mirror. The priestess was still standing at the gate with her right hand raised shoulder high in a kind of benediction that was neither a salute nor a wave. He was approaching the outskirts of Julia Springs when it hit him. Kedzia was making the sign against the Evil Eye.

Moss hit the brakes and pulled over on the shoulder, scaring the hell out of the truck behind him. He found he was breathing hard and sweat was breaking out all over his body in spite of having the air conditioner blasting. He rolled down the window and pretended to be writing a ticket. The sketchy traffic got the hint and went by him at a crawl.

Jeremy Fabulous Johnson was waiting in the office

when he got back. He was filling out an application when Moss walked in, pining for a dose of reality and a cold beer.

"Someone to see you, Chief," Earlene hissed as he went by her desk, to his office. "He wants to be a deputy."

"You know the drill. Tell him to fill out an application and leave his phone number. If he qualifies, I'll give him an interview."

"But—"

"Chief Moss?" Before Earlene could finish her protest, the young man appeared behind her. "Hi, I'm Jeremy Johnson." The young man holding out his hand, bypassing Earlene, was latte dark, handsome, and built like Moss used to be.

Moss wanted to hire him on the spot. Finally, someone who talked the same language, and looked reasonably like him except for the beer gut and the double chin. Somebody young and obviously with it who would build the trust of the black community after years of Jim Crowe.

But he knew the town council would have to approve the new hire.

He could imagine the conversation Ashton Asshole Clark would have with his cronies at The Springs, a golf club that had magically appeared outside town where the token black, beside the caddies, was a surgeon attached to the military base.

Mayor Clark, head of the Council and everything else, was well-known for holding the color-line, as it was referred to locally.

"Afraid blacks are taking over the town," was how Kenya rephrased it. "Old Jim Crow is alive and well and a member of the golf club." Despite the fact that Johnson had a spotless resume, had three years of college with a major in criminal justice, Clark would find some loop-hole.

Then Cody Reed announced he was quitting to get a full-time job preaching somewhere else god willing. Moss appointed Johnson to take his place in the interim until the Council could get their act together and vote on it.

JJ fit right in, coaching the boys fledgling basketball team, showing up with Halee for supper, cracking jokes, and looking like an NBA poster. Kenya, finally home for the weekend between tours, whispered to Moss one night as they snuggled in the king-sized bed, if he thought that maybe, just maybe, JJ could change Halee's mind about being gay.

"How do you mean?" Moss mumbled in her perfumed ear, the thought of Halee's sexual orientation being the furthest thing on his mind. He was more into his own sexual orientation at the moment.

"Oh, baby, you know what I mean."

Why did women always say that? Why would they say that if you knew what the hell they meant in the first place? But not wanting to get in an esoteric discussion just then, he dropped it, just content to hold his wife, messing up her hair to make her giggle.

Moss was deciding to follow up on Howland Corpora-tion's mysterious activities without the requisite com-plaint outside of town when the priestess of the Glory Road Church paid him a visit. He offered her the only other chair in his office, but she shook her close-cropped head.

"I like to stand. It makes me feel my roots through the floor. Makes me feel one with the trees."

Whatever, he thought. "What can I do for you, Miss..."

"No, I'm not Miss anything. Just Kedzia is fine. That

my only name." She looked behind her at Earlene who was talking on the phone. "I've came here to tell you there's going to be a plane arriving tonight out on the airstrip. I promised I wouldn't say any more than that, but the owner of the land the airstrip is on is expecting you. He'll guide you there."

"Who or what's on the plane? Can I know that? Does this landowner think it's something illegal—drugs, illegal immigrants, liquor? And when's it supposed to arrive?"

"About midnight. That's all I'm supposed to say. But I'd get there while it's still light. That way if they have lookouts, they won't see your headlights. It's really dark out there at night."

"Then how does the plane land?"

"You'll see." She turned to go.

"Wait, what's this guy's name I'm supposed to meet?"

"Tom. Just call him Tom. He'll be waiting on the logging road about two miles past the McDermott place. Remember your friend said he's got your back. Bye, Chief Moss. Do good work." With a whisper of bare feet across the office linoleum, she was gone, leaving behind a scent of patchouli.

Earlene interrupted her conversation to watch her go. "That girl's kind of strange, but she's real sweet. Makes you feel good just to be around her. Darn, I forgot to ask for some more healing salve for my mom's back. She's got arthritis real bad in L-three and four. That's from bending over so much picking and planting when she was young, you know."

Moss couldn't tell if Earlene were talking to the person on the phone or just talking. It was nearly five and getting dark already. "I got to go," he told Earlene as he went out.

"So you going to meet that plane she told you about?"

"Yeah, got to meet the plane at the airport in Macon in

case anyone asks. That's what you'll tell them, okay?"

Earlene gave a wink-wink as if to say they were in this together.

He went exactly two miles past McDermott's place and there it was on his left, just as Kedzia said it would be—the logging road cutting into a thick stand of trees. He could barely make it out as it wound across the sandy soil of the Piedmont Plains, keeping the car moving so as not to get stuck. The dark shape of a man carrying a shotgun stepped out, outlined by the setting sun behind him. He was holding up one hand in a kind of greeting or signaling him to stop right there, Moss couldn't tell.

He stopped the car, preparing to get the hell out in case this was an ambush and hoping his windshield was bullet-proof. If not, this was a helluva time to find out. The man with the shotgun tapped on the window.

"Hey, evenin', Chief." It was McDermott.

They sat in the woods for three hours, watching the strip of tarmac lined with weeds and speaking in whispers. Moss was beginning to get butt fatigue when McDermott grabbed his arm and nodded toward the road.

A pair of headlights coming from town swerved off on the logging road. An SUV whipped past Moss's car which he had pulled off in a dry creek bed, and camouflaged with branches. Several more cars arrived, turning on their bright headlight as they reached the tarmac, and in a few minutes, the airstrip was lit with battery operated lanterns as well. Then from a side road through the woods, a stretch limousine crawled beside the landing strip, adding its lights to the others. It was a beautifully organized operation that only professional criminals have the expertise and the hutzpah to pull off.

Moss realized whoever it was behind this had local boots on the ground. At least two cars had come from town, and he would bet anything at least half of those participating in this operation were local boys from some berg nearby. As he and McDermott watched from their hiding place in the bushes, a small twin propeller plane came out of the night, landing expertly on the makeshift runway.

Several men rushed out, got a briefcase each, and went back to their cars. Moss counted seven briefcases total. A chauffeur in uniform carried an envelope back to the pilot, carried on a brief conversation, and wished him a safe trip in a language that sounded to Moss like a cross between Italian and Spanish. The little plane taxied down the runway and took off into the night sky, blending in with the canopy of stars. The whole thing took less than ten minutes.

The lanterns were gone, the cars were gone, the limo took off, all in that brief time. *Commandos couldn't have done it better*, Moss thought.

Beside him, McDermott put his very thoughts into a series of questions. "See what we're up against, Chief? If the government worked that good, we'd all be sitting pretty, eh? Me and the missus would be living high on the hog, wouldn't we? Isn't that so?"

"I'm afraid so, Mr. McDermott. But then, if nobody tries to do anything, we're just going to be victims. And you chose to do something. And now I'm going to do something. That's two of us who are willing to stick our necks out. Whatever's going down out here is illegal, that's for sure. And I'm going to find out what it is."

"It's on my land, that's what worries me. That's why I've kept quiet up until now. Suppose the government thinks I'm part of it? It only takes some money to change hands for them to prove it."

"And has it? Have you taken some money to look the other way?"

"Do I look like I'm rolling in the green stuff to you?

Hell, last time I saw a penny from those people is the time they gave me twenty bucks for killing one of my cows that got out there on that blasted runway."

"Only twenty? Aren't cows worth a lot more than that?"

"Hell, yeah, they are. That was what was left over after they deducted for repairs to their gosh-darned plane." McDermott wandered off in the dark, swearing to himself.

Moss was uncovering his car when he heard the shot, followed by a low moan. Keeping his head down and running in the direction McDermott had gone, Moss found the farmer face down on the sandy road. He had been shot in the back and, from the way the blood was bubbling up through the wound. McDermott would die before he could get help.

Moss phoned for an ambulance to meet him on Alabama Road and picked up McDermott in his arms. Carrying the wounded man back to his car, Moss laid him in the back seat, covering him a blanket. McDermott was still breathing when the paramedics transferred him to the ambulance, after giving him first aid.

"Probably some hunter getting an early start on the deer season. They'll shoot at anything that moves, especially out here." The driver shut the doors, leaving two attendants inside with McDermott. "Better watch yourself out here, Chief. And wear a neon-orange vest next time."

He followed the ambulance to the hospital in Macon, filled out the report, listing the cause as a hunting accident, and went home. Whoever shot McDermott had intended to kill him. But who knew they were out there? Unless they routinely had somebody covering the drug-drop.

But who were "they"?

He passed by The Glory Road Church and saw there

was a light still on in the darkened town. Rapping on the double front doors, he was greeted by the cleaning crew who were cleaning up after a pre-Kwanza celebration. Kedzia was busy with some paperwork in the kitchen when Moss came in. She looked from his bloody shirt front to his face, betraying no surprise.

"Are you the one who's hurt?"

He shook his head. "McDermott. He's alive though. Barely. The bullet just missed his heart, nicking a lung as it passed through him."

The priestess shook her head and gazed at the candles placed on the countertops around the large kitchen. "First Mr. Segal, then Mr. McDermott. Both crusaders, both brave men. I'll say a special prayer for them, a healing prayer." Her gaze traveled back to him. "And definitely one for you." Indicating the chair across from her, she said, "Sit down, Grover. You could use a cup of coffee, I think."

Moss didn't argue. He sat down with a sigh of gratitude. "I don't mind telling you that was one slick operation out there tonight."

Depositing a steaming cup in front of him, Kedzia nodded. "Money buys power." She gazed at the candles as if drawn by their soft light. "I feel responsible for telling you about the runway. Some things are better discovered on their own."

Putting down his coffee, Moss met her eyes across the table. "You had to tell me because people trusted you to carry their burden, isn't that so?"

The light from the candles reflected the sorrow in her eyes. "And then I passed it on to you."

"But it's my job, isn't it?" Moss took a sip from his cup. "That coffee sure has a different taste. Chickaree, right? My mom's from Louisiana."

"And something else to make you sleep better." Her

eyes wandered back to the candles. "You have nightmares, don't you?" It was more a statement than a question. "Nightmares about something following you. Don't worry, you will emerge victorious. The thing will be conquered."

When he left, the light was still on in the kitchen. Moss had the best night's sleep he had ever had.

He awoke the next morning to an empty house. While cooking breakfast in the kitchen, Moss turned on the TV in the kitchen and let his pancakes burn up while he watched his whole family make a pitch for the Help Bernie Segal campaign.

First, Kenya sang "He's Not Heavy, He's My Brother." Then Halee announced that she, too, was gay Next Ashlee pitched a commercial for a line of T-shirts she had made. Modeling one of them, his sister-in-law turned entrepreneur strutted across camera. In big letters, were printed the words *I'm Not Gay But If You Are, That's OK, TOO*.

"See, Bernie, you're not alone," she said, boldly facing the cameraman so he got a good close up. Also in the lineup of Moss's kin were Sheldon winning a science award, demonstrated by Piglet, drowned in one of Ashlee's T-shirts and Wilson's kindergarten class with a poetry contest. The theme was Get Well, Bernie. Wilson rhymed the words Hell and Well.

Freddy even took out an ad for his new clinic, emphasizing the clinic was LBGTQ—friendly. Overnight, subscriptions doubled, no doubt in anticipation of more juicy gossip.

The talk show became a regular in the line-up of local programs, replacing the *Tour the Library Hour*.

When Faun came down from Atlanta for Christmas, Kenya pounced on the daughter of the former police chief for an interview. They were in the middle of discussing her biomedical company she had started while still in college when Reynolds Chapman happened to glance up at the TV. He usually kept it on with sound turned down as he worked on the layout for the paper.

A beautiful girl was moving her mouth and smiling, the camera loving every minute of the close-up. At first, he thought it was an ad for something, but since he had to approve all the ads and most were homemade jobs, he realized she wasn't selling anything. Next, he realized his mouth was open. He fumbled around on his littered desk and got the remote.

Before he even heard her voice, Reynolds Chapman was in love.

☙☙☙

As Christmas approached, a mood of charity engulfed the village because that's what Julia Springs was—a village where everybody was related to at least thirty other people and their entire immune systems rejected any other blood type as if it carried the Bubonic Plague virus. Which was why Moss was so amazed they embraced Reynolds Chapman as one of their long lost relatives.

Earlene said it was because Bernie Segal had survived the attack and was home from the hospital. "They want to make out like they're politically correct, see, Chief. They're ashamed of what other folks think about them. Some of 'em, anyway."

Kenya and Halee had a different take. "It's because we put Julia Springs on the map," Kenya said, looking particularly luscious in something cranberry-colored which plunged down to there. Moss was content to sit back and admire her legs as she stood on a stepladder in glittering heels. Trimming a tree that could have easily fit in the White House.

"No, it's because we made a statement." Halee was, by contrast, in the usual jeans and sweatshirt with Coach Moss on the back in large, yellow letters.

"Just because you announced to the world you're gay isn't making a statement. It's making a confession about your sex life nobody wants to hear anyway." Sheldon was pushing thirteen and a lot of buttons, most of which had to do with people's egos.

Halee fired back. "Like your klutzy moves on the court. When the benchwarmers make it to the court, that is."

"Now that's harsh, Halee." Moss was amazed at how easily JJ had adopted the role of peace-maker to family flare-ups. "You two sound like my sisters and brothers at home, always ragging on each other." At times, there was a hint of the islands in his rich voice, only slightly there like a soft breeze rustling through the palms.

"You've got a gay sister, too? What is it, an epidemic?" Sheldon looked at JJ in alarm.

With a broad smile, JJ shook his head with a glance at Halee. "No, not me. But if I did, I wouldn't go making a big thing out of it."

"Everyone will have a chance to put their words into action because Bernie Segal is throwing a Christmas party," Kenya called down from the ladder. "Have you seen his partner's house outside Atlanta? It makes Magnolia Alley look like an outhouse."

Moss snapped to attention. "Partner? Makes Bernie Segal sound like a law firm."

"Bernie's lover, Dad," Halee added with a smirk. "You left that part out, Auntie Kenya."

"What's the problem?" Kenya climbed down the step ladder to survey the tree. "He's a nice man, sharp dresser. Kind of charming, in a white people's way. Kentucky colonel-type. Little bitty moustache. *Atlanta Magazine* did a big spread on him a couple of weeks ago. He's an interior decorator to the jet set. "Name's Trevor Etheridge Spaulding."

"I believe they did an article on Bugsy Segal, too, that had the FBI seal of approval." Moss rattled the evening paper. "Mr. Trevor Spaulding and Mr. Bernie Segal are giving an open house on December twenty-fourth at their home…blah, blah, blah. All are welcome."

"Let's go, everybody! JJ?" Halee looked around as if she were selling tickets. "It ought to be a total blast."

"Count me in, that is, if it's okay with the Chief?" They all looked at Moss, expecting him to encourage Halee's straight love life.

Instead, he played the heavy. "Sorry but I need you on duty, JJ. Christmas Eve is when everybody starts tying one on around here. They don't sober up 'til New Year's Day."

"Can I go? I want to see how gay people live. Bet their pets are gay, too." That was from Sheldon.

"They live just like everybody else lives, you little nerd." Halee fired a plastic ornament at Sheldon which he caught and threw back.

Zeb piped up. "I wanna go to the party, too. I'm nearly seven."

Kenya took over the discussion at that point. "Listen up, boy. We're going to early church service 'cause I promised them I would do 'Go tell it on the Mountain.' After that, you all are going home to wait for Santa. Grandma Moss will be here to see you don't hunt for presents."

"Oh, no! She'll ruin our whole Christmas. Like 'Don't touch that fruitcake, it's for company! And don't go peeking at presents or Santa won't leave you none'." Sheldon stuck his lower lip out. "So you're going to the gay guys' party but we're gonna be stuck here at home, waiting for Santa who isn't coming 'til you get home anyway? That sucks!"

"Sheldon, button it!" Moss's reaction was automatic but Kenya intervened, putting her arms around Sheldon.

"Yeah, that's exactly what we're going to do. And don't talk about Grandma Moss that way. You know she's been good to you." He winced as his mother planted a kiss on his cheek.

Moss shrugged. "To say nothing of disrespecting her. But I got to be on duty Christmas Eve and so has JJ. Just in case."

The young man came over and sat beside him. "Do you think there's something going down, Chief?"

Moss was aware that everyone was watching him. He hid behind the paper again. "No more than some fools having too much to drink and thinking they can make a car fly. Last year some other fool tried to shoot down Santa's reindeer only he hit his in-laws' car who were coming for Christmas."

Zeb and Wilson gasped in horror but Sheldon muttered, "Too bad he didn't shoot at the Greyhound bus Grandma Moss was riding in. He couldn't have missed!"

Moss lowered the paper. "Say what, Sheldon?"

Kenya quickly smoothed over his twist on Christmas lore. "That's okay, boys. With your papa in the saddle, the bad guys will end up sober on Christmas morning with a bad hangover after a night in jail." They didn't look convinced.

"You make my job sound like a bad Western, Kenya."

Over Sheldon's head, his wife arched her perfect brows. "Welcome to Julia Springs, Grover, honey."

That was it, he thought later. Despite five years as police chief, he still felt like an outsider. You had to be born here before they'd accept you somebody had told him. Out of town was bad enough but out of state was even worse. And somebody who had played football for Alabama was no better than a Yankee.

Julia Springs was village where the entire collective immune systems rejected strangers as if they were viruses. Which was why Moss was so amazed they embraced Reynolds Chapman as one of their long lost relatives. Good-looking with a pedigree like a Kentucky-bred race horse, the suave young man showed up at all the holiday parties, including his Uncle Bernie's which the best one in town was by far.

He got a drink at the bar and cruised the rooms full of laughing people, nodding to the ones he knew, being introduced to the ones he didn't. Since seeing her on his uncle's TV station, he hoped he would run into Faun Walker.

On Christmas Eve, wandering through the Victorian mansion, he had to admit to himself the house was breathtaking, The rooms looked like windows of a New York department store at Christmas, a bit over the top with swags of red and green velvet atop the Victorian windows and a different style of Christmas tree in every room. That was Trevor's doing, Reynolds observed. Bernie's partner was a professional interior decorator with Hollywood stars and pro ball players for clients.

Reynolds had decided to stay in town instead of going up to Louisville for Christmas after Trevor told him he was going to take Bernie to the Bahamas tomorrow for a surprise Christmas present.

"After all, somebody has to make sure the newspaper goes out and the TV station chirps away with pathetic local stories and amateurish skits that make you want to gag. Otherwise Bernie will worry the entire time we're away." Catching his reflection in an elaborate mirror on the opposite wall, Trevor smoothed his carefully-styled blonde hair. "I told him this thing about being a small town newspaper editor wouldn't work out. But you know your uncle, he wouldn't listen. They don't like Jews here in Toonerville, not to mention gays. But a gay Jew? You've got to be kidding. So I'm going to convince him to give it up and move back to Atlanta over Christmas vacation."

Considering the rooms were packed, it didn't seem to Reynolds there were too many people in town that didn't like gay Jews. He went on from room to room in the vast downstairs, drink in hand, looking for pretty blonde girls. There were some Alabama redheads whom he admired from a distance and one gorgeous brunette on the arm of her escort. She caught him admiring her and flashed a Miss Georgia smile at him. That did it.

He moved away, looking for someone who ignored him that he would have to work to get. Someone who was a challenge. Somehow he knew that girl was Faun Walker.

He found her at last, surrounded by some of the most eligible men in town, explaining DNA to them. She was hardly into small talk, he thought, joining the group surrounding her. Maybe she was trying to bore them stiff, who knew? They didn't look bored. In fact, they were hanging on her every word as if waiting for the punchline of a good joke. She saw him, lurking on the outskirts of her admirers and immediately challenged with a look.

"Don't tell me you are interested in genetics, too?"

"Sorry, I bombed my high school science project." Reynolds eased his way into the circle. "That ended my scientific career, I'm afraid."

The young men turned to look at the newcomer who had attracted her interest. "Really? What was it on, your project?"

"Different kinds of mice. They all got loose—all a hundred of them as the judges were going around giving out prizes. A lot of the girls climbed on the tables and made them tip over, throwing the projects on the floor. Somebody had snakes. The snakes went after the mice. It wasn't pretty."

"At least it wasn't boring with all the nerds explaining dandruff or what makes zits." A tall good-looking man in a navy blazer and khakis with a beeper on his belt checked the phone in his breast pocket. "That's what I did."

"Sounds like a fraternity party I was at once," commented a red-haired guy, a dead ringer for the Crown Prince's brother. "Not the dandruff and zits, but mice and snakes. Guys were finding snakes in their laundry baskets and mice in their cereal."

The guy with the beeper said, "You should have said that was your science project, to see which mice the snakes would go after first. Sort of natural selection."

The group parted for him. "Yeah, I thought of that, but the judges were all beating it to the door. It did make the evening news, though."

Faun was laughing so he took the opportunity to introduce himself. "Hi, we haven't met. I'm Reynolds Chapman, Bernie's nephew." When Faun gave him her hand, he held it longer than he should which sent a signal to the bachelors around her they'd better get their game on. "And I didn't bring any mice with me."

"I didn't either," she said, still laughing. "The thing is, I could have. There are plenty in my lab."

The guys laughed appreciatively at the inside joke. She was not only beautiful, but smart as well and single. Her eligibility as a mate wasn't lost on the men assembled at her side. They were Carter Bates, the young district attorney, and Sterling Ross who everybody knew didn't have to work, having inherited a fortune from his father, but he played at being an investment banker just the same. The man with the beeper was Doctor Morrissey's new partner who ran the clinic in town, Jason Caldwell. Faun didn't look particularly interested in any of them, so Reynolds figured the way was clear.

Just then, a jarring explosion sent a shudder through the old house and the lights went out. "What the hell was that, a bomb?" somebody asked. Fortunately, there were so many candles as well as candelabras, the guests weren't completely in the dark. Then a voice yelled, "Fire!" and in the ensuing stampede, somebody bumped into a table, knocking a candelabra on the floor. That set the drapes alight, and the Christmas swags went up like fireworks.

Reynolds grabbed Faun's hand and pulled her back from the fiery wall of flame which seconds later, crashed down across the table. "Out the back way, everybody!" He herded frightened guests ahead of him, reaching for the fire extinguisher in the kitchen at the same time as Bernie. "Go with Trevor, Uncle Bernie!" They wrestled with the extinguisher until Reynolds jerked it away from his uncle's weak grasp. "Go, I said!"

It was like swimming upstream against a torrent, but cutting through the dining room around the stampeding guests, he made it back to the twin salons, spraying until the tank ran out of foam. Through the thick smoke, a man ran past him with a backup extinguisher and another one with a tank of his back, spraying the rest of the flames. They were the volunteer firemen who had been guests at the party.

"We can't do nothing about the front porch until the tank truck get here. So you'd better get out now, buddy, before the smoke gets to you."

Reynolds didn't argue. He could already feel the acrid smoke taking its toll on his throat and lungs. As he stumbled out into the chilly night, his lungs couldn't handle the impact and if Faun hadn't grabbed his arm, he would have tumbled down the steps.

"Here, sit down on the grass. You look like you're about to pass out."

"Thanks," he said, but it came out in a croak.

"It's the least I can do since you saved me from being toast. Stay here. I'll go get Dr. Caldwell."

"No, I'm okay. Just had to get unpolluted air in my lungs." He started coughing what sounded like his lungs coming up. She was one step ahead of him. "Here, can you make to my car?"

Surprisingly strong or just because he was so weak, she pulled him to his feet, still locked into convulsive coughing. They made it to her car, a sleek sports job. She plunked him down on the passenger seat and got behind the wheel.

"This wasn't how I planned to seduce you," he said as they roared away from his uncle's house.

The girl of his dreams laughed. "Didn't you know? There's nothing more sexy than a vulnerable man."

"Could I ask if we're going to you place or mine..." He trailed off in a fit of coughing.

"Sorry to disappoint you. I'm taking you to the hospital to get checked out."

It was Christmas Eve duty and Moss was on patrol, slipping around the hushed streets when he received a call from Prescott and Johnson who were scouting Bernie Segal's Christmas do, just to make sure there was no trouble.

"Hey, Chief, I think we got trouble. A couple of trucks just pulled up with their lights off. Two or three guys sitting in the bed. Don't look like party-goers to me."

"I'll be right there."

Then another frantic call crackled from Prescott.

The 911 dispatcher pre-empted the call. "Chief, officer

down at Three-Twenty-One Dobbs. Fire and paramedics are on the way."

Moss had always thought he was ready for trouble. But trouble came in like a hurricane on that Christmas Eve, sweeping every preparation before it like a flood tide.

The choir was revving up for the finale, clapping and swinging with the rhythm of the Holy Spirit when the hooded figures burst in the sanctuary doors. In the church foyer, Bobo Franklin was sinking to the shiny heart-of-pine floor, blood spurting through his fingers which still clutched the Christmas Eve program.

"Nobody move, understand?" A woman screamed and a bullet lodged in the wall over her head. "Just get down and shut up." There was a sudden collective thud as people hit the floor. A child remained standing, looking at the intruders but a hand snatched him back down.

At the altar, Kedzia interrupted her prayers to see what the disturbance was. In her crimson and gold robes, she was transformed into a queen. She didn't even flinch when she saw the three gunmen. "You are interrupting a Christmas celebration—"

"Shut up! Get on your knees, Mama, or I'll shoot you." One thug who seemed to the leader, strode down the aisle, brandishing his automatic rifle as though it were an extension of his manhood.

But she descended the two steps from the altar and kept moving toward the masked gunman, arms outstretched. "Welcome to the celebration of our Lord's birth. We forgive you if—"

She didn't finish. The gun spat and Kedzia dropped like a dying flame to the aisle.

From the choir stall, Kenya shouted, "You bastards!"

"That's the one we want! Get her and let's get out of here."

Kenya darted from the choir loft, trying to escape to the side door, but the leader caught her by the robe and held on to her until the other two got there. Then the three of them hustled her outside.

Moss was at Dobbs Road before the fire truck got there but he could see the worst had already happened. Flames were spilling out of the wrap-around porch of the huge mansion, and people in party dress were streaming over the lawn, racing for cover, while gunfire was coming from somewhere in the dark woods surrounding the house. A group of protesters had dropped their placards and banners and were heading back to the parking lot.

Using his SUV for cover, Moss rolled out into the dark and, skirting the manicured lawn through a forest of azalea bushes, ran at a crouch toward the spot where the shots were coming from. Seeing a flash of gunmetal through the azalea forest, he fired and someone yelled, "I'm hit!" He went on toward the spot and through the azalea branches, caught a glimpse of a hooded figure wearing night vision glasses, dragging a wounded person by the arms.

He should have just dropped the bastard then and there, but police protocol forced him to call out "Police! Drop the weapon and freeze!" That was a mistake because what followed was a round of fire he hadn't experienced since Afghanistan. Moss flung himself on the ground as bullets whizzed over his head. Then somebody returned fire in back of him and the thugs retreated, caught off guard.

Moss heard someone crawling through the bushes behind him. He didn't dare even raise his head to look, but relief spread over like a soothing balm. Whoever it was on his side.

"Chief, you okay?" It was JJ.

"Yeah, thanks to you." They listened as a truck started

up somewhere deep in the woods. "Who the hell are those bastards?" They rose cautiously to their knees, then to their feet. "Where's Pres?"

"On the other side of the house. I took this side." It didn't register at the time, but rehashing over and over the events of the night, Moss realized JJ was wearing night vision glasses, not standard equipment for a patrol office. Neither was the telescopic sight that JJ had tucked in his pocket when he thought Moss wasn't looking. Nor was the high-powered rifle in his hands not the standard issue.

The fire truck had arrived with EMTs who were tending to the guests. Moss kept looking for Halee who he knew was there when he ran into Sheldon who was supposed to be in church. From the look on the boy's face, he knew at once without hearing a confession, that Sheldon had something to do with the melee.

"Well, come on. Out with it. What're you doing here when you were told you couldn't come?"

"I can tell you that, Chief." It was Prescott, fresh from being a hero.

"Let me hear it from the boy first, Pres." Moss waited while Sheldon wiped away tears.

"See, Halee said come on with her so I figured I'd get back before you and Mom—"

"So what'd you do? Obey Halee instead of you parents?"

"I only wanted to come see—" There Sheldon broke down and sobbed, head in hands. "And when we got here she said don't come in with her, she didn't want to be seen with a dork so to get her back and put those gay-haters down, I—I—"

"Go on, what'd you do?"

"I tossed a firecracker—a cherry bomb in the back of their truck. And there was this big explosion and the truck disappeared and caught the one next to it on fire and the banners and all...”

"And the trees and part of the burning stuff caught the porch on fire," finished Prescott, thumbs in his belt. "That's arson, Chief."

"No," Moss replied. "That's just dumb-ass shit."

Their radios squawked. It was the 911 dispatcher. "Hostage situation over at Glory Road Church. Shooting. Two wounded. Possibly three. All units alerted."

Moss did a rapid triage. "JJ, get over there. No siren. Just red light on to clear the way."

He looked around for the young deputy. "I'm on my way now, Chief!" came over the police radio.

Deputies Owens, Lee, and what seemed like everybody with a gun which was everybody in Julia Springs, showed up. "Does anybody know an access road that leads into those woods?"

A couple of locals chorused, "There's an old logging road into those woods. You can reach it by Highway One-Seventy-One."

"Good! Cal, go and block any vehicle that exits the logging road. Be on the lookout for a pickup truck with a bunch of guys in it. One of them is wounded, so alert the hospitals. But be careful. Those guys are armed and dangerous."

The deputy ran back to his squad car followed by ten vigilantes who tore after him in a posse of trucks.

At the church, all was strangely quiet. No joyous hymns, no organ music, it was as if there was no one inside even though cars overflowed the parking lot on to the grass. As he pulled up in the turnaround behind the kitchen, Freddy thought that was strange. "Looks like Halloween," he commented to his date and fellow medical student Lelanie. "I'll meet you round in front, okay?"

Her perfect smile flashed in the dark. "Now, you not

going to take off 'cause somebody's calling you for an order of hot wings, are you?"

He was planting a kiss on her turned-up nose when some men came out a door. Kenya was between them, wearing a blindfold, arms behind her back. Freddy suddenly pushed Lelanie down on the seat, crushing the hot wings beneath him. She giggled. "You crazy? Not on Christmas Eve!" She laughed. "And not in front of the church."

He whispered in her ear, "Be quiet! Something's going down."

Something was going down, that was certain He had turned his lights off when he entered the driveway so as not to disturb the service going on inside, Freddy thanked God for that. Raising his head just over the dashboard, he saw the side door of the church open and four people come out.

One of those people was his cousin Kenya and the man beside her wearing a black ski mask held a gun to her head. They were followed to two more masked men holding automatic rifles, looking this way and that.

A car waiting in the parking lot moved forward to pick them up. No license plate or it was covered up. But as it passed under the lighted church windows, Freddy got a better look. Ford Fusion SUV. Somebody in the passenger seat exchanged fire with Deputy Owens whose truck was just pulling up.

In seconds, the SUV burned rubber, careened around the corner and was gone.

Sirens blaring, Deputy Owens and Lee followed in pursuit.

Sitting up, Freddy was on the phone to Moss. "They've got Kenya. At gun point. New Ford Fusion. No plates. I'm going after them."

The answer came back, calm and cool. "No, don't get

in the way. Get in the church and see what you can do. Somebody's hurt bad."

"Ten-four."

Moss took a shortcut, figuring the kidnappers were heading for the state highway when he got a message from Owens. "We've got a visual on the suspects' truck, no license plate, three men, and one woman. Headed out West Peterson Street—"

The highway patrol broke in. "This is the Georgia State Highway Patrol. We're coming east down West Peterson to head off the vehicle in question. We'll inform you when we've got a visual."

Lee was back again. "Whoa! We just lost them, Chief. They went around that dead man's curve on Peterson and just disappeared in thin air. Wait a second. Owens says there's a logging road in there somewhere. They probably took that. We're in pursuit."

Moss heard Owens shout "Hold on!" There was a horrendous crash. Glass cascading, then an awful silence. Then someone moaned. "Damn. Oh, goddam."

"Cal? Steve? What's going on?"

There was a groan then "We hit something." It was Steve Owens. "I don't know, a tree or something. Cal, you okay? Cal! Call an ambulance. Cal's hurt."

Cal was still in the overturned truck, hanging by his seatbelt. At the same time Moss was pulling up behind his injured deputies, the Ford SUV was driving up the ramp onto a semi-tractor trailer parked further along the logging road. Two men closed the tailgate after the SUV had been driven all the way inside and then jumped in the front seat of the truck.

Simultaneously, the highway patrol was following the same model Ford without a visible license plate heading out East Peterson Road. When they turned on their siren, the SUV kept going albeit at the same fifty-five miles per hour until they pulled it over. The exasperated troopers were met by a bespectacled senior citizen driving her even more senior mother to a church Christmas party. She turned out to be deaf as a fence post which is why she hadn't stopped. She hadn't heard the siren, she said. By that time, the semi with Kenya in it was well on its way south.

The first thing he saw when Freddy burst through the door of the Glory Road Church was blood on the floor of entrance. Bobo Franklin was sitting in a chair, his fine Sunday suit covered in blood. J.B. White, the undertaker was tending his wounds while his cronies looked on.

"Got our order of hot wings, young Fred?" Franklin managed a weak grin. "I could use some about now. With two fingers of Jimmy Beam to wash them down. Matter of fact, we all could."

"Amen to that, brother," was echoed all around him.

Freddy found Lelanie kneeling over Kedzia who lay in the aisle of the Glory Road Church surrounded by a pool of blood. The rest of the congregation stood back, humming, praying, and swaying, their faces wet with tears. "Two gunshot wounds to the abdomen. Blood pressure's dropping. She's lost a lot of blood. She'll go into shock if the EMTs don't get a drip in her pretty soon." Lelanie kept rubbing the wounded woman's hands as if she were frostbitten. "Damn guns anyway."

Freddy knelt beside her. "Kedzia, it's Freddy Jones. Can you hear me?"

The priestess opened her eyes and smiled weakly. "Yeah, Fred. Your grandmother can, too. She says this is what you were made for. Healing wounds."

"Hush, don't talk now," he said though his voice shook. "You're going to need all your strength. Just hold my hand and stay with us. We need you. The whole town needs you."

Kedzia closed her eyes, still smiling. "Oh, you have the gift. I can feel it." Her grip grew stronger. She opened her eyes. 'Ouch! That hurts!'" This time she grimaced.

"Blood pressure's coming up." Lelanie had her stethoscope to Karzai's chest, fingers on her wrist. "Pulse steadier, heartbeat stronger." She looked up at Freddy who bandaging Kedzia wounds. "What are you doing? She's coming back!"

"He's got the gift." Kedzia closed her eyes, this time in prayer. "Thank you, Lord. For life and for this healer."

The paramedics arrived and took both the wounded to the hospital. Freddy rode in the ambulance and held Kedzia's hand all the way until they took her into surgery.

Moss went through the motions of following police procedures like a man slowly freezing to death in a blizzard. The GBI arrived promptly on the scene and started taking statements from the church members. The whole time Freddy kept him informed of Kedzia's and Bobo's emergency surgeries and Cal's condition, the same thought kept passing through his mind again and again like a computer loop.

It's my fault. All this is my fault. The bastards have my heart. They have my heart, the bastards have Kenya.

Finally, at three in the morning, he stood outside the police station looking up at the same stars that looked down on his wife, wherever she was. It was a clear, beautiful night and he actually prayed to someone up there to make her safe. He hadn't prayed in a long time, since he first got shipped out to Afghanistan when he was eighteen. He was scared then, but not like he was scared now. He didn't care if his heart stopped beating but it just went on relentlessly thumping in captivity.

"Dad?" It was Halee emerging from the dark, her holiday clothes covered in soot. JJ was with her. Her arms went around him, but he couldn't feel anything and absently patted them.

JJ stood there, looking helpless. "Go get some rest, Chief. I'll take the night shift. Promise I'll wake you up if there's any new development."

Halee whispered, "Come on home now. The kids are asleep even that little shit Sheldon finally conked out waiting for you to come home. Ashlee is watching them, wide awake. Anxious to know where her sister is."

Moss suddenly clasped his daughter in his arms and they rocked back and forth in a grieving dance. "I wish I knew, baby. I only wish I knew."

He woke up in their king-sized bed, thinking he had to play Santa Claus. He reached for the lush body of his wife beside him and the whole ghastly nightmare of Christmas Eve came crashing in on Moss. He cannonballed downstairs still in his shorts and tee-shirt to a room full of people in the living room. About a half dozen phones snapped a picture of his face before he fled back upstairs. Sheldon and Halee were right behind him. Slamming the door in their faces, Moss locked it behind him.

Sheldon got there first. "Where's my mama?" he shouted hammering on the door. "Where is she, you lousy cop?"

Jerking the door open, Moss thundered down on the boy with a face like an Asian demon. "If you hadn't done something as stupid-ass as blowing up a truck, damn you, I might have been there to stop the bastards that took her. Now, all because of you, I've lost her!"

"Dad, that's not fair. He's only a kid. Kids do stupid things." Halee tried to comfort Sheldon who pulled away and ran down the hall. "Now get dressed and come downstairs. We've got visitors."

"Not now, Halee. I don't want to see anybody now. I

want to touch bases with the station to hear the latest, okay? Tell them to go away or give them some eggnog. Kenya—" He stopped there.

"I know, but it's Toya, Mom's little sister. She's come with a truckload of presents and she wants to take Zebby back to Atlanta. Says she's got a court order. And JJ didn't call so there's no news yet."

Zebulon still in his Christmas pajamas was playing in the black and white foyer when Moss came down stairs again. This time he was dressed, phone glued to his ear. "Watch, Pawpaw!" Moss slowed and watched while Zeb zoomed a remotely-operated dump truck around the foyer, much to the frustrated glee of his son, Wilson who kept chasing it. "Cool, huh? Auntie Toya brought it to me. Where's Big Mama? She better come see this, too."

"Cool it, Zeb. Big Mama's not here just yet. She's coming, though. Real soon."

Toya was clean, she said, after waiting for the period the judge assigned her, she got a job at an upscale Atlanta hairdressing salon as a manicurist, her own apartment, and a car.

"Your pimp set you up then?" Sitting on the stairs, Moss sipped the coffee Ashlee brought him, her large eyes sliding back and forth from Moss to her older sister, urging him to be cautious.

Toya's back went straighter like a cat on the defensive. "I'm not turning tricks anymore, if that's what you mean. I want my son back, and I've got the court order right here."

He fended her off with a bluff. "We'll see about that when Kenya gets here."

"Well, she's not here, and she won't be coming, will she." It was not a question, but a statement of fact. It hung in the air between them like an insult, too heavy to be dispersed. It sank in slowly as Moss processed it. Then with a lightning flash, realization burst through the fog like a spotlight. How did she know that?

He looked at Ashlee. "When did you tell her?"

Ashlee shrugged. "I haven't told her anything yet. She must have heard it on the way down."

"They never release the names of kidnap victims. You knew before that, didn't you, Toya? Because your boyfriend told you, didn't he?" He took a menacing step toward, his face like a storm cloud. "Didn't he? Name's Cory Williams, right? Last I heard he was in jail for assault and armed robbery. So this was planned way before, wasn't it? He told you way before you're going to get Zeb back, ain't that right? How much did you get for fingering your own sister, huh?"

"You're a liar!" But to his surprise, she crumbled into a sobbing heap. Zeb ran to her, holding her head trying to kiss her face. "Don't cry, Auntie Toya. Zeb will kiss it and make it all better."

Toya clutched her son to her thin chest. "That bitch isn't satisfied with raising one kid that isn't her own. She has to take mine, too."

"So you planned to get him back by getting your own sister kidnapped and maybe killed?"

A voice came from the landing above his head. "Cayman's Key. That's where he lives." It was Sheldon, looking through the banisters. "I can show you the map, if you want."

Ashlee went to the staircase where her nephew was sitting. "Who, little man? Where who lives?"

"Aunt Toy's boyfriend pimp. At least, his phone comes from there. Chief says he's still in jail, though."

Ashlee rolled her eyes. "Shelfish, you hacked into his cell phone plan? Sometimes you scare me, little dude."

"It's my mom we're talking about here and Chief thinks it's my fault she was kidnapped." To hide his tears, he said, "Here, I'll print out the map for you." He ran back up the stairs and disappeared.

Moss said, "Tell me who this guy Corey Williams works for, and I swear I'll do the best for you I can. Don't tell me and I will bring all hell down on you and him, too."

He actually found a soft edge of pity as Toya raised her face to his. He even saw a little of Kenya in her amber eyes. "Moss, believe me when I say I don't know his name. Some Brazilian guy…Wahoo or Waha, something like that."

Sheldon was back. "It's Arauja. He owns the island off the coast of Georgia called Cayman's Key, but he lives on his yacht because he's wanted in about half the countries in South America."

Moss was growing impatient. "Let me guess. For sex trafficking and drug-running, not to mention murder."

"And gambling. He owns a whole bunch of casinos, all on islands off the coasts of every country where they can't get him for tax evasion."

"Where did you learn that? Don't tell me online."

Sheldon shrugged. "You have to know where to look, that's all."

Saying no more, Moss walked past Toya and Zeb sitting on the floor. Passing by Ashlee with the cellphone glued to one ear, he said, "Hold the fort, Ash. I'm bringing your sister back." Behind him, little Wilson burst into tears. "And your mama, my main man."

CHAPTER 6

Heading out of town to the interstate, Moss was getting directions from JJ at the station, who was reading an online map, when a reedy voice from the backseat said, "No, that's totally wrong. He's trying to throw you off the track, big time."

Moss hit the brakes and swerved off on the shoulder. "Sheldon, what in the flaming hell are you doing back there?"

The answer was surprisingly weak for Sheldon. "Going with you? You'll never get there if you listen to him."

Telling JJ he'd call him back, Moss said, "This had better be good. Come up here."

Sheldon climbed over the passenger seat and slid down, looking humble for once. "And he's not who he says he is."

"Who isn't?"

"JJ isn't. That's not his real name."

Moss got back on the road to 75 which would lead to the coastal interstate. "Son, you got computeritis playing those video games. And it's gone to your brain."

"Got to keep up my skills." Sheldon instantly regretted the remark. It was like tossing the firecracker into the back of the pickup.

"It don't pay to be so cocky. Skills like that will land you time in Juvie for hacking into sealed records. You know who you'll meet in Juvie, don't you?"

Pinned under Moss's fierce gaze, Sheldon could only shake his head mutely.

"A lot of guys just trying to keep up their skills. Robbing folks, shooting and stealing from folks, that's who." Moss looked over and caught the frightened-out-of-his-wits look on Sheldon's face. "So what and where is this Cayman Key or whatever?"

When he could talk around the lump in his throat, Sheldon said, 'It's a private island that belongs to a Brazilian man called something like Fernando Arauja. It's somewhere off the coast not too far from Savannah. Probably have to take a boat there."

"Great. So you got a plan, I suppose."

Sheldon sat up and got out his tablet. "I got the map. And Arauja's yacht is registered in Liberia."

"Wherever that is."

"Dad." A sleepy voice from the shotgun seat sighed as though talking was a pain. "It's a country in Africa. And they're MMA fighters. The bodyguards, I mean."

"Okay, I get it. Like Bruce Lee stuff, right? So what's your plan, man?"

"You're the cop." Sheldon yawned and snuggled down in the seat. "That's your job. I'm just the tech guy."

"Oh, no, you can't expect not to have a real job, man. Even the radio operator in the Army is armed for combat."

Sheldon smothered a yawn. "This isn't the army, but I've got a plan anyway." His voice was getting slower. He hadn't slept the night before and the hum of the car was getting to him.

Moss's phone blurted. Checking it, he saw JJ's number and sent it to voicemail.

"Go on, what's your plan, man?"

Silence. The tech guy had fallen asleep at his post.

They hit Savannah about noon and checked in at a chain motel. Moss paid cash for the room and ordered pizza from a chain restaurant. With a large coke and two slices of gooey cheese pizza, Sheldon was revived. Sitting cross-legged on the king-sized bed, he put on his ear buds and listened to music while he hunched over his laptop.

Moss nursed a beer and ate the breadsticks that came with the large pizza, but he wasn't really hungry. On his personal cellphone, he had checked in with the hospital where the paramedics had taken Kedzia. Bobo had been released after he was treated for a shoulder wound. They would only tell Moss that after being stabilized, the priestess had been flown to Atlanta by helicopter to a bigger hospital. After that, he checked in with Ashlee.

"Moss, where are you? I've been on the phone all morning, fielding calls from the whole world. Your mom's here, and Isis and Faun. They're helping with the kids. And Sheldon's disappeared completely. Tell me he's with you."

"He's right here. Sheldon, it's your Auntie Ashlee."

Looking up briefly, Sheldon replied, "Tell her I said 'hi,'" and went back to his tablet.

"He says 'hi.'"

Ashlee hissed, "Wait 'til I get hold of that little shit!"

"You'll have to take a ticket and stand in line. The line forms behind Bernie Segal, Trevor Whatshisface, and everybody else at the party last night."

A weary sigh told him Ashlee hadn't had any sleep either. "And JJ. He's called every hour on the hour since eight this morning. Grover, where are you?"

"Believe me, Ash, you don't want to know. That way, you can't tell anybody, get me?"

"I get you. Thanks for letting me know you're okay. And Sheldon's with you. When you get back, tell him to expect a major butt-whupping."

"Check with you later. Hang in there. I'll bring your sister back with me."

After he got off the phone, he saw the tech guy had one earbud dangling, which meant Sheldon had been listening to his conversation all along. "She's mad, isn't she?"

"You would be, too if your sister had been kidnapped, you were left with my mother and two babies and your nephew had disappeared on you. That's bad enough, but the phone has been on meltdown all morning."

Sheldon hung his head. "It's all my fault, isn't it? People are saying I'm no good, aren't they?"

"Hey, man, you didn't kidnap your mom or shoot up the church, did you?"

Sheldon put on puppy dog eyes. "No, but I did blow up a truck and burn down Mr. Segal's house. That's about forty years in prison, isn't it?"

"Hey, listen up." Moss sat up and put his beer on the bedside table. "Nobody knows where that firecracker came from except Sergeant Prescott of the Yukon, and he's not going to say anything. Besides those guys were threatening Bernie by burning crosses on his lawn. That's a hate crime, and what were they doing with a truck full of explosives, anyway? That's a weapon in itself, man, you know what I mean? So don't beat yourself up about it, hear?"

"I didn't do it on purpose." Sheldon hid brimming eyes, pretending to read something on his laptop screen. He wiped his nose with the bottom of his Tee shirt. "You know something? I'm glad you're my dad now. I wasn't very nice to you when I was younger, was I?"

"That's kind of an understatement. You were a mean

little shit, but that's okay. I handled it. Now, you got a plan yet, tech man?"

"That was what I was working on. It hasn't got all the monkeys ironed out yet, but I'm going to print it out for you anyway."

"You can do that without a printer?"

Sheldon got a weary look on his face as if he were dealing with Wilson. "It has a built-in printer, Dad."

Moss found himself looking at an aerial map of Cayman's Key. It sort of resembled Afghanistan surround by water. *All that water*, he thought. *At least, you could walk on sand in Afghanistan. Slowly. But water. Only Jesus had the nerve to try that.* "Okay, I suppose we'll just pose as tourists who got their islands mixed up."

"Oh, great. That's called trespassing, isn't it? I can see the headlines now. 'Local Police Chief Caught on Zillionaire's Private Island.' That would just make old man Clark's day. I mean Mr. Clark."

"Hey, little man. Who cares about what old man Clark thinks? We're talking about getting your mom back. That's worth the risk." That said, he waited a few beats before asking, "So have you got a better plan?"

Rolling his eyes as if that were a rhetorical question, Sheldon shrugged modestly. "Glad you asked. Okay, you can relax about the trespassing charge. Cayman's Cay has a casino on it. Open to the public. We pose as tourists, check out the place first. See if they took Mom there. Maybe play the slot machines."

"Reconnaissance, you mean."

Again, the boy genius got his patient face on. "Dad, you got to get over the PTSD thing. This is not a military operation in Afghanistan. We don't go in there like we're going to rob the place, like with guns blazing. Be subtle."

They rented a Vespa to get down to the docks where the tours left. "This ride is subtle enough for you, son?

Nobody would be suspecting a police chief to be riding one of these jobs." Moss put on his helmet and got astride the scooter.

Sheldon just stood there shaking his head. "Lame," he said. "Very lame."

They got down to the docks only to learn the ten o'clock tour had just left and there wouldn't be another one until two in the afternoon. The man in the ticket window told them, "There's a guy down the river that takes private tours over to Cayman's Key. Maybe you can go with them. Name's Al. Better call him Captain Al or he won't take you." Moss got directions and went back to Sheldon waiting beside the scooter.

"Hey, Dad, can I drive now? I know how to drive. Freddy lets me drive his pickup. Besides Mom said it was okay, you being the police chief and all. After all, I'm going to be fifteen in January and I'm tall for my age."

Moss folded his arms. "Your point is?"

"I just mean you didn't have to rent the scooter, okay? It looks…well, it looks funny with you driving. These things are for kids like me. Poor kids who can't afford cars."

"I don't care how it looks, man. Like I said, it's on my credit card. Now get with the program. You can fake poor because I know I can and I wouldn't be faking."

Deciding which battles to pick and which ones to run like hell from was part of parenting, Moss figured. He was losing this one, having been undermined by forces on the home front. He let it go for now. When he got Kenya back, he would remind her how Sheldon drove her new caddy convertible into a peach tree at age seven. *You didn't talk down to this one, though*, Moss told his parental self. It would come back to bite you in the butt every time. "Anyway, we do that tonight when it gets dark, okay?"

"Okay, you're the boss." The moment the words were out of his mouth, Sheldon wanted to take them back.

After getting a burger and a shake, they cruised the boulevard down to the riverfront on the rented Vespa. Riding on the postilion seat, Sheldon grew uncharacteristically silent at the sight of deep sea fishing boats, sleek launches, and elegant sailboats riding anchor in their slips. His mother might be on any one of them, gagged and bound ready to be transported to a foreign shore. They left the Vespa in the parking lot and stopped beside it to survey what they were up against.

"So this is where the rich people play."

Even Moss who had battled many enemies was intimidated by the one he couldn't win against. That enemy was money. It could buy verdicts, pardons, commuted sentences, and even twist political outcomes—all of which cost poor peons like himself years of work, sometimes even their lives. He felt like that Spanish guy, the old knight that tilted at windmills with his ridiculous sidekick playing backup as he surveyed the sleek yachts and motor launches riding the river waves.

But they had his wife in that multi-million dollar net and that was motivation enough to take it by storm or by stealth to Moss. Moss was rooted to the pier, utterly transfixed with rage—it was as if a frozen fire suffused his entire body, freezing his feet where he stood. His eyes bulged with it, his fists longed to smash into those eyeless faces so badly his nails dug into his palms. Those bastards had taken his whole motivation for living away.

When Sheldon remained silent, he said again, "So that's where Arauja parks his boat?"

He knew by the sound of Sheldon's "Dad" that he had made an error. "You don't park a boat, you moor it, and a marina doesn't berth ocean-going yachts like Arauja's got. His yacht is moored somewhere offshore where it's deeper. But I would guess the crew will probably come ashore in a dinghy to drink and have fun."

Moss looked at Sheldon with new respect. "How do you know so much about yachts and dinghies and stuff?"

"When school was out, Mama did a lot of shows on cruises. I grew up playing hide and seek all over the ship with the crew. The captain even let me steer the cruise ship a couple of times."

"Bet the passengers were thrilled by that."

At the mention of Kenya, Sheldon grew suddenly quiet and they absorbed the sound of the ocean breathing for a long couple of minutes while he recovered his cool. "I sure do miss her."

Moss clasped Sheldon's thin shoulders. "You and me both, son. You and me both."

Walking along the dock, Sheldon snapped pictures of the boats bobbing at their moorings to send to Ashlee. Meanwhile Moss was surveying the sleek sailboats and motor launches, looking for someone to ask about Captain Al or just anybody who would take him out to Arauja's island. Finding no one, he went back to Sheldon who was still fooling with his cellphone.

Moss attempted to put a fatherly arm around the boy's shoulders but Sheldon shrugged him off. "I got to upload these pictures to my computer and send them to the FBI."

"Send some to my phone so I can send them to Earlene. She's got contacts with everybody, even the White House. Only just don't send the one's where you've got your finger in the way. Earlene will think it's the ghost of her dead father come back to haunt her because she put plastic flowers on his grave or whatever." Moss allowed himself a laugh but Sheldon ignored his attempt to be funny.

Continuing along the pier, Moss grew impatient. There were a few signs for tours but all the berths were empty, the boats having left. Leaving Sheldon eagerly framing shots with his camera of a manatee swimming behind a shrimper, hoping for a bite, Moss saw some men at the end of the dock unloaded boxes off a deep-sea fishing boat. He walked down to ask them about the private tour run by Captain Al.

"Captain Al?"

One grizzled fisherman looked him up and down suspiciously. "Who's asking?"

Moss shifted his weight to both feet. "I am. I take it you're not Captain Al. Could you please tell him I want to talk to him about taking me out to Cayman's Key, sir?" One of the crew left the group on the pier and ran across the gangplank onto the boat. He came running back while Moss did a stare-down with a ring of suspicious eyes. Only the young crewman had a welcoming grin.

"Cap'n said to tell you he would take you out there. But you have to come aboard to talk to him. He cooking lunch. Lunch is included in the price."

Moss could have kicked himself later for not recognizing a set-up. But he was so possessed with anger, so full of thoughts of revenge on those who had done such damage to his very soul, he wasn't thinking clearly.

He climbed aboard the boat, followed one by one by the crew.

The captain of the shrimper waved him on board with a huge smile on his bearded face, gabbling in some foreign language that might have been Spanish. Moss took two steps on deck before the crew surrounded him, talking in the same foreign tongue. They were all short and muscular so he figured he could take them on with ease until somebody hit him in the head from behind.

The blow didn't quite knock him out and the men laughed when he sprawled across the planks. He grabbed the ankles of the man closest to him and yanked his feet out from under him. Driving his legs out like pistons, he managed to knock two more down and was almost on his feet when somebody choked him with a rope from behind. Moss tried to fight his assailant off but lost the battle. Everything went black, and he fell to the deck. His last thought was the wooden planks smelled like fish.

"Dad?" Trailing behind Moss as he went down the pier, Sheldon got the whole thing on camera—the smiling fisherman welcoming Moss aboard then proceeding knock him out while the rest jumped on him. Then young one shouted and pointed at him. Sheldon didn't need a translation to know what that meant. It meant "get the kid" in any language.

He turned tail and ran like an Olympian in the time trials. The young thug following was gaining on him as he headed out of the marina into the busy street nearby. Dodging blaring horns, he ran across to the boulevard in the middle where there were police patrolling on bicycles. The young thug stopped and shouted something, making an international gesture of drawing one finger across his throat. Sheldon snapped his picture just as a car passed in front of him. Nevertheless, he got the guy's picture from behind. He was wearing a bandana tied around his head that had something printed on it.

During the long walk back to the motel, Sheldon tried to zoom in on the shot of the young fisherman who had chased him out of the marina. But his battery was low and he had to recharge it. Arriving at the motel, he asked for an extra key at the desk, making up a lie that his father had an accident water-skiing and was in the ER. He thought the desk clerk would be sympathetic. Instead she just handed him the key saying, "Don't leave the key in the room next time, kid."

He opened the door to the room and gasped. It had been ransacked. His laptop was lying on the floor smashed to bits. Even the mattresses had been over-turned. Moss's suitcase and his backpack were lying on the floor, emptied of their contents. He grabbed both the suitcase and the backpack and ran out in the hall. A man with grey hair wearing baggy, khaki shorts was passing by and Sheldon shrank back inside the room, opening the door a crack to see what the man would do.

The man pushed the elevator button, saw Sheldon peeking through the door, and said, "Want me to hold the door, son?"

Having seen enough movies where the elevator door opened, revealing some poor guy with a knife stuck in his back, lying on the elevator floor, Sheldon slammed the door shut and waited until the elevator door closed. Then he took the stairs, dragging the suitcase and ending up in the lobby at the same time the elevator emptied its pas-sengers.

The man in the baggy shorts saw him and grinned. "Let me carry that suitcase and I promise not to run off with it. My kids have enough Lego blocks and I keep stepping on the damned things."

At Moss's SUV, the man deposited the suitcase, said "Have a good one," and went to his own truck, putting his suitcase in the back.

Sheldon waited until the truck pulled out of the park-ing lot and fumbled in the ripped lining of Moss's suit-case for the extra money and set of keys that Moss al-ways hid in case of emergencies. This had to be the mother of all emergencies.

Breathing a sigh of relief when he felt a bump beneath one of Moss's sneakers the robbers had missed, Sheldon located the keys, an old watch with a compass, and a hundred dollars wrapped in a pair of dirty shorts.

He threw his knapsack in with it and got behind the wheel. The first thing he had to do was move the car because that was a sure clue as to where they were. Sheldon started the engine and put it in reverse.

The car shot across the parking lot just inches away from a truck bumper before he remembered to take his foot off the accelerator and put it into drive. He sat there at the entrance to the parking lot waiting for his heart stopped beating a reggae tune and slowed down to normal.

Then turning on his turning signal, he drove into the traffic, keeping his speed down to twenty miles per hour, creating a line of cars behind him two blocks long with furious drivers. He cruised along the boulevard as drivers sped by him shaking their fists and giving him the middle finger. Seeing a supermarket parking lot, Sheldon did a left turn that left the driver behind him standing on his brakes, parked and, making sure there was no one waiting for him with a baseball bat, got out with shaking knees. Satisfied he hadn't been followed, he went into the supermarket and got a sandwich and a slushy drink. Back in the car, Sheldon ate the sandwich and fell asleep while the slushy melted in the cup holder and a neon sign advertising car insurance flashed in his face.

First thing he did in the morning, after peeing in an alley next to the supermarket, was call his Aunt Ashlee. She sounded as if she'd been awake for two days, living on black coffee. When she heard his voice, she screamed. "Sheldon! Where the hell are you?"

"I can't tell you that. I only called to say I got everything under control, except—" It suddenly hit him that he was all alone in a strange place. Sheldon took a deep breath and his voice squeaked up several octaves. "Dad's missing." He gulped back the unbidden tears. He had to hold himself together yet he still couldn't trust his voice to cooperate in this conspiracy. Gradually, it skidded up the scale and into the stratosphere.

Ashlee didn't help by screaming, "Say what? Did you call the police? Whoever kidnapped Kenya has kidnapped him, too."

"I know that. Just wanted you and everybody to know I'm okay."

"Sheldonnnn!" was the last thing he heard before he hung up. His phone rang and rang but he turned it off, fighting tears. His last link to home was gone. He put his head against the steering wheel which smelled like Moss and bawled.

Deciding that Moss's SUV was definitely on the bad guys' radar, Sheldon took his backpack and walked to a bike shop where he rented a bicycle. It was about two miles back to the marina where Moss had disappeared, but as he threaded through the traffic, Sheldon was planning how he would get to Arauja's island, Cayman's Key. It was past ten o'clock and the first cruise had left the dock by the time he got there. He looked on his phone which he had recharged in the car and struck pay dirt.

There was a ferry leaving for the islands at eleven fifteen, Cayman's Key being one of the stops. He had to be on that boat. Beyond that, he didn't have a clue what he was going to do. He parked the bike in the weeds around the marina, making sure to put on the lock. Stuffing the watch and money in his baggy shorts, he slipped the lock through the straps of the backpack. If anybody wanted to steal his dirty laundry, they were welcome to it.

He bought a hot dog and sods at the little kiosk on the dock and sat on a bench to eat. As he waited for the ferry to arrive, a stretch limousine oozed through the entrance and parked across half a dozen parking spaces. It disgorged two crewman carrying stacks of takeaway boxes which they carried to a sleek sea-going launch. Then what looked like two MMA fighters followed by a short, fat man. Next came a woman who looked like a spin-off of Miss World, followed by a black-veiled woman wearing red heels. It was Kenya. Sheldon knew his mother's shoes anywhere. They were the ones she wore to church on Christmas Eve, to make all the women in the congregation jealous, she said with her wicked laugh. He had to put his hand over his mouth to silence the inadvertent yell rising to his throat. *Mama! Look over here, Mama!*

But she looked stiff-backed like she had slept wrong or something, he thought. Kenya was accompanied by a woman dressed in black Spandex exercise clothes who looked as if she were holding a gun under a big shawl. Quickly Sheldon got out his cell phone and snapped a picture of the whole parade getting in the launch.

Then he heard a shout. "That's him! The negrito!"

The whole entourage quick-stepped on to the launch, leaving the two MMA fighters behind on the dock. They grinned and nodded when the young thug with the do rag shouted something in a foreign language which Sheldon took to mean "Relax, dude! We're going to beat the shit out of the kid who just took your picture!" He was followed by two more of the thugs who had jumped Moss. Sheldon took off but seeing they had the element of surprise on him, hid behind the limo still parked in the parking lot. The door to the back seat was open and the chauffeur was walking a tiny white dog, smoking as he did so. The crew of the bogus fishing boat slowed down when they saw him, hesitating to converse in a huddle. Sheldon took advantage of their distraction and, assuming the limo was empty, was about to climb through the back and out the other side, when he saw there was a girl in the way.

"Hello," she said. "Are you the one they're chasing? My name is Olivia. What's yours?" She was about his age and pretty in a plump, wholesome sort of way. She was eating from a Styrofoam box in her lap.

Sheldon jumped nervously. "Just call me Flash. That's better than what most people call me." He hunched down so the men wouldn't see him.

"Are you American boy?" She went on without waiting for him to answer. "Finally, I meet one. I've been in America two years and all I meet are Brazilian boys. So boring! Now, when I'm just about to leave, I meet one who creeps into my car like a hunchback Romeo. Dios, you are not a cripple, are you? Because it would be shame if you are although Sister Monica tells me I must feel sorry for cripples."

Sheldon eyed her from the floor. "Hold it right there. I'm not a cripple. Let's just get that straight, okay? I couldn't have run here if I was crippled, could I?"

"Why are you running? Oh, I see why you are running. It must be from the men there who are talking to Marcelo. By the way, I am forgetting my manners," She held out her plump hand. "I'm Olivia Arauja."

Still crouched down. Sheldon shook three well-manicured fingers with a stinky one of his own. "Pleased to meet you. Now could you please move your feet so I can get out the other door?"

"You stole something, yes? How exciting! What did you steal? A fish for supper?"

He decided to go with the flow. "Yeah, yeah, that's it. I stole a big tuna fish from that guy's boat and now he wants it back. He's got twenty more just like it but he just wants this one back. Can't even give a poor kid a break."

"Pobrecito! Are you very poor?"

Stuck at knee level, Sheldon adopted the posture of a supplicant. "See, my mom is very sick with cancer and all our money goes for her medicine. So there isn't enough money left over for food. All she can eat is fish and rice. So I come down here every night to steal some fish for her so she can get better."

Olivia looked down at the take-out box in her lap. She fastened the lid shut. "Here, Flash. Take this to her. I've hardly touched it. It's Brazilian—sort of like lasagna but with plenty Brazilian spices."

"No thanks. She can't eat spicy stuff and, anyway, I can't get away from here if I'm carrying a Styrofoam box of lasagna, can I? But thanks, all the same. I've got to split now because—"

He was interrupted by a man's deep voice behind him. "Here's Poochy back, Miss Olivia." A little dog jumped up on the seat above him and immediately started barking. "What're you doing here, kid?"

He turned and looked up at the hard, battered face under the chauffer's cap. "Olivia said to wait here so I'm waiting."

The driver looked at the girl for confirmation. "Miss?"

Before she could speak, Sheldon thought of a sales pitch. "You want a fish? I got one I could sell for the right price. It's in the bushes though. Didn't want the dog to get it."

This time, it backfired. With a snarl, the chauffeur grabbed him by the tee-shirt. "Get outta here! Scram or I'll stuff the fish up your—"

Olivia was surprisingly authoritative. "Marcelo, he's my guest. Leave him alone. Come on, Flash, I'll walk around the marina with you."

Sheldon looked at his protectress with puppy-dog eyes. "No, I can't. Those guys want to kill me for taking their fish."

"Marcelo, take care of those *bastardos,* eh?"

Maybe Marcelo had been a *pobrecito* once himself or maybe he just did he was ordered. He growled and gave the thugs a dirty look. They melted, backing away rapidly, casting menacing looks over their shoulders.

Sheldon couldn't wait to tell Moss what had just transpired. Then he remembered Moss wasn't there. "Must be nice to have protection," he said wistfully as they emerged from the limo with Marcelo riding shotgun.

The girl made a so-so noise which sounded like Brazilian for "whatever." "Sometimes I feel like a prisoner. Arauja is not my father. I don't know my real father but my mother is a beautiful woman and his fourth wife. I should be grateful to him, but I was born in a *favela* and I'd rather be poor than live in a prison."

He was surprised at the vehemence of Olivia's words as if she were voicing them for the first time. "No, you wouldn't. Being poor sucks."

At the entrance to the marina, she took his hand. "What does 'sucks' mean?"

She was becoming annoying and he tried to extract his hand from her grip. "I don't know. It's just something that everybody says. Like you don't have to know what it means just to say it, okay?"

"Flash, you have become my only American boyfriend. Will you come back tomorrow?"

He had a sudden thought. "If I could get to one of your dad's casinos, I could win some money and take you out on a real date. How about it?"

He thought he was dead in the water the way she frowned, her large eyes filling with suspicion. "How did you know my dad owned casinos?"

Shrugging off the question, Sheldon tried to look worldly. "Everybody knows your dad owns casinos. It's been on the TV and everything. No kidding, it's common knowledge."

"What you mean is, I could be famous? The nuns never let us watch TV and neither does Monica. She is Mom's bodyguard. Dad says there are black people who are robbers." When she saw his hurt expression, Olivia realized her mistake. "Oh, I didn't mean you, Flash!" She was still carrying the Styrofoam box. "Here," she said, shoving it at him. "Take this home to you mother. I have to go on…how you say?…a crash diet. Right now! I have to crash so no food for me. My mother say I'm too fat. Here nobody like fat girls."

He stretched for a compliment. "I like you, Olivia. I think you're fine."

Her face lit up with a brilliant smile. "Really? Then take the ferry to the island. A lot of our workers take it because it stops at Cayman's Key On there is the casino. You will be my date tonight and we will win big money all for you and your mother, eh? You will leave rich! Here, take this." She reached into her handbag and pulled out a wad of bills. "You'll need to pay for the ferry and something to eat beside fish. Take it. Marcelo is watching."

Sheldon replied in a strangled voice that cracked just when he wanted to sound cool, "Sounds like a plan. See you tonight." Looking over her shoulder, he saw the hard-eyed bodyguard watching them from a discreet distance. "Only don't tell anybody, okay? Especially not Mr. MMA."

"Who?"

"Never mind. Thanks for the food. My mom will love it. See ya."

He hid in the bushes until the girl got back in the limo and they drove away. He waited until the island ferry pulled into its berth, disgorging passengers. Then mixing with the crowd waiting to get on, he looked back again at the pier. The thugs had returned and kept walking up and down as though they were looking for somebody. Sheldon threaded his way to the front of the line. "My mom and dad are already on board," he told the ticket taker. "Can I join them?"

He gave the man his ticket and went to stand by the

first black couple that looked old enough to have children. It turned out they were total strangers, but Sheldon didn't care. At least, he was safe while the trip lasted.

CHAPTER 7

Moss woke up feeling as if his head was being used as a drum. At first, he thought he had realized his dream of being a drummer in a rhythm-and-blues band—tump tump, ch-che, cheche-che, cheche-che. Then he realized he'd make a lousy sober drummer. He realized then that the pain in his arms was cause by his hands being tied behind his back and the throbbing in his head was because he was lying against a wall with a diesel engine chugging on the other side.

By using the hard surface of the wall as a brace, he managed to roll over on his stomach, and again, on his back. From the rocking motion under him, he figured he was on a boat, a small boat though one with an inboard motor like a tugboat or shrimper. But how did he get there?

Moss was trying to sort out the events of the past hours and got as far as going to look for that little shit Sheldon when something hard hit him from behind. There was a metallic taste in his mouth. It was familiar, but he couldn't place it. He tried to spit, but only managed to drool blood.

Daylight momentarily blinded him as someone opened a door in the ceiling and a shaft of white light seared his eyes. "I see you are awake, Chief." He squinted with one eye. Whoever it was, his voice was familiar but his back was to the sun and Moss couldn't make his face out, plus something had changed. Moss couldn't put his finger on it until the man spoke again.

"Water. Could I please have some water?"

"Sure you can, providing you don't try something."

There was that accent again, almost imperceptible, like the breeze through palm trees. "JJ?"

The same mirthless chuckle. "It's me, Chief. The real me, like Sheldon found out."

Help had reached him even in this hellhole. "Sheldon? Where is he, JJ? Did you find him? Did you call the FBI?"

"Sheldon is still loose, but he'll show up eventually. We've destroyed his computer and, no, I told Earlene I would call the FBI myself. But alas, I failed in my duty." JJ climbed down the steps and emptied a bottle of water on Moss's face. "Let me introduce myself. I am Charles Jabar. I work for Mr. Arauja, and I shot your farmer informant. And I will shoot you if you don't cooperate."

Despite the fog in his head, Moss put two-and-two together. JJ was one of Arauja's men. "Go ahead, just free my wife. I guess those were your buddies who shot up the church and kidnapped Kenya."

"Also those who set fire to the queers' house as a distraction."

"Some distraction. They could have burned alive half the people in the town, including my daughter Halee."

JJ only shrugged. "Queers repulse me, especially girls. They only need to have babies to change their minds. Come on, get to your feet. We're approaching our destination right on schedule."

JJ's casual American language had changed to a clipped accent only the British could manage. The pronunciation of some words and a sing-song speech pattern gave him away as coming from somewhere in the Caribbean Islands. Moss wondered whose identity he had stolen to have a record like Jeremy Fabulous Johnson's on the books.

"You got the gun. It would be a lot easier if you took these handcuffs off me."

"Oh, no, sir." JJ faked a smile. "That's an old one. Get up yourself."

Moss made a mental note to slam this cocky SOB's head against something hard a few times once he got to him, but then agonizingly slowly, sliding up the splintered wall, he got to his knees and then to his feet. "Now up the ladder to the deck. I'll uncuff you so you can hold on but one wrong move and you're dead, okay, Moss? Paolo, are you ready? We're coming on deck."

A shadow appeared and then a muscular man with an automatic weapon stood above them. "Ready."

"I wouldn't try anything, Moss. One round and you're in cut in half," JJ's voice behind him said. "Start climbing."

When Moss was on deck, JJ put his handcuffs back on, but it was a relief to feel the sea breeze, however warm, on his sweat-soaked body. They were approaching a small island with a few structures on it, one of them being a boat dock. "Cayman's Key. You won't find it on any map. Too small. By the time they realize that's where you are—if they ever do, you'll be gone."

He didn't ask JJ what he meant by "gone," he was too angry. And, as always, Moss had to rely on rage to get him out of a mess. This ingrate had weaseled his way into a job, and then into his own family's affections, Moss thought. He, the cynic, had been had. All the time JJ was posing as the all-American minority made good.

"Looks okay to me. Anything that doesn't move is

better that a boat." JJ translated rapidly for Paolo and the muscle man laughed, showing white teeth against his dark face. He said something to JJ and JJ joined him, laughing at an inside joke.

Meanwhile, Moss took advantage of their amusement to get a good look at his surroundings. There were two other boats at the dock—a small sailboat, a speedboat, and a fishing boat like the one he was on, except in better condition. There assorted rowboats scattered around, though most were pulled upon shore.

The rest of the island had the usual palm trees, scrubby palmettos, and marshes. Paolo prodded him off the boat with the nose of the automatic, laughing, and exchanging jokes with JJ. As they had to climb the ladder to get to the dock, JJ had to uncuff Moss's hands. Moss considered giving his captor a hard right to the jaw, knocking him into the water. But figuring that punch wouldn't kill JJ and would cost him his own life, he decided to put his revenge on hold. *Revenge is a dish best served cold, somebody said once.* It hadn't made sense at the time, but JJ was a trained killer, and there had to be plenty of people before him who wanted a piece of the man he knew only as JJ.

The house was spacious enough in quasi Spanish revival style—long and low, its terra cotta walls blending in well with the scenery around it. A pool glistened in a back courtyard, and a fountain splashed in the front drive. A gardener raised his head above the hibiscus in front as they pulled up in a golf cart. He ducked down again as soon as he saw JJ and Paolo with the rifle.

JJ led the way around the house to a small garden shed. He shoved Moss through the door and shackled him to the wall. As he looked around, it was obvious to Moss they had kept more than one prisoner in the small room because a lot of them had left something behind. There was a set of false teeth on the dirt floor and a strand of long dark hair adhering to the rough beams above by a patch of dried blood and skin.

"This your little house of horrors, then?"

JJ looked amused. "You could say that. It will be for you, Chief, if you don't cooperate." He explained the joke to Paolo who did a good job of laughing, pointing to the piece of scalp hanging from the rafter.

"No cooperate," he said, shaking his head.

They left him, sweltering in the small shed until the sun went down. Moss thought of tearing the shackles out of the wall but they were anchored in cement blocks. In Memphis, he had learned to pick any lock with a piece of wire. The only piece of metal he could reach was his belt buckle and was worrying the small clasp back and forth, when he thought he heard a sound outside. He stopped and listened to the sounds he had grown familiar with back home, the night sounds of the swamp and somewhere far away, there was music.

The frogs and the cicadas had kept him awake when he first moved in with Kenya and she had teased him about being a city boy. Kenya. The thought of her spurred him to redouble his efforts to escape. He heard the sound again, above the music. This time it was louder.

"Psst, mister?"

His captors had left the door open, saying they had a security camera on him, but judging from the music and the sounds of laughter, somewhere there was a party going on. The cool night air flooded in with the perfume of jasmine.

The invisible speaker went on. "I am work in garden. Don't worry, I get you out."

"Water. Could you give me some water?"

"Later. Sleep now. Come later."

Sometime in the night, a figure kneeled beside him

and pressed a water bottle to his lips. Water ran down his chin to his chest. Then the figure slipped out of the shed into the dark.

೮ഏ৩

The island ferry was loaded and interminably slow. Most of the passengers were locals working in Savannah going back home for the night, only to repeat the trip in the morning. There were a couple of kids with book bags on their backs who obviously went to school on the mainland. Sheldon couldn't imagine going through this every morning, considering the school bus at home drove him nuts.

Nevertheless, the passengers talked happily as if they were meeting in the evening for drinks. A few played cards and there was a chess game going in the bow of the boat. At last, Cayman's Key was the next stop. As they approached the island, some passengers dressed in uniforms lined up and behind them a few tourists. He attached himself to a middle-aged couple who asked him about school, thinking he was one of the islanders.

Adding a pair of cool sunglasses, he ditched his own prescription glasses in case the Brazilian thugs recognized him. He couldn't see three feet in front of his nose without them, but who cares, he thought? Cool is everything. Turning his cap around, Sheldon went into cool mode.

೮ഏ৩

Faun heard Ashlee scream into the phone and came running from the dining room. "You've found him?"

"That little shit wouldn't tell me where he is." Ashlee was sitting on the stairs, holding her head as though it was threatening to fly off. "And now he says Grover is missing!"

Taking Ashlee's phone away, Faun pressed the Call Log. "That area code is Savannah. I know because I've dealt with a lab there." Sitting sat down beside Ashlee on the stairs, Faun took out her own phone and called Reynolds Chapman. She would be the last to admit she'd been looking for an excuse to do that ever since the disaster at his uncle's house. The sound of his voice was hurried, though polite. Even so, it sent a strange thrill through her.

They went through the usual how-are-yous and then she cut to the chase. "We've heard from Sheldon and Chief Moss has gone missing. Any ideas?"

"Hold on, let me connect you with my uncle Bernie. He has to hear this. And are you available for dinner tonight?"

"Put him on, and yes. Pick me up at seven unless you get off earlier."

"I will make sure to do that."

There was a click and Bernie answered. "What's going on, beautiful?"

Faun handed the phone to Ashlee. "There's been a development. I just got a call from Sheldon. He sounded scared and said Grover is missing. And wouldn't tell me where he was..." Her voice rode up the scale to high C then trailed off. "Faun says he called from Savannah. I wish I knew what was going on."

"Just take a deep breath and listen. It's going to be all right. I checked with Earlene at the police station last night. Moss is chasing down Kenya's kidnappers. Some guy called Arajoo or Arau...hell, I don't know. Anyway he's into all kinds of crime including Howland Enterprises. It's one of his fronts for drug and sex trafficking."

"Did Earlene say she's got a fix on his car?"

"I didn't ask because she said JJ went after him so

he's got backup, and I assume she's notified GBI and everybody else including her mother for fifty miles around here. Keep it under your hat for now, darling. I want to be the first to break the story, okay?"

Ashlee sat down on the stairs, suddenly feeling weak. "But why'd he leave Sheldon on his own like that?"

Bernie was silent for a moment. "I've just been to see Miss Kedzia, the preacher at Glory Road Church. Anyway, she told me Moss was looking into Howland's Enterprises because he thinks old man Howland is innocent."

Relieved to drop the subject of Moss and Kenya, Ashlee got control of her voice again. "Yeah, he's obsessed with that case. He even had me digging around to find out the dirt on Howland Enterprises. He should've asked Sheldon. Wonder Boy can get around the net to find dirt on anybody. Go on."

Segal went on. "She said Moss was there when Mr. McDermott was shot after they saw something was going down on McDermott's land. McDermott was taking kickbacks for looking the other way because his wife was sick. Something about an airstrip somewhere off Alabama Road. That's when that Nazi nurse ran me off without letting her finish. So that could be a lead. I'll follow it up and get back to you."

Faun had already looked the name Howland up in the business directory on her laptop. "There's an Arlen Howland listed as the president of Howland Enterprises."

Bernie sighed into the phone. "Tell her I've already tried that, but he's retired some place in the Bahamas. Anyway, he's only a nephew or something. And Ashlee, tell Miss Science of the Month to stay out of it. These guys are mean and ruthless. They'd kill their own grandmother and probably already have. So leave it to me, okay?"

"Okay. I'll tell her." She covered the phone. "Faun, Bernie says...Faun?"

Faun's car spat gravel and had disappeared down the drive of Magnolia Alley before Ashlee could make it to the door. "Damn! Damn and double damn!"

"My sentiments exactly," said Bernie's voice from the phone dangling from her hand.

An hour later, Faun got off the plane in Savannah and immediately booked into the luxury hotel where she had already reserved a room. Changing to shorts and a tee-shirt, she brushed her long, silver-blond hair back into a pony tail. Picking up Moss's spare set of keys she had plucked off the hat stand in the hall of Magnolia Alley, Faun went down to the information desk.

"Could you tell me where the central police station is in town?"

The girl behind the counter's smile froze then automatically restarted. Whipping out a map, she drew a small circle on a green space. "Or it's on your phone under city services in the yellow pages. Is there a problem?"

"No, I just had a wild night and forgot where I parked my car." Faun rubbed her forehead.

"Oh, that's easy! Tourists do that all the time. We have a shuttle service, a guy in a golf cart just to help you."

Before Faun could stop her, the girl was on the phone. "He'll be right in front when you get ready to leave. Anything else?"

Nothing except my friend and her husband have been kidnapped, and their kid is running around the city thinking he's Superman minus the cape.

"It'll be a lot faster if I just rent a car, thanks anyway"

"Sure! There's a kiosk in the lobby right over there."

After driving along the main boulevard pressing Moss's car alarm, Faun passed the supermarket mall where Sheldon had parked the car and gave it one last try. Moss's SUV lit up like a Christmas lawn display gone berserk, flashing its light and honking to a recorded message that squawked "Security breach, security breach. Please step away from the car!"

Smiling, Faun turned around at the light and drove back to the would-be crime scene. Turning off the security alarm, she opened the car with a pounding heart, half expecting to find Moss's body inside. Instead, she found the remains of a chicken sandwich and Sheldon's backpack. Moss's suitcase was in the back.

Sitting in her car, she put the location of the parking lot into the Moss Missing algorithm she had worked out on her laptop. It changed everything. Moss was somewhere within fifty miles of Savannah, and Sheldon was somewhere nearby.

Figuring she had either constructed her algorithm wrong or was missing some vital detail, Faun called Kedzia's room in the hospital. The priestess answered, "Faun, where are you? In Georgia?"

"How did you know it was me?"

"Your area code and phone number. I've been lying here worrying about you."

Faun related finding Moss's car but not Sheldon.

Kedzia's voice had a smile in it. "The boy will come back, don't worry about him. It's Moss. He's in a dark place. It's him you need to find. I feel so responsible. It was I who told him about McDermott about Howland's dirty tricks, and about the airplane runway on Mr. McDermott's land. I just figured he'd pass it on to the right people."

"What airplane runway?"

Faun listened to a story that was so similar to the one which cost her father and her stepbrother their lives that it sent shivers through her entire body in spite of the heat.

Kedzia paused. "I know what you're thinking. That's how we met, isn't it?"

"At Holly's funeral. I remember. In fact, I relive the whole thing—the rape, Biopharma, Michael, and my dad all the time."

"Then this is your turn to make it right instead of being a victim."

"But how? I keep running into walls everywhere I turn. I'm missing something big, but I don't know what." She told Kedzia about trying to fit every component into a mathematical formula and ending with Moss and Sheldon being in the area. "But now I have to no idea where to begin looking."

Over the wire, there came a painful giggle. "Don't make me laugh. It still hurts."

"Sorry. That's the first time anybody's thought trigonometry was funny. So what am I missing?"

"Trust your intuition, girl. Your mother and grandmother do, so why don't you? You have the gift, use it. Don't depend on formulas. They only disguise the truth. The truth will come to you."

Faun rang off when the nurse came in Kedzia's room. She was plugging in the airstrip into her equation when there was rap on her car window. Reynolds Chapman was peering in at her, laughing.

Lowering her window, she asked, "What's so funny?"

"It's just that you're always at work even in the playground of the rich and famous. Can I get in? It's hot out here."

She unlocked the doors and he got in beside her. "How'd you find me?"

"I asked Earlene and she showed the pictures Sheldon had sent her. I recognized Savannah right away because I kind of grew up here, off and on."

She smiled, sending his heart on an ascending ride. "I

bet there's a story about the off-and-on bit."

Chapman shrugged. "My mother was my father's third wife. He's kind of a serial groom. The off-and-on bit takes a little more time. Over dinner maybe?"

They were so absorbed with each other they didn't notice the skinny kid pedaling down the street, dodging the traffic.

"Depends." She hadn't felt this way since she had met Chris Bjorn four years before. Four long years since they had gone through hell twice. Faun played for time. "Who's running the studio?"

"Halee's got it under control. She's quite a photographer, too. You should see her pictures of Uncle Bernie's house fire. She's even got photos of the KKK guys burning the crosses and the truck blowing up. It's a wonder she didn't get hurt. CNN picked them up and they've gone viral."

"Thanks again for getting me out," they said in unison, then both burst into laughter ending fits of coughing.

Faun sobered first, thinking about Kedzia saying laughter hurts. Reynolds watched her face as she told him what the priestess had said about Moss being there when McDermott was shot and what they saw.

"Sounds like drugs or dirty money or both. Stands to reason, though, if they got old man McDermott, they must have suspected Moss was there, too. Maybe they had the place under surveillance so nothing would interfere with their operation. You hungry?"

Faun smiled. "That was a fast switch. Yes, as a matter a fact. I haven't had a bite except a *latte* at the airport, but I can't leave the car in case Sheldon comes back."

"I've got an idea." Chapman did on a quick take around the strip mall." Be right back."

Before she could say anything else, he was out of the

car and hurrying toward the stores. Faun watched him go—a six-foot dynamo of electric energy whose synapses worked even faster than hers. It didn't hurt that he was good-looking, too.

But wait until he heard about her maniacal half-brother who made a sport of torturing and killing women and tried to blow up a plane full of people, costing her father his life. She sometimes looked at herself in the mirror thinking how by some twist of DNA, she could have been him, brilliant but insane, hideous instead of beautiful.

No, she was defective goods and when Reynolds Chapman learned her family history, he would go the way of Chris Bjorn and all the others who had been attracted to her like flies to honey.

If she thought about the past for too long, it always put her in such a depressive funk that she would be useless for days. She usually could avoid that by going for a long run, then working out for hours at the gym. That and a couple of lattes usually gave her enough endorphins to stave off the bouts of depression. Faun looked longingly at the shady park just behind the strip mall. Here she was in an historical paradise and stuck in the car.

She could hear her father now. Quade Walker would say, "Suck it up, baby girl, and just get on with it."

That was her dad. Faun grinned to herself and got to work. Reynolds was back at the car window. "See that picnic table over there?" He pointed to a table under an awning. "That belongs to a little Italian place. Come on, you can see Moss's car from there."

They were deep in discussion over antipasto and Campari cocktails when Faun looked up. "Look! What are those guys doing around Moss's car?"

Two men and a woman were examining every inch of Moss's SUV. They were dressed in shorts, sweatshirts, and sneakers. "Probably store security. Or they could be the kidnappers, come to see if Sheldon's left some clue as to what he's hiding in there."

"We've got to find him before they do."

Faun suddenly got very interested in her antipasto. "Don't stare, Rey."

He grinned. "That's the first time you've said my nickname."

"You know what? While they're…whoever they are… are there, Sheldon will never show. But I bet he's around here somewhere, just watching and scared to death. We've got to look for him."

"Even before the main course?"

"I thought that was the main course."

"It can wait. Meanwhile, I'll call the police. That'll scare them off, whoever they are. Tell the waiter to hold up on the lasagna, okay?"

CHAPTER 8

Moss squinted at the dawn through slits of eyes. Mosquitoes had done a number on his eyelids when he drifted off during the night.

"Wake up, Chief. Time to shake, rattle, and roll."

Moss groaned, aware that he was resorting to one of Sheldon's put-downs. "That's so yesterday, JJ."

JJ hit him a blow in the gut. "How's that? Better?" Behind him, Paolo with the machine gun laughed

During the next two hours, they worked him over good, in between asking him to write them a check for a million dollars.

"We know your wife has that much and more in your joint account so you can write us check and stay here until it's cashed. Be stubborn and we'll double it."

"You're crazy, JJ. What's your guarantee you won't kill her?"

The answer came as another gut punch. "Don't call me that, stupid! I'm not your woman now, understand? Do this, do that, JJ. Do you know how much I hated you for that? Like a slave hates his master, that's how much."

Paolo interrupted JJ, saying something in Portuguese. "Paolo says you'll get your guarantee because your wife will be here tonight. Watch yourself, Chief, or she won't be so beautiful to look at anymore. Take him back, Paolo."

"Can I have some water first?"

"Sure thing, Chief!" JJ reached for a bucket beside the patio, and threw sea water over Moss's open gashes and bug bites. It felt like he was engulfed in flames. JJ and Paolo laughed. "Feel better, Chief?"

Then and there, Moss decided the world would be a better place without JJ in it.

But Paolo still had a spark of humanity in him. Back in the shed before he shackled Moss to the wall, he left one hand free. There was a bottle of water and a packaged roll filled with meat sitting beside the door outside. Still cradling the automatic rifle, he handed them to Moss one at a time. Moss wolfed the roll down and followed it with the water.

"Thanks."

Shrugging, Paolo shackled his other hand to the wall. "It's nothing. You die anyway."

After the guard left, Moss felt nausea overcoming him and he vomited everything back on the dirt floor. Dizziness overcame him, his knees buckled and he fell to the floor. Moss was a big man and his dead weight pulled the chains out of the wall. Unfortunately, the concrete block they were mounted in came with them and fell on his head, knocking him unconscious.

Some minutes later, he came to, finding someone kneeling beside him. He tried to focus but his vision was blurred. "Quiet, everyone is still asleep. I will free you, but don't move. When I return, you follow me."

As soon as he was free, Moss followed what he'd learned as a soldier. When the power is with the enemy, run like hell. He crawled through the open door, and around the back of the shed. He lay there awhile, gathering enough strength to go on. Not trusting his legs quite yet, he crawled into the thick brush just beyond the clearing surrounding the house and passed out.

Somehow, the afternoon had crawled to its conclusion amid swarms of flies, and mosquitoes fighting for space on his open cuts. JJ would come out soon and discover he was gone. On his elbows at first, he continued snaking through the underbrush, dislodging snakes and lizards at every move. When he had put a good distance between himself and the house, he got up and started to run, falling down repeatedly at first as his legs gave out. As adrenaline kicked in, he began to gain speed, knowing death was at his heels.

On the map, Cayman's Key was a small island no bigger than Memphis. Moss figured by running in the direction the sun was setting, but away from the villa, he would reach the sea. But, as he leaped over roots and green ooze, Moss discovered that route only brought him deeper into the jungle of the interior.

Then hearing shouts of alarm behind him, and gunfire, he knew they'd discovered he was gone. Given JJ's accuracy with a gun, coupled with what Arauja might to do him for letting Moss escape, he and Paolo would be on him like white gravy on rice. Both men were half his age and could cover more ground than he could. The only option was to hide. He looked up and found himself looking at a giant water oak tree like the one Kenya called the Mama Tree at home. *It cradled me in its roots and protected me until Root Woman found me.*

With that thought tattooed on his conscious mind, Moss started climbing although he hadn't climbed anything since boot camp. That had been twenty years and thirty-five pounds lighter ago. But his life was on the line, so he climbed up and up among the leaves with Kenya's voice repeating those words in his head, as if she was a drill sergeant. From his perch in the strong branches of the tree, he had a good view of the ground just below and very far away to the sea. Afraid any movement would attract his pursuers' sharp eyes, he remained very still and listened. The birds stopped twittering in the canopy and, in the silence, Moss heard footsteps approaching.

In just a few more minutes, JJ passed a few yards from the tree, rifle with the telescopic sight under his arm, absorbed in talking to Paolo on his Blue Tooth device. Presently, he heard a shout from Paolo and then a burst of gunfire across the island that sent JJ running at top speed in the direction of the noise.

That gave Moss the chance he needed. He climbed down and moved on in the opposite direction from the gunfire. Presently, the sound of a boat approaching reached his ears, and he crouched down among a clump of palmettos. It must be Arauja bringing Kenya to this hellish place where possibly they both might die. But it was only a tour boat, joined by several more with deep sea rigging.

There was a rasping whisper behind him. "*Americano, no me moleste. Soy jardinero*. Gardener." The man crawled forward, using his elbows. It wasn't until he collapsed flat on his face on the soft sand beside him, that Moss saw the blood covering his back. His worn shirt had split open, revealing a blood-soaked bra. The gardener was a thin, brown woman!

"Lie still." Looking around for something to stop the blood flow, and since neither one was wearing a shirt, Moss did the only thing he could think of. Lying flat, he shucked off his jeans and since there was a big hole in the knees, he ripped the legs off in strips, tied the strips into knots, fashioning a tourniquet around the woman's shoulder. She was very still for a long while.

Presently, she made a motion to get something out of her pants pocket. He took out some strange brown leaves, and held them out to her. She selected some pieces, putting them into her mouth. "Gracias," she said around the wad.

Curious, Moss smelled them before putting back in her pocket. He was close enough to smell the leaves which he figured were some sort of native remedy for pain. The smell was familiar and yet strange. The woman smiled, brown drool coming from the corners of her mouth. "Cacao. Quiere?"

Figuring she was offering him some, Moss shook his head. "No thanks. Lie still. You have to rest. Restey, okay?" He figured Spanish was just another version of Pig Latin.

The woman made the effort to explain. "Me from Honduras. I see you run. I go other way. They follow."

He regarded her as she lay beside him, blood slowly soaking her clothes. In spite of her sinewy muscles, she couldn't have weighed over a hundred pounds. "So they were shooting at you? Why in hell would you do that? You could have identified yourself and been safe."

She nodded and lay face down for a while, chewing slowly. Presently, she spoke again. "You help my brother, please, Americano, His name Miguel, and he go to Los Estados Unidos con coyote."

Moss recognized the words brother, Miguel, and coyote. "You mean, he's illegal, right?"

The woman beside him was silent.

Presently, he heard a different kind of engine, this one with a high whine that meant it was coming fast. He recognized Arauja's motor launch, the one he had seen pulling out of the slip in the Savannah marina the night before. When it pulled alongside the dock, five twittering, giggling women emerged from below. The sunlight shone through their brightly-colored hair and through their skimpy party clothes as the crew helped them to climb to the dock while taking the opportunity to look up their short skirts.

The woman beside him raised her head to look at them. "*Putas*," she whispered. "Whores."

Figuring this was a chance to escape, Moss said, "I've got to make a move," but the gardener dashed his hopes. "All boat come here belong to Arauja. He has many boat."

Keeping his voice to a whisper, he said, "I know. I know he has a yacht."

"Nothing. Arauja has many same. Maybe ten. Ship, too."

"You sound like you know a lot about him."

"Father fish. *Muy pob*re. He carry drug for Arauja, too. Arauja say Father keep some drug to sell to street. Say he owe money, but Father, he don't keep none. He say Arauja's men, they short him, but Arauja no believe him. They take Father here, and I follow. I hear him scream for five days before they kill him. They feed body to *crocodilo*. I have one shoe, I bury that." Her eyes filled with tears which glistened in the moonlight. "Now he kill me, too."

"No, he won't. You're going to live to see Arauja put away for the rest of his life."

She smiled. "I like America. *Tierra de esperanza*."

They were quiet while the girls trooped noisily down the dock, their high heels clattering on the wooden planks, and up the path into the house.

"What's your name?"

"Mimi." The woman beside him winced in sudden pain. "I can do nothing for my father."

In the stillness that followed they heard a dog bark. "Paolo," the woman beside him said. "With dog, he follow the blood."

"Did Paolo shoot you?"

She gave a little sideways nod that he had learned

meant no. "He try. Bullet come from other gun. Hit me in back."

JJ strikes again, Moss thought. "Come on. We better move."

"No, leave me here. I die with Father. You go."

"That ain't the way it works. You save me. I save you. Come on, I'll carry you."

Knowing it was a risk to move her, he had no choice but to put her over his shoulder, and run through the dark away from the beach. As they approached the pool area, Moss stopped to get his breath.

Putting Mimi down beside him, he dropped flat behind the banana plants that grew in the sunny spots just before the wooded interior and looked around. They had ended up behind the large patio of the villa. Moss planned to move around the pool. Hot loud music and the girls laughing guaranteed their movements wouldn't be heard by anyone other than the dogs

There were other men who had joined the party, probably from the boat crew, and two guys who worked in the villa. And of course, there was JJ, wearing a shoulder holster under his Cuban shirt. He was wearing a thong which the girls were trying to take off, chasing him around the pool, alternately turning and pushing one another into the pool.

Putting her hand on his arm, Mimi pointed to a small metal shed. "Pool stuff."

Suddenly JJ stopped playing, slipped on his shorts, all the while talking on his Blue Tooth. When a girl tried to grab him, he pushed her roughly away, sending her backward into the water. Then he loped off into the forest.

CHAPTER 9

When they reached Cayman's Key, it was half past three. Sheldon followed the ferry passengers off the boat on to the island and up the hibiscus-lined stairs to the luxurious casino. On reaching the building, he immediately sought the restroom and there, ignoring the gold appointments which would stop adults from urgently having to pee, hid in a stall. Locking the door, he climbed onto a gold-washed bidet, rested his skinny legs on the toilet, his head on the side of the stall, and fell asleep playing a game on his phone. An hour and a half later, when he ventured out, he spotted a phalanx of what looked like MMA fighters, going around the main floor, looking under tables.

Escaping from the casino, Sheldon spent the next hour sitting in the gathering dark on the beach, letting the warm tide curl around his toes. He hoped he would be mistaken for a fisherman's son, waiting for his father to come home with the day's catch. His whole body ached for his mom—for her pillowey chest when she put her arms around him, her perfume, her voice singing in his ear. Even her unsolicited kisses that left the scarlet imprint of lips on his cheeks for hours. Amazingly, he missed Moss, too. He missed his stepdad's gruff humor, his man smell, and even his occasional yelling fits.

After an hour, a powerful motor launch pulled into the small, brightly-lit harbor and docked. Thinking Olivia might be on it, he stood up and took a few steps in that direction. But it was only a few drunk girls, laughing raucously as the crew—all rough-looking characters looked up their skirts while helping them off the boat. As they teetered on high heels up the dock, one of them turned and looked at him through oversized sunglasses. He turned around and walked back the other way up the beach, but he was sure she would tell somebody she saw him.

In the dark, he could move around more easily looking for Moss. There was a party going on somewhere behind the casino so Sheldon decided to look there first. He was sure whoever had jumped his stepfather wouldn't have been invited to a party on the island unless they had a hard time getting guests out here, which didn't seem likely.

A steady stream of inter-island ferries and tour boats came and went from the docks, disgorging loads of passengers. Cayman's Key carried on a brisk trade in gamblers and tourists as well as kidnappers.

As he started in the direction the girls had gone, Sheldon toyed with idea that maybe, just maybe Moss had gone over to Arauja's side. Money and power did that to people. He'd seen it happen over and over again on TV— good cop gone bad. With Moss out of the way, he'd have his mother back again all to himself—except for Wilson and Zeb. And Ashlee and Toya and the whole rest of the world.

Sheldon put away the thought, chalking it up to his evil twin that his mother would say took his place when he did something bad. He was stumbling up the sandy bank toward the party going on in what appeared to be a

Spanish-style motel when a voice from the casino veranda stopped him in his tracks.

"Flash! There you are!"

It was Olivia bellowing from the balcony of the casino on the hill like some over-nourished Juliet. It was loud enough to wake any zombie lying in wait behind every rock and tree. He saw a man come out of the Spanish motel carrying a high-powered rifle. An equally dangerous-looking dog barked and snarled, sending him up the slope to the casino as if he were storming up San Juan Hill.

As he arrived breathless on the terrace, Olivia was waiting with open arms and hugged him to her prickly self. "You came! Oh, when you weren't on the dock, I thought you stood me up! And I bought this dress and got my hair done just for you." She twirled around like a pink nylon *pinata,* a matching pink camellia tucked in her hair. "Like it?"

He stumbled over the words. "Uh…uh, yeah. I do. You look—"

"Never mind," she gushed. "I know it's cool not to give girls compliments in the States. But then you can't believe guys in Brazil. They're only after one thing. Come on." Grabbing his hand, she pulled him away from the brightly lit casino.

"Where to? I thought we were going in here so I could win some money."

"But first, we have to make love. I'm tired of being a virgin, Flash."

"Whoa!" He planted his feet, jerking her backward. "Say what?"

Looking up through fluttering lashes, Olivia snuggled against him. "It's just that all the girls at school tease me about being a virgin at fifteen. They're already having sex with their boyfriends, and I haven't got anything to talk about."

He was aghast. "But I thought you went to a strict Catholic school where they train you to be a nun."

Olivia brushed the objection away. "But lots of us are townies. We live at home so the nuns can't control everything we do."

"But…but what about your mom and dad? What will they think?"

She pulled him along by the hand. "Oh, they won't care. Come on, we're wasting time. Let's go make love, and then we'll get down to the blackjack tables before Fidelio's shift is over. I told him you were coming so he's setting you up to win big."

They entered the huge casino through the kitchen which looked like a session of the UN. At least five different languages were being thrown around like golf balls on a driving range. Only a few sous-chefs stopped what they were doing as Olivia pulled him through the maze of waiters with loaded trays, bus boys with tubs of dirty dishes, chefs barking orders and cooks slicing, chopping and mincing.

Introducing him as her date, Olivia navigated the kitchen with remarkable grace in spite of swinging her hips samba-style and knocking over two loaded trays.

"There are the stairs the upstairs servants use," she said, pointing to a steep, winding staircase. "Follow me, Flash, and don't look at my behind," Olivia added with a coquettish giggle.

As if I could avoid it, he thought.

⋐⋑⋐⋑

Seeing the stake-out of Moss's car still ongoing, Faun and Rey went back to the hotel to get to know each other a little better. Much better, it turned because when Faun woke up beside Reynolds in the king-sized bed, it was already nine o'clock. She leaped out of bed and headed for the shower.

"What?" Rey reacted like he'd been shot. "What's wrong?"

"Nothing, only it's ten past nine. Sheldon's got to have gone back to the car because a kid can't get a hotel room by himself." She stood in the doorway of the bathroom, totally unaware of the paralyzing affect her nakedness had on him.

Rey was dazzled by the perfection of her body as Faun turned to get into the shower. "Hurry," she called. "We don't have much time."

Needing nothing more than that invitation, he leaped out of bed and into the shower with her where they made love one more time.

"Don't get any ideas," she said breathlessly. "I'm not always like this."

"You have no idea about Jewish mothers, do you?"

Drawing back, Faun scrubbed herself off. "What does that mean?"

"It means I've had every Jewish princess pushed on me since my mom enrolled me in the cotillion of every country club from New York to Georgia."

Faun smiled, as he hoped she would do, and rubbed up against him. "So you can dance?"

"The samba, the meringue, the waltz. You name it, I can do it."

"Then dance with me." She danced naked out of the shower and then, giggling, grabbed her clothes, and ran into the dressing room. When Faun came out, she was all business. Rey marveled at the switch.

"What about that dance now?" Holding out his arms, hips swaying to a silent samba, he danced around the room.

Faun laughed. "You look like a gigolo. Come on, we

have to get going. Sheldon's bound to come back by now. He's probably asleep in the car."

"Good theory." Rey pulled on shorts and a white cotton shirt which he left open. "Then let's go."

They got to the parking lot and saw Moss's car but no Sheldon. Faun took Moss's second set from her purse and unlocked it. It was a mess—seats with deep cuts, stuffing pulled out, glove compartment gaping, its contents scattered. Moss's suitcase and Sheldon's backpack cut open and stuff strewn around the car.

A patrol car cruising through the lot pulled up. "Evening, ma'am, sir. What's the problem?"

"My car's the problem. It's been vandalized."

He took one look at the car and was on his radio immediately. "Can I see both your driver's licenses and the car's registration, please, ma'am?"

"That's just the problem, officer. The registration is gone."

The policeman walked to the back of the car and told the dispatcher the plate number. Then he unfastened his holster and took out his pistol.

Pointing it at both of them, he said, "But your hands up where I can see them. Now!"

Rey dropped his wallet as he getting out his license and put up his hands. Faun just stared at the policeman appalled. "Step back against the car, ma'am."

"But you don't understand, officer—"

The cop looked at her with eyes as hard as bullets. "Back against the car. Now!"

"Faun, do what he says. Explain later, okay?" Rey said in a low, urgent tone.

The police officer explained, "This vehicle is on the all points list. Raise your hands and get against the car, ma'am."

By now they had drawn a crowd from the all-night

grocery store. "They don't look like car thieves," a woman said to her friend.

"You never can tell these days. Thieves come in all sizes and shapes," replied her friend.

By that time, the backup squad rushed to the scene, sirens blaring, Rey and Faun were hustled away in cuffs in separate squad cars, and the crowd cleared off. Except for one man watching the whole thing from his table outside the small café. He picked up his phone and called a number. "*Policia*," was all he said and then rang off.

CHAPTER 10

In the half-light from the patio, Mimi started shivering next to him as the gunfire from the beach moved to the interior of the island. JJ and Paolo raced off in their Speedos, leaving the girls still trying to get the drunken one out of the pool.

Finally, one of the crew of the speedboat had to dive in and get her out. Then, as one, the crew all jumped into their shorts and bolted leaving just the waiters to cope with the five women.

Moss held the shivering girl against his own sweating body. She felt no bigger that a bird he had rescued as a boy back in Memphis, her pulse fluttering against him. Recognizing the symptoms of shock, he thought if she didn't get help soon, she would die.

The thought drove him into action. Leaving her behind the pool house, Moss rushed at the two waiters who saw him coming and bolted for the house. Knocking one down, he got the other one in a chokehold. "You're gonna show me where Arauja keeps his guns, or I'm gonna tear another hole in your skinny ass."

"I'd tell you to go right ahead, but you don't really have to get your hands dirty, Chief Moss. Here, take my gun. I've another one in my…you don't want to know."

As the voluptuous blonde in the string bikini pulled a pistol from somewhere behind her, she introduced herself. "Special Agent Copeland, FBI undercover." She looked more like the centerfold of a men's magazine than a federal officer. The feds recruiting office was definitely getting up to speed, Moss thought.

He took the revolver, the size of a toy pistol but deadly. "This will definitely help. I won't ask you how you got this past the guards."

"Then don't." From her secret stash, Agent Copeland produced another gun the size of the one she had given him.

Moss still had the waiter collared and added the gun to his back. "Look, while I scope out the inside, there's a girl behind the pool house that's been shot." He nodded at the beach bag. "Do you have anything for first aid in that thing? I think she's going into shock." He jerked his head toward her tote bag.

"Will this do?" Agent Copeland pulled a hypodermic syringe from her beach bag. "I've got some adrenalin somewhere." She fumbled in her bag, "Ah, here it is. From the sound of it, the guys should be here any minute, once they take the defensive team out." To the cowering girls, she said, "Go inside and find somewhere safe, like a closet or a bathroom. I don't want anyone to get hit in the crossfire, okay? And put some clothes on while you're at it. This isn't the time to advertising your stuff." They scurried indoors in a twittering flock. Turning to Moss, she nodded. "Okay, go ahead. I've got your back."

Before she could make a move, JJ ran up on the patio. Seeing Moss, he fired the gun he was holding. The bullet flew harmlessly a foot away as JJ fell on his side and rolled into the pool, blood streaming from the hole in his chest where Agent Copeland had shot him.

The waiter sagged in Moss's grip, fainting dead away.

"Going to check on the girl now," she said, replacing the gun in her bikini bottom.

Going inside, Moss found another man cowering in the kitchen. He raised both arms in surrender. "Don't shoot, mister, please. I've got a two month old son at home. I'm just the chef anyway."

"Then you'd better show me where Arauja keeps his guns, or your kid will grow up without a daddy."

The man showed him to a locked gun cabinet in the sumptuous living room, and saying, "But I don't know where he keeps the key."

"No key needed." Thinking Agent Copeland was right behind him, Moss prepared to smash the glass with the gun butt. As he turned toward the gun case, he caught the reflection of the man producing a butcher knife just as he brought it down in Moss's back. Moss turned and shot him. Ignoring the knife, he got a semi-automatic rifle from the cabinet with a round already in it just as Paolo's automatic rifle rattled outside on the patio.

Moss got ready for the guard to come running in the house for cover. But when Paolo didn't show up, Moss waited for him, crouching behind a chair, training the rifle on the doorway, hoping for a lucky shot. Otherwise, it would be his last. He could hear people talking in staccato bursts which sounded like English, but it could just more of Arauja's men.

Instead of Paolo, a man wearing a blue bullet-proof vest cautiously peered around the doorway. When he saw Moss crouching behind a chair, the man said, "Hello, Chief Moss. Nice to see you alive. Your wife and son are safe, you'll be happy to know, except your car is a little messed up. Do you know there's a knife in your back?"

Moss passed out cold.

He and Mimi rode together on the launch back to the mainland, Mimi with a drip in her arm and an oxygen mask on her face. Moss was lay on his stomach while the paramedic treated the wound in his back, alternately debriefing Agent Copeland and the CIA guy while talking to the unconscious girl beside him. "Hang in there, little Mimi. You going to be all right, hear me? Now, where were we?"

Copeland went on. "So we get these pictures and an e-mail from somebody named Prescott in your office with a picture of Charles Jabar, AKA Raymond Toussaint, AKA a lot of other fake names…"

She looked at the CIA man called Bill to explain further. The man who calls himself Jeremy Johnson alias a bunch of other names had been on our radar as one of Arauja's boys. But when he showed up at your station, asking for a job, we wondered what his game was. We wanted to catch the big fish so we just watched and waited to see what he'd do."

"So you were watching and waiting when he shot the old farmer McDermott who showed me a shady deal going down on his land? Who has a wife with cancer from the toxic stuff Howland Enterprises dumped in his backyard. Is that what you guys call collateral damage? I call it using private citizens as bait." Moss shook his head in disgust.

"JJ was trained back in Nigeria as a sniper. That's where he was born, but his family moved to Brazil when he was still a kid. That's when he went to work for Arauja. No telling how many people that guy has killed since then." Bill, the CIA guy, shifted his six-foot-something frame on the hard ambulance seat. "You were lucky, Moss. Prescott said in his message that you were in the process of investigating a shooting when they kidnapped your wife."

"Yeah, I was. But it would have been nice to know Big Brother is watching. I bet you guys were in one of those SUV's with tinted windows, weren't you?"

Bill nimbly leap-frogged over the question. "Arauja is a top priority on our list of international criminals. I'd advise you, Chief Moss, to let us go after him. He's got operations in practically every state in the union."

Moss, stinking with sweat, his clothes smelling of vomit, let the rage show in his face. "I didn't fight in Iraq and Afghanistan to back off a threat to my family at home, Bill. You can crawl around if that suits you, but I'm going to find him and get rid of him, you hear? Even I get killed in the process."

The CIA agent sighed and shook his head. "You must have a death wish."

CHAPTER 11

With Olivia leading him through the upstairs halls of the elaborate casino, Sheldon looked longingly at the crowded tables below. "Couldn't we try our luck at the slot machines? I've got a pocketful of quarters. We could strike it big."

"Not when we've got this opportunity to make love. I've even reserved a room just for us, except I don't remember which one it was." Dragging Sheldon down the carpeted hall, Olivia kept opening doors, revealing the occupants in various sexual positions. One nude woman astride an equally nude man invited them in. "Hi, kids, want to make a foursome?" she called.

"I've paid for an hour," said the guy under her. "I don't want to share it with some kids."

Olivia shut the door, giggling, but Sheldon was mortified. Just then a man's voice behind them shouted, "Olivia! What the hell you doing?"

It was Arauja followed by a phalanx of bodyguards.

"Papa! Meet—" She turned to see Sheldon belting down the hall in a blind panic.

"After him, boys," Arauja shouted, launching the phalanx like a javelin at Sheldon's back. "The little horny bastard!"

Turning a corner in the corridor, he tried the door of the first room he came to. It opened and he ducked inside, closed the door, and locked it, letting the rumble of Arauja's men go by. There was a familiar smell—he'd recognize his mother's perfume anywhere. He was exploring a little deeper in the room when there was an urgent knock on the door. He ducked in the coat closet just as a key turned in the lock and the door opened. Sheldon found a coat on the closet floor and curled up under it, not daring to breathe.

A male voice speaking in a foreign language demanded something and a deep female voice answered a curt "No!" The door closed again and, on the floor of the closet, Sheldon breathed again. There was that perfume again, his mother's scent. Kenya was somewhere nearby, he was positive of that. Then he heard her voice ask, "Who was that, Monica?" His heart did a little dance and he almost called out to her.

But he swallowed the sound when the deeper female voice answered, "Just some guy asking if we had seen a lost kid." Immediately, Sheldon pictured the woman who had escorted his mother to Arauja's boat at gunpoint. As the woman's voice faded into an echo chamber which he assumed was the bathroom, he crawled out of the closet to the door. On his knees, he reached up and opened the door to the hall.

Arauja's goons were nowhere to be seen. Sheldon got to his feet, and beat it down the hall toward the stairs leading down to the enormous kitchen. On the way down, he saw a fire alarm and an idea stuck in his evil twin's mind.

If a fire had worked at Bernie's house to scare away the KluKluxers, why not here where the whole place was surrounded by water? What could go wrong?

Remembering the time he had tried to make his own

breakfast and set off the fire alarm, Sheldon sneaked into the back of the busy kitchen. All the action was taking place up in front, closer to the grand dining room. All the older equipment had been moved to the back of the kitchen. Finding a stove that worked, he found an empty pan nearby, and turned the gas up as far as it would go. Filling the pan with cooking oil somebody had left on the counter, he watched until it started smoking. The pan burst into flames a few minutes later. In a few seconds, the smoke reached the smoke alarms. They went off all over the casino, setting off the all-too-efficient sprinkler systems.

The arsonist joined the herd of dripping guests fleeing down to the ferry docks where the tour boats were waiting. Inside the casino, the smoke reached the rooms upstairs, sending naked people out of the smoking building, clutching their clothes.

One man stopped and looked behind him in Lot's wife fashion. "Boy, the firemen must be getting an eyeful."

The woman beside him said, "It ain't nothing you've never seen before."

Back on the mainland, Sheldon took a cab back to the parking lot where he had left Moss's SUV. The taxi driver was mildly curious what a kid was doing out by himself at midnight especially in a supermarket parking lot. He'd seen kids a lot younger as runners for drug dealers.

The cab driver eyed his young passenger in the rearview mirror. "Do you want me to wait here 'til somebody picks you up? I don't mind."

The supermarket was the only brightly-lit building in the mall which gave Sheldon an excuse. "My mom works at the supermarket. They're doing inventory, that's why she's working so late. I'll just run up there, and she'll let me in, okay? Here, keep the change."

He gave the cabby forty dollars which convinced the

driver he was doing a drug-drop. When he reached the front door of the supermarket, Sheldon waited until the taxi drove away before returning to Moss's car. Unlocking it, he opened the door and found the interior unrecognizable. The entire vehicle was trashed, all his stuff was mixed with Moss's. His backpack had been emptied along with Moss's suitcase, and the contents strewn everywhere as if a tornado had somehow combusted inside the car.

With a resigned sigh, Sheldon climbed in behind the wheel and turned the key in the ignition. The engine rumbled satisfactorily and he was in business. Exiting the parking lot at fifty, Sheldon drove right past a police car parked with the lights off, waiting to ticket some clueless driver.

Seeing the blue light flashing behind him, he clutched the wheel in fear. He stepped on the gas at the same time because the SUV sped along the boulevard, running red lights, as if programmed to follow the only route it knew, down to the river marina. A comet's tail of police cars followed it, blue lights flashing.

Behind them came Rey and Faun in Chapman's sleek sports car. They had just gotten back from the police station by convincing the arresting officer that Rey wouldn't be caught dead driving Moss's tank-like SUV when he had the Porsche in the same parking lot. The officer saw his point. Seeing Sheldon exit the parking lot like something shot out of a cannon, police car in pursuit, Faun said, "That little shit!" and raced to Rey's convertible, vaulting over the passenger door.

Just as Sheldon careened down the driveway to the marina, Arauja's limo was just oozing out of the parking lot. Sheldon squeezed his eyes shut as the SUV bore down on the stretch limousine like a mad water buffalo about to gore a python. The last thing he saw was the horrified face of the limo driver before everything blew up.

The next thing he knew, he was in his mother's arms. "Am I dead?"

"My boy!" Kenya was sitting on the curb next to him. "My brave, brave boy!" she said, kissing his face all over. "My hero."

"You know this kid, ma'am?" The patrolman who had been following Sheldon came up with his pad and pencil, ready to write a whole raft of tickets.

Kenya gave him a victorious smile. "Of course, I do. He's my son, my little angel, my Sheldon."

Having heard that from mothers before, the patrolman rolled his eyes. "Then is this car yours?"

"No." Kenya only glanced at the crumpled SUV. "I have a Cadillac convertible which I'm going to give him when he passes his driver's test."

"Then I got news for you. I have to arrest your son for stealing a car. And you're liable for all the damage he's done to the one he's stolen and the limo."

That got Kenya's back up. "I'm not paying for the limo. Listen here, that man kidnapped me and shot two of my friends! Arrest *him*, not my boy, you idiot!" Seeing the police, Marcelo and Monica who were following the limo in an SUV, turned around, and went back to the marina.

Three ambulances arrived. The policemen handcuffed Arauja and his wife and hustled them into the patrol car, leaving Olivia to wander over to the curb where the EMTs were checking Sheldon's head wound.

Sitting down beside Kenya, she asked, "Can I come with you, Miss Kenya? I'll be no trouble."

Suddenly recovered, Sheldon straight up. "You crazy, girl! Your dad kidnapped my mama! Tell her no way, Mom. Please, please, please!"

"Why, Sheldon, that's so unkind of you." Kenya put

her arms around both children. "Sure, you can, sugar. Never mind what ol' grumpy says here. You're always welcome at my house. Now, baby, about this driving your daddy's car and running into folks. Where is your papa anyway? Did he let you borrow his car to go cruising down the avenue at past midnight?"

"I bet I know the answer, Kenya." Faun had settled beside Olivia.

"What are you doing here?" Kenya stared at her for several seconds. "Where's this place? Where is Abe?" She looked behind her at the marina and shivered. "I hate boats!"

The EMTs exchanged glances. "You better get checked out, ma'am. You and your son here."

They motioned the gurneys over and put Sheldon on one, but Kenya refused, saying she would sit beside Sheldon in the ambulance. "You coming, Faun?" Her voice sounded wobbly like a child who was on the verge of tears. 'I'm so confused, I wish Abe were here."

"Where you and Sheldon go, us groupies will follow." Faun looked at Reynolds Chapman surveying the damage to his car. "Even if we have to walk. By the way, Sheldon, that was good work, racking up an SUV and a stretch limo in one night. You even beat my little brother's record."

He struggled to sit up. "You all don't get it, do you? I did it on purpose. That was the only way I could stop him from kidnapping my mama again."

"Oh, you think you're so smart, Flash." Olivia hooked her arm though Kenya's elbow. "You haven't fooled me. I knew who you were first thing. I took you there to the casino so you would see your mother was all right. Only I didn't know you'd set the place on fire."

Kenya looked her son with wide eyes. "That was you? You did that?"

The spurned lover smugly drove another nail in his coffin. "And he and I were going to make love, only we couldn't find a room."

As they were loading him into the ambulance, Sheldon started moaning and clutching his head. "I'm hurt bad, Mama. My head!" He glared through his fingers at Olivia. "Snitch!"

Kenya sucked in her breath, the sound of a coming tsunami. "That's nothing that a good butt-whupping can't cure." The comforting mother switched to Momzilla. "Shacking up at your age and crashing cars. Just wait 'til I get you back to the house, young man." As if she'd just come awake, Kenya suddenly looked around. "Where's my husband? That's his car, but where is he?" Then she winced and clutched her stomach. "Where is my husband? I want to see my husband! Don't tell me you've arrested him, too."

When Faun tried to comfort her, one of the EMTs told her that was normal. "She might have hit her head on impact. Better check it out just to be sure. You can follow us to the hospital."

Faun looked at Chapman. "You don't have to. I'll call a taxi."

"I gave him money," shouted Olivia desperately. "We were going to make love." That stopped the conversation. Satisfied that all eyes were turned to her, she simpered, "Only he was scared my dad would find out and kill him."

"She looks a little young to be paying a gigolo," said one of the EMTs under his breath.

Doors slammed behind the row of smashed vehicles, and a woman wearing a FBI cap came running up, flashing her badge at the patrolman. "I've got it, Officer, okay? Miss Arauja, we want to ask you a few questions, okay?"

"I'm not really his daughter, you know." Olivia, suddenly prim, brushed off her skirt. "My mom was a Miss Universe contestant and his third wife or his even his fifth wife. He's like King Henry the Eighth. We don't know what happened to the others. For all we know, they're on one his islands or in the sea."

The agent smiled warmly. "We'll find out if we have your help, honey."

"Have you got my dad yet?" Sheldon shouted to the FBI agent from the ambulance where the EMTs were helping Kenya aboard.

"Yes, this is his car," Kenya said, indicating the smashed SUV. "But where is he?"

"You should be hearing from him real soon." The agent walked over to the ambulance. "From what I hear, he's a tough guy like his son, though."

Sheldon grinned in her direction, even though he wasn't exactly sure where she was. "He's most likely undercover."

Her smile grew wider. "Most likely,'" she said.

☙❧

Down at the docks, Moss waved off the second ambulance. Instead, he got into a waiting car with AKA Bill. He leaned out the window to talk with Agent Copepland. "What'd you say to her? You must've said something because she was smiling."

"I just told her you were some kind of a butthead. And she said, 'I know, but he's a brave butthead.' See you, Chief. Pleasure working with you."

His last glimpse of Agent Copeland was a good one. The woman walked away, still wearing her bikini under a long yellow shirt, the high gold heels of her sandals clicking across the dock, ignoring the whistles she evoked as she strutted passed the boats moored there.

AKA Bill stuck to him like glue as they prepped him for surgery. "Have you ever heard of Howland Enterprises, Moss? That's one of Arauja's shell corporations that operate around your area."

"Howland? That's exactly what I started to look into when JJ came on board." It was hard to talk lying flat on a gurney being pulled ass-backward at top speed by three attendants. However, Moss was determined to contribute as many pieces to the CIA puzzle master as he could. Enough to get a guy like Arauja put away for a long time. He could tell AKA Bill was, too. The agent was jogging along beside him, hanging onto every word.

"Good timing, wouldn't you say?" Bill stood at the Surgical Wing door as it swung wide to let the attendants pulling the gurney roll on through.

That's when Moss felt a needle stab his buttocks, and he dropped off a cliff into the dark,

When he woke up, two moons, one large and the other small, were hovering over him. "Abe?" The bigger moon was wearing Kenya's perfume and had a voice like melted chocolate. "He's coming to, Sheldon. Daddy's going to be fine."

The moons traded places, the smaller one coming close to the bed, peering at him. "You sure, Mama? He looks like he's gonna die."

"That's no way to talk, Sheldon. He's just lost a lot of blood…" Kenya's voice trailed off into a muffled sob. She grabbed Moss's hand and held it to her soft cheek. He could feel her whole body shaking through her fingers.

"Sorry, it's just that he looks like Darth Vader with that mask on. Sorry about your car, Dad."

*This must be Sheldon's virtuous tw*in, Moss thought. He'd never known the other Sheldon to apologize for anything. Moss squeezed his eyes shut, then opened them, rolling them toward Sheldon so that he looked like a mad bull about to gore a runner at Pamplona. "Say what about my car?"

Sheldon took a step back from the bed. "See, I told you, Mama. I'm gonna be grounded for life."

CHAPTER 12

After the surgery to close the knife wound, Moss was hospitalized for, among other things, a ruptured kidney, suspected concussion, four broken ribs, dehydration, infected insect bites, and of course, diarrhea.

"Hell, I had all of that, but the skitters when I played for Alabama," the reluctant patient moaned. "I got to get back to work. No telling what's going down back there."

Sitting beside his bed, Kenya patted his arm. "Relax, honey. I kinda like the ambience down here. I even told Ashlee to line up some gigs around Savannah. Wouldn't it be kinda nice to a little place on the beach where we could all go during the winter?"

With his good eye, he glanced at his wife. She had on her fake smile like those wax lips with perfect teeth kids put on at Halloween. She seemed to have forgotten Christmas night and her kidnapping ordeal, or the fact that her son had been running around Savannah by himself at night, crashing into crooks.

That could be a good thing, he thought, so better not remind her of it now. In could be a Scarlett O'Hara moment of irony, Kenya would put off thinking about unpleasantness today until tomorrow. When she felt less vulnerable, she would re-visit the whole scene. The thought sickened him by the feeling of dread that came with it. What would the scared child within her do then?

The room was filled with flowers which made Moss feel like he was at his own funeral. To stay real, he kept tabs on Mimi's progress, shuffling down to the ICU, pulling his IV behind him.

"She's hanging in there." The charge nurse nodded toward the door that had a big *No Entry* sign on it. "That girl is a fighter, but she has a frail constitution even without the collapsed lung. See that sign? That's because she had an active case of malaria when she came in. That would weaken anybody's immune system. The bullet wounds didn't help. Neither did malnutrition, poor teeth, parasites, you name it. Poor thing will always be on disability, probably for the rest of her life."

Moss almost resented the contrast presented by Faun and Reynolds when they stopped by on their way to the airport. Looking tanned and happy, they were holding hands when they came in his room, but Faun broke away to come kiss him on the cheek.

"Daddy would have been so proud of you." Tears sparkled in her clear blue eyes.

Moss raised his free hand and stroked her bright hair. "You know something, baby? I think your dad was right there, behind me all the way. The last thing he said to me before—on that plane, he said, 'I've got your back, Moss.' I believe he's still doing that." Looking over her head at Chapman, he changed the subject. "I see you've finally got you a man. 'Bout time, too."

Faun wiped the tears away. "Oh, you sound just like Dad. Always trying to marry me off."

"He just didn't want his daughter ending up like poor ol' crazy Dr. Frankenstein, okay? Like 'I have created life!' or something." Moss grinned at Faun's expression of disgust. "Let's have a word with the man to see if he passes muster."

"I'm ready to make an honest woman of her, but she just wants my body." Rey took Faun's place at his bedside as she went to hug Kenya.

"I know the feeling," Moss said.

He shot a look at Kenya who just let out a hoot of laughter.

"Some body!"

"If you don't mind my asking, how did you get the glamorous Chantal West—" Rey nodded at Kenya who was whispering to Faun. "—to marry you?"

"If I knew that, I would've figured out what the hell Faun is talking about when you ask her what she does for a living. I'm gone after the first three words."

Rey Chapman winked conspiratorially. "Know something? Me, too. I just nod when she slows down to take a breath. By the way, I have a message for you from Uncle Bernie. He says for you to get well fast because Prescott is becoming a neo-Nazi, ordering everyone around. And he forgives you for trying to burn down his house because he thinks Prescott did it. Anyway, he says not to worry, the insurance covered everything, and they wanted to redecorate anyway. But the guy who owned the truck is suing him because he didn't have insurance and it was on Bernie's property."

Laughter hurt, but Moss couldn't resist a chuckle. "Same old Springs."

"And something else. Uncle Bernie said to tell you he did some investigating into Spencer-Howland's corporation. Turns out old Howland retired long ago after some corporate raider bought him out. Bernie couldn't even identify where the corporation was based. Said their office was a vacant building on Atlanta's west side."

After they left, Kenya came and snuggled beside him.

"They make a cute couple, don't they? I feel a wedding coming on."

"Where? At your little beach hideaway?" Moss thought he had made a joke, but he could tell Kenya took it seriously.

Kenya sat up. "Now, that's an idea. How come I didn't think of that?"

"I guess 'cause you're not crazy enough to suggest it. Will you stop moving around? You're jiggling the bed."

Kenya snuggled against him again. "Poor baby!"

The following day Arauja was arraigned by a judge who set his bail at one million dollars, pocket change for Arauja, who quickly coughed it up. His lawyer said he had an EB5 visa which made him eligible for a green card. The whole issue of deportation was bound over to ICE, the immigration authorities, and so into infinity.

Arauja and his wife walked out of the Savannah courthouse and, sometime in the middle of the night, boarded their yacht, taking off for places unknown. They left the nuns in charge of Olivia. Monica was charged as an accessory to kidnapping. She, too, vanished with Arauja.

Marcelo came to the hospital to pick Olivia up and take her to school, but the girl had other ideas. "I really want to go home with you," she said to Kenya. "And Flash."

Kenya hugged the girl to her, "You have to go to school, baby. You can come see us this summer, how's that?"

"Oh, no," Sheldon moaned. "That means we'll never get rid of her."

Agent Copeland paid him a visit, this time fully clothed in a short orange linen dress and silver sandals with matching toe nails. "I can't stay long. Just wanted to let you know Arauja gave us the slip, thanks to a judge that was on his payroll. But we'll shut his bogus operations down in the States. That will dry up some of his dirty money. Mimi will be a big help in fingering his contacts in the Caribbean and Honduras."

Moss quirked an eyebrow. "What's she get in return? Beside a bullet in the back and malnutrition."

"Look, Moss, we don't do charity. We can give her asylum and she has a brother in detention ready to be deported for illegal immigration. We'll get him a lawyer and see if he can get a case in court before they deport him. And since one of Arauja's coyotes transported him and left him and about a hundred others stranded in the Arizona desert, in exchange, the brother can help us nail that leg of the octopus."

Considering the current political situation, Moss thought that was the best case scenario. "The land of the free and the deal, I guess."

"You got it. I'll let you know how it turns out, okay." Uncrossing her exquisite legs, Angela Copeland got up and came to his bedside. Bending down she kissed him on the cheek. "Be good," she whispered. "Not many men like you around." With that parting shot, Agent Copeland walked out, leaving a trail of musk and patchouli in her wake.

Sometime during the night, Moss had the dream again. He was running through the dark, menacing death right behind him. He woke up with a yell in a cold sweat.

A nurse came in and covered him with a light blanket. He noticed a dark mole on her left cheek the size of a quarter. "You had a bad dream," she said in a voice with a heavy accent. "Go back to sleep." He glanced at the clock on the bedside table and saw it was two in the morning. There was a hypodermic needle in a tray behind it.

"I have to use the bathroom," he said.

"Okay," the nurse answered. "Be careful."

He noticed she didn't offer to help him to the bathroom like the other nurses had done. When he came back, she was gone and so was the hypodermic needle. About three-thirty, Moss fell into an uneasy sleep. When he awoke, Angela Copeland was sitting there, a Styrofoam cup in her hand, looking like a less-than-perfect angel.

The first thing she said was, "Mimi is dead."

CHAPTER 13

Moss had to look away for a moment. "So much for deals."

"I'm sorry, Moss. Somebody, who knew what they were doing, put something in her feeding tube in the middle of the night. The lab is analyzing it now, but they think it was arsenic because of the symptoms."

Moss made a disgusted sound in his throat. "Rat poison because she was going to rat on Arauja's operations. Sounds like something he'd do. You'd better get her brother out of detention before Arauja's boys find him."

Copeland looked into her coffee cup. "We're working on that."

"Damn it. Why does the law have to work so slow and let scum like Arauja get away with stuff like that? I never will understand that if I live to be a hundred."

Copeland countered that with, "Why do you have to get a search warrant when you know somebody's got an arsenal in their house? Or a meth lab? Or a body in the backyard?"

"I swear the laws are only for us, and not the criminals." Moss threw back the bed covers and pulled the IV needle out of his arm, "I'm out of here," he said, striding barefoot across the floor in his pajama bottoms, his chest still swathed in bandages.

"The doctors okay with that?" Angela knew what the answer would be before she heard it. She knew a determined man when she saw one and Moss, determination was a force to reckoned with.

"The hell with them if they're not. I'm going anyway."

The Moss family took the plane home, and Ashlee picked them up at the airport. Zeb and Wilson were in their car seats in back and Sheldon climbed in between them, feeling suddenly mature. Ashlee looked like she hadn't slept in days, but she hugged Kenya and gingerly kissed Moss who had a twenty-four hour growth of stubble on his face.

"I want to hear all about it when we get home."

"Not all of it." Kenya began humming a little tune. "Only the good parts."

Moss looked at his wife quizzically. "There were good parts?"

"Yeah, like when I crashed Dad's car into the bad guys' limo. That was so awesome!" Sheldon hung over the front seat, ignoring the clamor of the two boys on either side of him.

"We'll have a talk about the awesome parts when we get home." Moss fixed Sheldon with an eye still swollen from the beating and mosquito bites. It gave him clout only Cyclops and professional wrestlers had. Sheldon melted into the back seat.

"Yes, sir."

The personal welcome was almost as exhausting as running through the jungle on Cayman's Key.

Moss dared someone to clap him on the shoulder good-old boy style and had some near misses as people piled into the house where Saranjii had laid a spread big enough for a wake of somebody important. Halee filmed the whole reception, directing the TV cameraman and interviewing guests.

She even got her father to say a few words into the mike, a very few. "Good to be home again. No place like it." Off the mike, she asked about JJ.

Moss figured, although JJ didn't deserve it, he would hide the truth about the man now that he was dead. "Last time I saw him, he was cooling off in the swimming pool."

He had no clue that a perfect storm was about to burst. When he arrived at the office the next morning at eight, there was no Earlene in sight. Instead, a cute, snub-nosed blonde girl was sitting at her desk, examining her eyebrows in her compact mirror.

Tommy Lee was sitting on her desk and leaped to attention when he saw Moss standing in the doorway. "Chief! We didn't expect you back, I mean, I just thought you might want to rest up from your ordeal."

"I'm fine, Tommy. Where's Earlene? She out sick or something?"

"Oh, guess you hadn't heard. Earlene quit. Miss Tina here is her replacement. Miss Tina, this is Chief Moss."

Miss Tina batted her eyes. "Nice to meet you, Chief. Tommy has been bragging on you, how you went down and saved your wife from the kidnappers. I think that's so romantic. It just really gives me the chills."

"Believe it was anything but romantic, Miss Tina. Where's Ears, Tommy?"

"Oh, he quit when Earlene did. They're related, you know. On her mother's side I think."

"So who's dispatching?"

"I guess I am. Unless Prescott's got other ideas."

Moss went into his office and found Prescott's mug on his blotter, Prescott's fat wife's picture on his desk and

Prescott's microwave on his sideboard. "Get Prescott, Tommy. Pronto."

Tommy breathed a sigh of relief. "I'm on it, Chief."

A few minutes later, Prescott came into to the station and stopped short when he saw Moss at his desk.

"Chief! How the hell are you?"

"Let's drop the niceties and get Earlene back here and Miss Daisy out the door on the double. And take your damned coffee cup off my blotter. It left a stain."

His first call was to Bernie who was in his office at the Julia Springs Journal. "Fill me in on all the latest earth-shattering news, Bernie. I hear there was a big-time rumble going down in the ladies Quilting Club."

There was a long silence while Bernie sucked his pipe to fire up the tobacco. "I guess you hadn't heard, the gays and blacks are taking over The Springs. At least, that's what Mayor Asshole Clark said at the town council meeting Thursday night. That's what has brought this wave of crime into our fair city and the police chief thinks he can just take off any time he feels like it, leaving our town wide open to criminals. Anyway, Moss, you get the picture. He's got a referendum going in front of the council tonight to fire you and hire Prescott, the moron, in your place. So other than getting canned, beat up, and stabbed, how the hell are you?"

"No sweat. Getting fired is the least of my worries. I'm really ready to pack it in, anyway, Bernie. No, what worries me is, if Arauja still has operatives in this area, I'm a moving target for his hit men and so is Kenya. We both know he's linked to Spencer-Howland through his casinos, drug-trafficking, and his other illegal operations. That's where he gets his money for his legal businesses like building a huge development outside of Savannah using Wynnton Spencer as his front man."

Moss pictured the editor shoving the pile of papers on

his desk aside and putting his feet up. "If I were talking to anybody else, I'd tell you to be careful. But since it's you, I know I'd be wasting my breath. This is like an undeclared war, and the other side is winning."

Moss imagined Bernie blowing the smoke from his pipe skyward.

"I got the feeling Asshole Clark has something to do with Howland Enterprises," Bernie said. "You know why? 'Cause he went to see Frank McDermott in the hospital right after he got shot, and they had a very short, very intense conversation, according to a nurse who I made friends with."

"I don't see what's wrong with that, he's the mayor. Visiting crime victims is his job."

"Huh. Did he visit me or Miss Kedzia or Bobo? We were all victims of crime. And Miss Kedzia said she has seen him talking to McDermott and other farmers out Alabama Road."

"Probably foreclosing on farm loans they've made at his bank. That's how he makes his money. Some of it, anyway. That's what Kenya says."

"How 'bout this? I paid a visit to the corporate office of Spencer-Howland Enterprises."

"Rey told me."

"Did he tell you I went by Arlen Howland's old place on West Paces Ferry? Big place. Estate really. Knocked on the door, asked to see Arlen, said I was an old friend. An exaggeration really." Bernie's nasal accent spoke of Atlanta's old money.

"Really?"

"Don't get smart with me, Moss. You ain't the only detective around here, you know."

"Did you get in the front door?"

"Yeah, that was the surprising thing. This foreign guy—Japanese or Asian, let me into the big living room and lo and behold out comes Arlen. Or at least, somebody who looks like a Howland, anyway."

"I thought he was retired and living in the Caribbean."

"That's what I said to him and he corrected that in a hurry, saying he flew back and forth to take care of some business interests he had here. So we chewed the fat, he asked where he met me, I said we had gone to the same university but I was a freshman, yadda, yadda. But the whole time I got the feeling he wasn't Arlen Howland. For one thing, his voice was lower, with a kind of accent showing up occasionally. Arlen always had a real twang, a Jimmy Carter type drawl. Another thing was the nose. Arlen had a beak like a hawk. This guy's nose was straight. I know people have nose jobs all the time, but I saw a picture of Arlen in the *Constitution* taken ten years ago. He had the same beak, same bald spot, and this guy looked ten or fifteen years younger."

"I don't know, Bernie. They say those margaritas down in the Caribbean can take years off you."

"No, Moss, you don't get it. The man wasn't Howland. I swear it wasn't him." Bernie fumbled among the paper stacks and pulled out a newspaper clipping. "I've got it right here. I'll send it over."

"I got to be going, Bernie. Fax me a copy of the picture. I want to show it to somebody."

"Be my guest. You going to be at the council meeting tonight?" Bernie sat back with a grin. "Here's your chance to tell Clark what an asshole he is and you're going to miss it?" A roll of ashes landed on his shirt unnoticed.

"I know it's a real shame but just say I'm recuperating if anybody asks."

"Oh, I'm sure they'll ask. Shame you'll miss the party, though."

"Party?"

"Yeah, everyone in town will be there, And I hear they're bringing refreshments. Shame you're going to miss it."

He scanned the photo and sent it to Agent Angela Copeland who shot back an email. *That's not Howland, all right. Besides, he's not been home in Charlotte Amalie in months. Least that's what his housekeeper says. And he hasn't flown out either. Let's talk. Call me at the number on the card I gave you.*

He took the card out again. The name on it was *Angel Bordeaux, personal trainer, masseuse, and cosmetologist. All-In-One Glamour.*

That's the way she answered the phone number he called. "All-In-One Glamour, Angel speaking. Hello, Moss, how're you doing? I hear they're giving you the old heave-ho for being AWOL"

"Good news travels fast. What's your take on Howland? I've got a friend who went to school with Howland and he says the man living in his house is not him. Let's say Arlen made a stink about something and threatened to go public with it. We both know what would happen then. But his bank account shows large withdrawals of cash, thousands at a time from banks all around Panama and Honduras so maybe this man is an imposter and old Arlen is lying low, keeping one step ahead of Arauja's boys. If I was going to keep one step ahead of Arauja, I'd make it one giant step up to Alaska, not play finders keepers in backyard."

Angela exhaled invisible cigarette smoke into the receiver. The sound was meant to be sexy and it was. "Yeah, I thought of that, too. Come down and work with me, Moss. You belong in Miami, not po-dunk hollow or wherever. We could use a good man like you."

"We? You kidding me? I'm too old to work for the feds and, besides, I couldn't pass their physical. No, my home base is here. They've got enough gators and snakes to make Cayman's Key look like a twelve-hole golf course. Is there any way you could get hold of the real Arlen Howland's finger prints or even his DNA. I've got a friend who runs a laboratory in Atlanta."

"Faun Walker, I know. I'll go you one better. I can get into Howland's Saint Thomas house and get his finger-prints and his DNA. My mother is his housekeeper."

"That's convenient." *What game was Copeland playing?*

"I'll run them through the FBI lab and send you a copy. If you can get a set of prints off the bogus How-land, we'll compare them. How's that?"

Moss tried an end run. "By the way, what's with the glamour trip? The card says you run a masseuse parlor and all."

There was an explosion of laughter on the other end. "Not a parlor, sweetie. I choose my clients very carefully. Only the most talkative ones preferably."

He hung up, thinking, *What the hell am I getting into, and how in the hell am I going to do that? I've just been kicked off the police force.*

When he got home, he found there was no one there. Not even Sheldon who had slept around the clock on his arrival back from Savannah. Moss was making himself a sandwich and looking forward to his first cold, long neck beer when the phone rang. It was Kenya.

"Abe, honey, you'd better get down to City Hall right now. Listen!"

There was chanting in the background. "We want Moss. We want Moss."

Kenya was back. "And guess what? They're throwing tomatoes and stuff at Mayor Clark! Quick, turn on the TV. Halee's filming the whole thing! Kedzia's here and Earlene and her mama and—" Suddenly, Moss could hear gunshots and Kenya screamed, "Oh, my God! Oh, my God!"

And then she dropped the phone. The phone recorded a pandemonium—people screaming "Run, run!"

Moss ran back to his car. It was a rental from the airport in Macon, and he had to drive one-handed because his arm was still in a sling so his wound wouldn't separate. But he burned rubber, tearing out the driveway and on the road to town.

When he got to City Hall, Moss saw three things— Interim Police Chief Prescott and Deputy Cal Lee with rifles and a body lying face down in the street. It looked like a scene from the war in Afghanistan.

Getting out of the car, he checked the wounded man's pulse, called 911, then, sprinted passed Prescott up the steps of the city hall and into the meeting room. Mayor Clark and the council were hunkered down behind their desks.

"Is it safe to come out?" If it had been 'Stan, he would have the soldier court-martialed for cowardice. But Ashton Clark had learned to save his skin first as befits the privileged. He got to his feet, assuming the role of city official.

"Ah, it's you, Moss. Glad to see you."

"Did you order this massacre?" Moss clenched his fists to keep from hitting the man.

Clark's cheeks turned bright red as if he were about to explode "Now, just a minute, Moss. You have no right to—"

"Did you?" Moss stuck his face right in the mayor's red one.

"I can tell you that." It was Bernie Segal behind him, pointing a shaking finger at the Mayor. "He did, Ashton Asshole Clark ordered Prescott and Lee to fire into the crowd, and they did just that."

"If you heard me right, I told them to *disperse* the crowd, didn't I, gentlemen?"

The rest of the council nodded mutely, except the only black member who stood up. "You said 'Shoot the bastards!' I heard you very clearly, sir."

"Moses, you couldn't hear a hound dog cornering a coon without your earpiece, I guarantee it." Nevertheless, Clark looked shaken at the signs of a mutiny. "Gentlemen, this has been a terrible event and I move to adjourn until next month. All in favor?"

Moss turned on his heel and walked out, followed by Bernie. The whole family, including a strange puppy, streamed out of the house even before he had opened the car door. They converged on him in a babbling mob while he shouted, "Watch the shoulder! Watch the shoulder!" to no effect whatsoever. Finally the policeman in Moss took over. "Okay, okay, break it up. Let's all take a deep breath and go in the house. I need a beer."

Sheldon got him a beer from the fridge while the ladies gathered as close to his big chair as they could. Wilson climbed in his lap while Zeb nestled beside him. He felt Biblical, like some old prophet gathering his children around him.

"Bang! Bang!" Wilson introduced the topic and what followed was like pulling a champagne cork out of a bottle. The whole room seemed to erupt in laughter. The strange puppy ran and hid under a chair.

Moss sipped his ice cold beer, enjoying the scene. Wilson, encouraged his audience's reaction, kept bang-banging away until Moss stopped him.

Then Zed spoke up. "I don't think that's funny, Wil. Someone could have been killed."

"Actually, someone was." Halee had been watching something on her cell phone then handed it to Moss. "Look at this, Dad."

Holding it away from Wilson, he saw a real time video of the man lying in the street and himself checking the man's pulse with his free hand.

Next shot was the paramedics loading the body on to a gurney and then taking off. "I guess someone filmed that at scene."

Kenya was abnormally quiet. "I was afraid this was going to happen. It's been coming for a long time. It's a real show down."

Moss took a sip of his beer. "This isn't the wild west, baby. There has to be an orderly way to protest. That's what our Constitution and just plain common sense says. Otherwise, somebody like this poor guy gets hurt."

She came back with that fire in her eyes that meant trouble. "But if the people in charge won't even let you speak—"

"Or they brush off what you say," Ashlee chimed in.

"If you'd been there, Dad, it wouldn't have happened." Sheldon leaned in the doorway, suddenly taller than Moss had ever noticed before. "I want to be a lawyer so I can help people who need justice." If he had said he wanted to climb Mount Everest, it couldn't have produced more shock.

Unimpressed by bravado, Moss said, "In that case, you'd better not keep driving without a license and crashing into folks."

Sheldon rolled his eyes and faded back from the doorway. "That again."

"Yeah, that again, and don't go rolling your eyes at me, son." Moss took another sip of his beer, looking around at his assembled family who were looking back at him with adoring eyes. "I'm just glad you're all safe. By the way, whose dog is that?"

They all looked blank. "I brought him home because he was running around loose in the crowd." His daughter dragged the puppy into to her lap. "I was afraid he'd get trampled, he was so scared."

"Is that why he just peed under the chair? 'Cause he's scared?"

೧೨೧

The whole thing was all over the morning news, television, radio, and in the Julia Springs Journal. Editor Bernie Segal couldn't miss a big story like this, Moss suspected. It even made the state coverage and Moss's phone was ringing nonstop. Then he heard Halee's familiar ring.

"Dad, got the TV on? Hal's got some fabulous shots and Atlanta's picked them up!"

The pretty anchorwoman was saying, "Apparently, a grass roots movement to support the local police chief turned into a riot last night when the mayor tried to force his removal and replace him with an acting deputy. The mayor, Ashton Clark, then ordered the council chamber cleared and the police forcibly removed some of the most unruly protesters."

Fresh from her morning shower, Kenya slipped in bed beside him. "Brother Benjamin singing 'We Shall Overcome' was unruly? Didn't hear her mention that the mayor ordered the deputies to fire into the crowd, now did we?"

There followed a shot of Tommy Lee wrestling with a man waving a sign hand-printed in big letters *Moss is Boss*. The focus now was on the sea of placards and signs saying *Dump Clark, I (heart) Moss, Moss Is The Man* and a shot of Earlene holding one that said *Moss Is My Boss*.

The news commentator's ambivalent voice continued. "When the protesters gathered outside the city hall and continued to protest, the police fired live bullets overhead to disperse them. One person was killed, but the cause of death is still unknown. Grover Moss, the former police chief, could not be reached for comment."

He flicked off the TV. "At least they got that part right."

"They want you back, Abe, baby." Kenya purred beside him, snuggling close. "Sweet Jesus, did I miss this when Arauja had me down there. I was so scared. I didn't know what was going on. And that butch guard wouldn't let me out of her sight. I think she was gay or something. She even wanted to come to the bathroom with me. Lucky for me it was a big bathroom."

"You don't even want me to do that." He kissed the top of her head which smelled of honey and roses. "You know something, baby? I missed your smelling good after they threw me in the bottom of that fishing boat."

"Oh, really? You thought I smelled better than dead fish? Well, thanks a lot!"

They both burst out laughing. When she laughed, Kenya was back to normal, he thought. The bedroom door opened and Zeb, with Wilson trailing, came speeding in, jumping on their bed. Wilson tried to get on the bed, but fell back and began to wail.

There were some drawbacks to having little kids, Moss thought, lifting Will on to his lap and making him smile. But the benefits sure outweighed all the drawbacks. It was then he found out Wilson's bottom was soaking wet.

"That's why I was running from him," said Zeb. "Because he smells like pee."

Bernie Segal arrived downstairs with an armload of newspapers. "He's owes me an exclusive interview for setting my house on fire. Where is he?"

Moss was flushed out of hiding to be skewered by Bernie's questions. They were in the big living room when the front door opened and a TV camera on a dolly with Halee behind it came rolling across the black and white marble foyer.

There Moss was, caught in an Alabama tee-shirt with the words *ROLL TIDE* big as life printed across his chest and blue jeans, sipping his morning coffee, and Reynolds Chapman asking him questions. "Chief Moss—"

"I prefer just plain mister, given the circumstances."

"Okay, Mister Moss, what is your take on community policing a town like Julia Springs?"

Of all the questions Reynolds Chapman might have asked, that one was the farthest from his mind. He answered off the top of his head.

"Well, in a town like Julia Springs where everybody knows each other there is no we-they thing, it's just us. If it takes a village to raise a child, then it takes a village to keep that child safe. A whole village, not just the police. But everybody's got to play their part. If you see something, say something. That's the only way it works. When I was growing up in Memphis, the neighbors would tell my mama everything I did at any given time of day. 'The Neighborhood Eye' they called it. I try to keep that in mind when I'm policing. We're all neighbors here."

The interview went viral, on every station in the country. People were as much fascinated by his lifestyle as his character. Here was a black man living in a mansion that had rescued his glamorous wife from kidnappers and gotten wounded in the process. The public ate it up with a spoon. Here was a new made-in-America icon.

After the interview, Moss collared Bernie just as the editor was leaving. "Oh, no, you're not getting off that easy. Now, you owe me. Bernie. You're the only one that can do this, and it's the least you can do for disturbing my peace." He showed Bernie the set of fingerprints Agent Copeland had sent him. "These are the real Arlen

Howland's prints. Your job is to get a set off the fake Arlen, and we'll compare them. The real Arlen hasn't been seen in months, they tell me."

The editor wasn't buying it. "Uh-uh, Moss. I've already on their radar. Next time they'll shoot to kill. Anyway, just how in hell am I supposed to do that? Say 'Arlen, old buddy, would you mind shoving your right hand into this inkpad. Oh, it's a real shame you got ink all your lovely suit. Here, let me wipe it off with alcohol wipes I just happen to have with me.''

"No, Bernie, nothing so dramatic. Just bring back something he's been holding. Like a glass or something." They waited until the camera crew filed past them to their van parked in the driveway.

When they were gone, Bernie resumed their conversation. "Oh, I see. So I walk out of his house with a glass in my hand. 'Here, Arlen, hold this' Next, they'll be accusing me of stealing the silverware."

"You'll make something up. Bernie. Get your inner Sherlock going. And remember, the FBI is waiting to bust him. They just have to make sure their case sticks. He's the one that set those hoods on you because you were getting too close. I bet anything he's Arauja's eyes and ears and boots on the ground."

That built a fire under Bernie. "If I don't come back, I'll haunt you with the smell of fish the rest of your life. People will say 'What's the weird smell?' And you'll say, 'That's just my old friend Bernie stinking up the room.'"

Later that morning, Moss got a visit from the FBI agent investigating the shooting at the church and the burning crosses on Bernie Segal's lawn as hate crimes. Moss assured him they were not and told the agent, whose name was Brian Whitman, what JJ had told him. The fire at Bernie's was just a diversion to pull him, Moss, away from preventing Kenya's kidnapping.

Whitman said he'd already got that figured out. He just wanted Moss not to make any statements jeopardizing the case against Arauja.

"Don't worry. I wouldn't do anything to interfere with an ongoing case, especially one I have a personal stake in." He indicated his arm sling and Whitman just laughed.

"You're lucky, Moss. Most people taken out to Cayman's Key have ended up dead, I hear."

Nodding, Moss grew silent and the agent noticed. "I'm sorry about the girl," Whitman said. "There are lots of unknown soldiers out there. More than you or I know. And they'll never be acknowledged. Never."

"There is one thing I can do for Mimi. She told me she had a brother in detention somewhere in Arizona or Texas. He made the long trek from Honduras and then some hustler dumped a whole truckload of illegals in the desert to make the crossing alone. If the border patrol hadn't found them, he would have died. He's waiting to be deported back to Honduras where Arauja will surely kill like he did her father. I'd like to see that he gets a good immigration lawyer to get him asylum. But I have to find him first."

"I'll see what I can find out and get back to you," the agent said.

Not very convincingly, Moss thought. When Agent Whitman left, Moss found his son in the kitchen.

Wilson was studying his face intently. "You mad, Daddy?"

"No, Will, just thinking."

"You mad thinking?"

"Why? Do I look mad?"

His son nodded. "You always look mad when you're thinking."

CHAPTER 14

That afternoon was New Year's Eve. Ordinarily, he would be out patrolling the city looking for drunks getting an early start on the new year. But since he was restless, and Kenya was busy recording in her studio, he decided to pay a visit to the Regional Psychiatric Hospital where John Howland had been taken.

On the way over, he was listening to the radio get everything wrong about the demonstration in Julia Springs, except the name of the dead man. He was an eighty-year-old resident of the county named Elton Brown. The medical examiner had said he died of an apparent heart attack then fell, cutting his head on the pavement. He had come by bicycle to protest the removal of the police chief, said his sister, Ella Purvis, when reached by phone.

"He would have been happy to know that Chief Moss was the first person to find him and call nine-one-one."

Pulling over on the shoulder, Moss had to blow his nose and dab at his eyes at the unexpected tribute. The radio went on. "…an emergency meeting today, New year's Eve, to discuss recall of Mayor Clark and appointing an interim mayor to run the city until an election can be held in the spring. Meanwhile…"

He turned the radio to a country music station and

drove on. Passing a big house whose front lawn looked like a superstore parking lot, he thought nothing much had changed. He would be out patrolling, tonight just as he always did on New Year's Eve.

When he got to the hospital, an oasis of light in the dark countryside, Moss asked the smiling woman behind the information desk to see John Howland and was told he was in the great room.

He shook his head. "Which one is that? I'm not familiar with that term."

The woman said sheepishly, "Neither was I. When the new corporation took over, they just renamed the old cafeteria." The woman shrugged. "Got to be politically correct these days, don't we?"

Somewhere in Moss's head, there was an alarm triggered by the word corporation. "Sorry? The new corporation? Who's that? What's their name?"

In an answer to Moss's questions, she picked up a brochure from a pile on her desk and handed it to him. "Here, knock yourself out then come back and explain it to me."

He glanced at the brochure in his hand then, doing a double-take, stared at it. At the bottom was Spencer-Howland's logo, the S winding around the H, except the name of the company was Southern Healthcare—another shell company.

Getting a choking sensation rising in his throat, Moss fought off the feeling that the S in the logo had turned into a snake, wrapping around his neck, and was gradually strangling him. Collapsing into a chair nearby, he only pretended to study the brochure while he tried to get hold of himself.

Presently, the feeling subsided, and he stood up again, saying, "Interesting. Are there many more of these Southern Healthcare hospitals?"

"As far as I know, only three so far. Macon, Atlanta, and Savannah, although there's more in the pipeline, I hear. Now you better go see Johnny before they wake the patients up for the party, Chief Moss," the information lady said. "Oh, I know who you are. I watched the whole thing on TV, the way the deputies fired into the crowd. Awful! I'm glad you're back and in control."

He didn't trust himself to say more than, "Thank you" to the woman who led him to a knot of geezers dozing in their chairs in front of a giant TV. "Which one is Howland? I only brought him in four days ago."

The lady from the information desk pointed to the only one watching the television with interest. He was wearing thick glasses. "Johnny's changed a lot since then. No wonder you didn't recognize him."

"Where'd he get the glasses? As I remember, he blind as a bat."

"Miss Doreen paid for them herself. He was almost blind without them. Here, I'll go with you. He's kind of shy of strangers, especially ones in uniform." She placed a gentle hand on Howland's shoulder. "Johnny, there's somebody here to see you."

Howland's face lit up when he saw Moss. "It's the big, black policeman. Did you come to my party?"

"Looks like they're getting ready for a big one." Moss looked around. There were great clusters of balloons and streamers all over the place. Banners saying Happy New Year were festooned in every corner of the room. All this was lost on the dozing patients. "Is there somewhere I can get a cup of coffee? I got a late night tonight."

"Snack stand's still open," the nurse sitting nearby with a patient said. "But nobody's in there."

"How 'bout it, Mr. Howland? Want a cup of coffee?"

"You buying?"

Just then, Doreen Murphy walked in and saw him. "I

heard about the mayor trying to oust you and the riot that broke out." She nodded at his arm. "How's the wound healing? I heard about that, too."

"You and the rest of the world." He deliberately avoided talking about how he got the knife wound. "Thing is, there wouldn't have been any riot except for that moron Prescott firing live ammo over the heads of the crowd." They pushed Howland's wheelchair to the elevator, Moss using his free hand. He nodded at the man in the wheelchair. "How's he doing?"

"He can see, that helps his disorientation a lot. And so does good nutrition." Doreen was wearing a glittery sheath that clung to her curvaceous body like a second skin.

"So does the haircut," Moss said. "In fact, I didn't know him. Can I buy you a cup of coffee or are you on your way somewhere? Silly question. You're looking good, by the way."

Doreen grinned. "Thanks. I do have legs, you know. My boyfriend's picking me up, Chief. It's New Year's Eve. Don't tell me you're working."

"Somebody has to do it, and I drew the short straw. Throwing vomiting drunks in jail for the night, breaking up fights, handing out DUIs. Very exciting stuff. The good thing is I get New Year's Day off so I can watch the games."

"Be careful what you wish for," she said, laughing at his ho-hum expression. "A little quiet is a good thing sometimes. At least, around here."

"Doreen?" He thought about the boyfriend who was waiting for her. "Forget it, you're in a hurry."

She shook her head like a high school girl, making her red curls bob. "I know that expression, Moss. What do you want to know?"

The man in the chair looked up. "What year is it?"

They told him the year coming up was 2019.

"That makes me one hundred years old. I was born on New Year 's Day, you know."

"You look mighty good for your age, Johnny." Moss winked at Doreen who nodded as if that was the way it was with Howland. His progress was mostly exterior. His mind remained where it was, hiding in back of the mill.

"Now, out with it," she said. "What'd you want to know?"

The elevator opened, revealing what looked like the entire staff in party hats waving noise makers. As they streamed by, one of the nurses pushing a cart full of me-diations, said, "I thought you were going to a party, Do-do."

"I was just leaving when this big handsome policeman threatened to arrest me. I'm trying to bribe him."

"Then plead the Fifth and get going." The nurse with the cart saw Johnny and stopped. "Time for your pill, Mr. Howland. Now don't give me a hard time."

Moss took the opportunity to ask Doreen about South-ern Healthcare. "This new corporation, Southern Healthcare, do they have their own pharmacy?"

Ordinarily, she would asked why he wanted to know, but since she was in a hurry and was helping the nurse coax Howland to take his medication like a good boy, Doreen replied, "Yeah, why? You want some pain meds?"

"No, I can't take them and drive. I was just wondering for future reference." He was thinking of Mimi's sudden death in the hospital in Savannah. Supposing somehow the medications had been switched.

Finally, Johnny swallowed the pill, making a face, and Doreen straightened up, cleaning her hands with a disin-fectant wipe. "Yeah, they took over from the private pharmacy, promising cheaper rates. But if anything, their rates are higher. The cost of rooms went up, too. And they're getting rid of Medicaid patients left and right." Nodding at Howland, she whispered, "Poor Johnny. I think he's happy here." Doreen gave Howland a hug. "Happy birthday, Johnny. See you, Chief. Don't be a stranger, hear?"

She walked away with more than one man's eyes following her.

"She smells so nice." Howland adjusted his new glasses and looked at the crowd. "Damn fools, making all that fuss about my birthday. How did you hurt your arm?"

Moss didn't hold out much hope John would remember Arlen, but Howland was full of surprises. He took over wheeling the wheelchair over to the one free table. "Get me coffee and a donut and get one for yourself. We can have birthday cake later."

Over coffee, Moss asked John about his cousin, Arlen. His face lit up. "Is he coming to the party? I'd love to see him. He always brings the best presents like the baseball bat—" Breaking off abruptly, Howland sipped his coffee gingerly. "That's a good cup of coffee. They have the best coffee here."

Tread on neutral ground for a while, Moss thought. *Don't ask too many personal questions.* "Is the food good?"

"The best, only this hotel doesn't have enough cornbread. I'll have to fix some myself when I get back home." Johnny got on topic again. Why did you ask me about my cousin, Arlen Talley?"

That came out of the blue. Moss tried to hide his confusion. "I just wondered what kind of presents he always brought you so I'd get something you like, that's all."

"Mama won't like it if I invite you to my party. No colored, don't you know. She put all the presents away so

I couldn't break them, she said. She said I don't appreciate anything nice."

"Well, that was kinda unfair. You ever find them and play with them anyway? I used to do that when my parents hid things from me."

A guilty expression passed over Howland's face. "Oh, I did once, when I should have been filling the corn meal sacks. Mama, she beat the tar out of me and—" He shifted in his wheelchair as if something hurt him and put a trembling hand to his head.

"And?"

"With the baseball bat. My cousin Arlen brought me a baseball bat and baseball. That's the worst beating I ever got. It's still there, in the closet. She locked me in with it for days so I would hate the sight of it. But I never did. Even though it had my blood on it."

The only thing Moss could think of to say was, "No kidding."

Howland looked at him, his glasses magnifying the pain in his eyes. "Thank you for the donut and the coffee. I better go to my party now. They'll be wanting to cut the cake."

"Before you go, do you know this man?" Moss showed him the photo of Arlen Howland that Bernie had faxed him earlier.

Johnny looked at it with a blank expression on his face. "Who's this?"

"Don't you recognize him? That's your cousin Arlen, except he's all grown up now."

Howland shook his head. "No, it ain't. That's not Arlen. Never saw that man before in my life. Now I better get to my party before they eat up my cake."

Moss wished Howland a happy birthday and headed out into the crisp evening. The leaves were spiraling down in colorful ribbons from the deciduous trees that dotted the pines along the highway. Fireworks occasionally blended with the red-gold of the setting sun melting along the horizon like butter on a hot biscuit. The silhouette of trees was lost in creeping fingers of fog as he pulled into Julia Springs. Funny how he had gotten used to having trees as his skyline instead of the towers and domes of Memphis.

On the way home, he played "what if" with himself, trying out different scenarios with the new information he had just learned. What if, since Howland was nearly blind without his glasses, he would recognize his cousin's voice if he heard it? What if Southern Healthcare's pharmacy somehow had switched Mimi's medication and was planning to do the same thing with John Howland?

Why would they do that? He was obviously not mentally competent and wouldn't make a credible witness. Even if he identified the man posing as Arlen Howland as an imposter, that wouldn't admissible in court. But if Bernie Segal got his fingerprints and they didn't match Arlen's, it would be all over except for the legal battle that would inevitably follow. And John Howland's deposition just might tip the scales in favor of justice.

Over his dashboard phone, he called Bernie on speed-dial.

"What now, Moss? Can't you leave me in peace on New Year's Eve when the rest of the world is partying?"

"One question, Bernie. I just saw John Howland out at Southern Regional and he didn't recognize the picture you sent over."

"Does that surprise you? He's as loony as a catbird from what you say. Plus he's blind as a bat, didn't you say? What'd you expect? Instant recognition?"

"He's got glasses now but he still said he'd never seen that man before. By the way, did you happen to record Arlen Howland's voice when you met with him?"

Bernie sounded tired. When he did that, everything got to be a question. "I thought that was coming. Look, I'm a newspaperman. Of course, I did, whadda you expect? So you want to see if poor demented John Howland will recognize his cousin's voice, right?"

"Bernie, did I ever tell you you're a genius? I'll bring him home tomorrow. Can you and Tommy come over for some drinks after you have your bloody marys?"

"We were planning on getting away to the Bahamas, but sure, Moss, as long as there's a story in it, the Bahamas can wait. About two then? And I'll be recording you and Howland, okay?"

"But no TV cameras this time, you hear me?" As Moss drove up to the gate of Magnolia Alley, a gaggle of reporters and camera crews was waiting for him. "Tell you what, Bernie. I think we're even for disturbing your New Year's Eve celebration. There's a whole pack of newshounds outside my house."

"I know. I sent them over there just get them out of my office. See you at two tomorrow."

The house looked so pretentious and grand, he was almost embarrassed. The reporters were huddling in the growing chill outside its wrought iron gates like poor children come to beg a wassail from the manor house.

He stopped the car, rolling down the windows, as the questions started tumbling in.

"Why don't you guys go celebrate the new year? Only better yet, have a designated driver if you do or you might spend the night in our only jail cell, standing up if I recall last year."

A reporter with a red nose asked, "How does it feel to be police chief again, Chief Moss?"

"Like I never left off. Which I don't think I ever did because the council didn't get around to voting yet."

"What do you think of Mayor Clark's way of dispersing a crowd?" came from a pretty girl who looked like she was fresh out of college.

"If I said what I think, you'd have to bleep most of it out, so I'd just say look at the results."

"Chief, how did you break your arm? Did that happen when you were trying to rescue your wife?"

"My arm isn't broken, I just had surgery on my back, and the docs don't want me to move my arm,"

"From a knife wound, the hospital in Savannah said." The pretty girl grinned when she said it.

"I see you've done your homework, ma'am. Bet you guys know more than I do. Look, I got to eat something before I go out again tonight. We're short-staffed as it is with two deputies suspended."

"Did you know a highway patrol car is parked at both entrances to the town?" asked the one with the red nose.

"See, Ya'll know more than I do, Rudolph. But I'm glad they are."

"About that stab wound in your back, Chief." The cute co-ed hurled her question over the shoulders of her male colleagues.

"The one Mayor Clark tried to give me, you mean?"

A ripple of laughter went through the reporters gathered in front of his gate. "No, the one you got in Savannah. How did that happen?"

"Let's just say that one came with the territory and leave at that. Now, you all go and have fun somewhere else. And Happy New Year!"

He clicked the gate opener and drove through the gate to cries of "Happy New Year!" but he knew they wouldn't go away soon.

When he got back to the station, he was surprised by the number of cars and trucks that were parked there. There was Earlene's battered Ford pickup, her nephew Ears's Chevy coup, Cody Reeds shiny 150, and Kenya's

Caddy convertible. Inside, a chorus greeted him again with "Happy New Year!" Inevitably, Halee was there with a camera to catch the gob-smacked look on his face.

"We thought we'd keep you company." Kenya came up and slipped her arm through his.

"And man the fort." Cody Reed caught the keys to the squad car Earlene tossed him. It had been repaired with a new radiator, but the bumper was still on order. "I'll take the first shift. The graveyard shift is yours, Chief. I've got to preach in the morning."

"Who's gonna get religion on New Year's Day?" Ears detached a head phone from one ear so he could hear the conversation.

"The people who don't party all night. Like us, for instance." Earlene took out her knitting. "I hope it's going to be a quiet night. I've got to clean up the mess Miss Tater Tots left my desk in."

It wasn't a quiet night. Supporters of Mayor Clark clashed with supporters of his recall, both factions being drunk as skunks. Some of the combatants carried the fight over the city limits and were arrested by sheriffs' deputies.

"They were so drunk they couldn't even do much but throw fireworks at each other." Ears gave them a blow by blow narration of the fight. "That must have been better than the dumbest home video on TV."

Moss had to provide back-up for Cody in a least a half a dozen domestic calls when someone reported they heard screaming. One turned out to be a family watching a zombie movie, another was girls being thrown into a pool by guys, and a third, a drunk husband threatening his wife with a knife after she switched the pro football game to the shopping channel. The rest were nuisance calls from high school kids. "Just wanted to see if you were on the job, Chief. Happy New Year!"

They locked up the drunk husband to sleep it off while he muttered that his wife was a compulsive shopper. Then Moss took the graveyard shift. Ears, Earlene, and Halee kept him company. The young people alternately dozed and played games on the computer while Earlene kept knitting as if she were sitting at the guillotine, waiting for an aristocrat's head to fall into the basket.

Kenya, always the night owl, went home to check on the kids then came back with coffee, eggs, and pecan rolls. About four, they all went home, except Ears who slept on the sofa in Moss's office. "Just in case there's an emergency or something. Glad you're back, Chief," he muttered, curling up so his long legs didn't touch the floor. "Prescott was such a jerk."

Taking the graveyard shift, Moss sat by the phone, thinking about John Howland, Jr. and what he had said about his mother. Arqueta must have murdered his father, but how? She had placed the burden of guilt on John's young shoulders, telling him he had been the one responsible for his father's death. No judge in his right mind would convict him of murder, anyway. But if Howland kept confessing to murdering his father, he could be kept in the state asylum for the rest of his life instead of a nursing home.

At six, Moss drove home to get some sleep. The automatic gates were closed, no doubt because of the media. As usual, Moss clicked the remote key and the gates started to pull back but stopped part way as if a stick or something had fallen on the track. He got out a flashlight from the glove compartment and went to see what was blocking the track.

As he walked toward the gate, a shot zinged by his head and through the metal bars. Instinctively ducking back behind the car, he waited for whoever was out there in the dark to come around in back of him. The single shot had come from the direction of the woods across the road. Beyond that, there was a swamp and then the great thicket went that for three or four miles. The sniper could easily get away if he knew how negotiate terrain like that.

Turning out the flashlight, Moss took out the phone from its holder on his belt and dialed Ears. No answer. Next he called the sheriff's office, hoping maybe there was a patrol car somewhere in the vicinity. The county dispatcher answered and Moss told her there was someone firing at him just outside his home. As he spoke, Moss took his arm out of the sling and crawled to the front of the car.

Ditching the phone, he took out his service .38 and fired a couple of shots straight at the woods. He knew his pea-shooter was no match for a sniper's telescopic sight with night vision but maybe that would let the bastard know he was armed. He had a shotgun in the car, but that wouldn't do him any good unless the shooter emerged from the cover of the woods.

It was JJ's style and expert marksmanship, but Moss knew JJ was very dead. The last he had seen of him, JJ was floating face down in Arauja's pool on Cayman's Key. A couple of long minutes went by and then in the pre-dawn stillness, a distant siren came screaming across town.

The whole family was awake and streaming onto the front porch until Moss shouted, "Get in the house! Back-up's coming!" They melted back inside just as another shot rang out somewhere over his head. He heard screams and the front door slamming.

The shooter was aiming at his family! Moss responded with a withering round of gun fire which wasn't returned. The shooter had been scared off. For now, at least.

Behind him, just as the morning sky grew light, he heard car doors slam, and muffled voices as vigilantes poured into the woods. Moss sat back against the car, closing his eyes, back on Cayman's again. Someone was hunting him down, and he had a good idea who it was.

☙☙

Freddy, looking very surgical, was checking the knife wound on Moss's back when he came to. He was lying on the couch on his stomach. His whole family was across the room on the sofa, mute and wide-eyed as if they were watching a horror movie on TV.

"Morning, Chief, looks like you're going to have a scar."

"I'm hardly beauty contest material anyway." When his eyes focused, he was looking at Wilson who was looking back with fright in his eyes.

In a wobbly voice, he asked, "You not dead, Daddy?"

What kind of a world is that when your kid thinks you're going to die on him any minute?

Freddy gave him the answer. "No, your daddy isn't dead, Will, but he's trying hard to be."

Hugging his teddy bear, Wilson edged closer. "Don't try so hard, Daddy."

"Thanks, Freddy. I think that reassured him a lot." Moss sat up. "Holy cr—Is that the time?"

The grandfather clock in the hall struck eleven. "Yes," Freddy said, repacking his instruments in his surgical bag, "I'm afraid you're still police chief, in spite of your date with death last night, Cinderfella. Right now, you better stay right where you are and let the sheriff do his job. I replaced the stitches you tore loose last night being a hero. Now, I got a hot date with my sugar Lelanie for a champagne brunch."

"Where's Kenya?"

Freddy nodded in the direction of the fireplace. Kenya

was asleep in the big chair in front of the fire. Sheldon was on the floor in a sleeping bag, with Zeb beside him. "You scared the hell out of them last night. I got to hand it to you, Moss. From what the boys tell me, you did one helluva job."

Moss sat up and looked for his shirt. "What boys are you talking about?"

Freddy continued putting his instruments away. "Seems a whole lot of guys are on the fuzz buster channel around here and heard your call for backup."

"And?"

"Moss, I know what that look is saying. 'Don't take the law into your own hands,' right? But people around here are independent as hell. They're used to defending themselves. And good thing, too, 'cause they chased that shooter through the woods like a pack of hounds."

Moss sat up painfully. "And like a pack of hounds, they probably tore up all the evidence. If you recall the lynchings back in the day—" His new uniform shirt was hanging in strips. "—geeze, Freddy, did you have to do that to my new shirt?"

"We had to tear it off you, it was so bloody," Freddy said with a wry smile. "You don't need it anyway, not where you're going. Halee, help me take him upstairs to bed."

"Sure thing." Halee was halfway across the room when Moss struggled to his feet.

"Now where're you going?" Freddy grabbed his arm.

Moss grimaced at the sharp pain any movement cost him. "Got to get there before they do. Where's my shirt? Get me a clean shirt, Halee, honey."

She hesitated looking from one to the other.

Half-heartedly, Freddy tried to reason with him. "Look, Moss, it's New Year's Day. Everybody's too hung over to do anything."

"Amen to that," came from the chair by the fireplace.

"Look, Fred, you're the doc, I'm the cop, okay? I don't tell your job, and you sure as hell don't tell me mine."

Freddy sighed and made a gesture of giving up. "Just tell me what you want to do, Moss."

"I have to go someplace as soon as I get a clean shirt."

"Okay, I'll drive you. I'll just call Lelanie and tell her I'll be a little late. She's used to that." He took out his phone and saw the blood spatters on his white coat. "I'll make it lunch instead of brunch. Looks like I'll have to change."

In Freddy's car, Moss kept checking his gun.

"Mind not doing that?" Freddy gave him a nervous glance. "I don't want to get shot. The student loan people will donate my body to science to get their money out of me. You're going to city hall where the action is, right?"

"Action? What kind of action?"

"Grover, have you been living under a rock? They're dumping Asshole Clark and the city council is running the city until a new election. You get to hire two new full-time deputies, man, without Clark and his buddies putting them under a microscope to see the color of their skin. There's gonna be one big party in city hall."

"All that can wait. I got to go out to Georgia Regional, Fred."

Behind the wheel of his old Mercedes, Freddy did a double take. Then he cut his eyes at Moss as if he suspected insanity. "You're kidding me, right? I got to put Lelanie off because you got business out there?"

"I can drive myself."

Freddy shook his close-cropped head slowly. "Oh, no, you can't 'cause I'm not sewing you up again."

"Okay, I promise not to stop you for speeding for six month, how's that?"

"A year. Once I get the MD on my plates."

"Done."

❧❦❧

At the hospital, Moss—with Freddy in trailing behind, apologizing on the phone to Lelanie—hurried into the reception area where the same woman who was there last night greeted them with, "Happy New Year, gentlemen. Chief, you're back again, I see."

"I made a date to pick up John Howland and take him out for a ride. And this is my friend, Doctor Fred Jones, who is going to accompany us. Can you show us where he is?"

At his shoulder, Freddy breathed, "I am? I haven't passed the license exam yet, so you can't refer to me as doctor."

"My bad."

The receptionist meanwhile was threading her way among wheelchairs parked around the big TV. "Same place he was last night, watching TV. But you'll have to wait until he's had his meds, I'm afraid. He wouldn't take his pill this morning because Miss Doreen wasn't here and he had a strange nurse giving it to him."

Moss recalled their previous conversation about Southern Healthcare. "Strange? How so?"

"I don't mean strange, I meant just not his usual nurse. See, we're always short-handed on holidays because the girls call in sick so the new company sent some over."

"You mean Southern Healthcare?"

The receptionist nodded and said in a conspiratorial voice, "Some of them don't speak English very well."

As Moss watched, a nurse approached Howland and bent over him, urging him to do something. Rushing across the cafeteria to where Howland was sitting, Moss said, "Hi, Johnny! You didn't forget we had a date, did you?"

A puzzled look crossed Howland's face. "No, I didn't. Did you come to take me to jail?"

"Sir, he's not going anywhere until he takes his meds." The nurse looked up at the two men. Her dark eyes were as hard as olive pits. "May I ask who you are?"

The receptionist was hovering nearby. "This is Doctor Fred Jones and Chief Moss of Julia Springs Police Department."

To Moss's surprise, Freddy stepped up to the plate. Talking gently to Howland, he said, "Could I see those pills, Johnny?"

The nurse snatched the little cup of pills from Howland's hand and held them tightly. "It's only something to keep him quiet. For his dementia."

Doctor Jones took over. "What *specifically*, Nurse? What kind of medication are you giving him?"

The nurse's defiant glance wavered. "Not sure. Something psychotropic, I guess."

"You're not an RN, I see. Or an LVN. Only a CVA? You do know it's against the law for you to dispense medication, don't you?"

Her eyes dropped to Freddie's name badge. "No, Doctor."

"Then unless you want to lose your job, let me see the pills you're about to dispense to this gentleman."

Moss was surprised at the authoritative tone in Freddy's voice.

Her nervousness apparent, the nurse's aide handed the pill container over. Freddy studied the contents. "This enough to put down a horse," he said. "Let me see his chart."

The little aide appeared to become more flustered. "It's back at the charge nurse's desk. Shall I go get it?"

Freddie was getting ready to tell somebody off, Moss could tell. "You're supposed to have it with you at all times. Moss, look here. This is Fentanyl." He held up an oblong capsule. "If he took that, it would kill him."

Howland was looking from one of them to the other. "Can we go now? I want to open my presents."

"Hang on just a tic, Johnny. I want to talk to somebody." Moss followed Freddy as he strode back to the nearest nurses' station. "Are you the charge nurse?" he demanded of the woman behind the counter. She shook her head and pointed to a rapidly retreating figure down the hall. "No, Doctor, that's her just leaving. There she goes, down that hall."

When Freddie called to her, the dark-haired nurse turned around. When she saw Moss, her eyes widened with fear and she took off running. He stared at her retreating back, thinking she looked familiar but couldn't place where he'd seen her before.

Freddy was back at the desk, slamming his fist down on the counter and looking for all the world like an outraged physician. "I want her name and nursing license number for starters. If she has one. She was trying to give that patient a cocktail of pills strong enough to kill an elephant."

The nurse shrugged. "What do you expect? This new company must be scraping the bottom of the barrel. Incompetent—some can't even speak good English. That one—" She nodded in the vanishing nurse's direction. "—was straight off the boat."

Suddenly Moss broke in. "Did she have a big mole on the side of her face?"

"Yes, how did you know? Is she wanted somewhere?" The nurse shook her head. "Wouldn't surprise me one bit."

Freddy and Moss exchanged nods. "If she isn't, she

will be real soon. And you say she's working for Southern Healthcare? What's her name?"

The nurse ran her finger down a clipboard. "Luckily, we've still got a sign-in record. They installed a punch-card thingie down in the hall, but I still keep a record at the station." Looking up, she said, "Here it is. Veronica Perez. Phone—that's funny. That's just Southern Healthcare's general number. And the switchboard is closed on holidays."

"I'll call. They've got to have an answering service for medical staff." Freddy was on the phone, dialing the number on the sign-in sheet. "Hey, I'm Doctor Fred Jones. I'm looking for a Veronica Perez. She's a nurse who works for you. She just tried to give a patient some Fentanyl, and I'm trying to get hold of her. Got her home number?" He started circling the hall, pacing around on the polished floors. "No, I'm not on staff here at Georgia Regional, and I don't have a patient here—" The phone call ended abruptly, leaving Fred with a dead cell phone still glued to his ear. "They only deal with the doctor in charge."

In his wheelchair, Johnny Howland began to cry. "I'm gonna miss my own birthday party. They have cake, too."

On the way home with Johnny, Moss got out his pistol.

Fred rolled his eyes, feigning horror. "Okay, I won't annoy you, man. Just tell me what's the gun for?"

"Just in case we get ambushed," Moss mumbled, looking out the window.

"What is this, the wild, wild West? I admit that hospitals are a great place for a murder, but did you ever stop to think the girl might have just made a mistake? Happens all the time."

"This wasn't a mistake. Let me fill you in, Doctor Fred." Moss told Fred about Mimi and the dark-haired nurse who paid him a visit at two in the morning. "When I woke up, she was leaning over me, close as you are to me. I saw the mole on her left cheek plain as day. And that was the night Mimi died. I'm on their radar, Fred. But don't tell anybody what happened down there. Kenya's had enough trauma. It's not good for the baby."

He felt Freddie's eyes on him. "Gotcha. What about you? You okay, G.?"

Moss gave his version of a chuckle. "As good as can be expected, isn't that what you docs say?"

"That's what they say, all right," Johnny chimed in from the backseat.

Freddie joined the chuckle. "That's only when we're hedging our bets, man."

At two, Bernie and his partner Trevor came over to sip bloody marys on their way to the airport. The rest of the family was watching Johnny Howland open his birthday presents wearing a left-over New Year's party hat. He looked up at the visitors briefly, saying, "I never had such a nice birthday. The whole town came to my party."

"Open my present next, Mr. Howland," Kenya said. "Sheldon, bring it in here."

Sheldon, on cue, entered the dining room, carrying a large box tied with purple ribbon. The smattering of applause died down to anticipatory silence during which Bernie turned on the tape of Arlen Howland's voice. At first, Johnny didn't look up. He was intent on seeing what was in the box, but when the fake Arlen launched into describing Atlanta traffic, Johnny looked around with childish fear behind his thick spectacles. "Is my brother here? Is that Julian?"

"Open the box, Mr. Howland! See what's inside!"

John Howland, Jr. looked torn between Zeb's imploring him to finish opening his present and paralyzing fear.

"Okay, hold your horses, little one," he said. Then,

looking over his shoulder at Moss, he asked in a trembling voice, "You won't let him hurt me, not on my birthday, will you? He always said that. 'Like hell for leather,' he always used to say that. Excuse my French, ladies. But that's what my big brother Julian always used to say."

Moss shook his head. "No, John. He won't hurt you, not ever again. Now go on, open up your presents so we can have cake and ice cream."

Bernie turned the recording off and the adults were silent, watching Howland open the box with help from eager little hands. Beside him, Kenya whispered to Bernie, "Bless his heart, poor thing. No telling what his life was like growing up."

There was a loud commotion as John saw what was in the box. "Great jumping Jehoshaphat, it's a puppy! You got me a puppy?" The puppy tinkled happily down the front of Johnny's shirt as he swept it to him. "What's your name, sweet thing? I never had a dog before. Do you think the hospital will let me keep it?"

Nobody answered, except the kids all shouting out names like Bullet and Rover. Ashlee got up in a hurry and left the table, dabbing her eyes. Kenya followed wiping away tears, and both women had a good cry in the kitchen. Later, after ice cream and cake, Johnny changed his shirt to a new blue one that Kenya said matched his eyes. Bernie and Moss grabbed a quick conference in the kitchen while they waited for Johnny to come back from walking the kids and the puppy out in the driveway.

As usual, the newspaperman was the first to put it succinctly. "So that was Wynnton Spencer masquerading as Arlen Howland who is his cousin? Damn, Moss! What a story! This is Pulitzer stuff."

"Was his cousin, Bernie. Key word being 'was.' Copeland says Arlen Howland's dead. Never even got to the Bahamas or wherever he was going to retire. Just plain disappeared."

Bernie's eyes gleamed behind his horn-rimmed glasses. "That figures. Just to make sure that he didn't come back to bite 'em in the ass. So Spencer is working for Arauja?"

Moss idly munched the last of the popcorn. "Yeah, but we got to prove it. What do you want to bet they got their tracks pretty well covered with a paper-trail as high as your head?"

"But we have his DNA and his fingerprints. That ought to count for something."

Trevor tapped his Rolex. "Time to go, sweetie. Don't get him too wrapped up in detective work, Chief. Otherwise, he'll cancel on me again."

He was as smooth as brandy and cream softening Bernie's raw edges. They made a good couple, Moss thought—Trevor in his custom English-cut jacket and designer jean and Bernie in whatever Bargain Barn had on the sale table. Kenya hung on his every word as Trevor dispensed decorating advice as easily as fake Santa Clauses dispensed candy at Christmas. In return, Trevor called Kenya his goddess. It was a mutual admiration society for two, a mirror-image of narcissism.

While walking Bernie to the door, Moss took up the thread of the conversation. "So they were cousins, right? Who's to say that before he left for retirement, Arlen signed the whole enchilada over to his cousin Julian. So Julian runs the company, nobody ever sees Arlen again, and Arauja laughs all the way to the bank to launder his dirty money."

That was the moment Bernie said in a low voice, "I hope you know you're speaking to the Jewish James Bond of Julia Springs. Not only did I get a plastic cup the fake Arlen drank out of, but also his snot. I didn't want

Tommy to hear I was playing detective."

It was too tempting. Moss played straight man. "No kidding, he used his cup for a hanky? Gross."

"No, a napkin, and then he stuffed it in the cup, then put the cup down, and got a fresh drink."

"Those poor waiters. The things they must find when they're cleaning up after one of those soirees. Where was this bash anyway?"

"At the Far Hills Country Club, a New Year's Day champagne brunch I made sure I was invited to. For alumni of Princeton."

"Bernie, I had no idea you moved in those circles."

"I don't, but Trevor does. That's why I didn't want him to hear. I went as his date."

Moss told him about the bat. "It clears Junior as his dad's killer. He was only six years old at the time. Blackmon is closing his case and then Georgia Regional is going to find him a place in a nursing home. He isn't mentally competent anymore."

"Anymore? I wouldn't be either if I'd been living in a hole all my life. What kind of mother would do that to her own child?"

"The kind that would murder his father and let him take the blame for it, I guess. Anyway, nice going, Holmes. Let me ship the stuff to the police lab and get it tested for DNA."

"Oh, no! I don't trust anybody anymore except I got a friend, Jewish guy, who'll get it tested for me. Independent lab, that's what's called for now. None of this hanky-panky in police labs where they get the DNA mixed up and pin the case for murder on some poor shmuck. No, I'll tell you when the results come back."

"So the most they can get Wynnton Spencer for is forgery, and I bet they've got away around that, too. Power of Attorney or some such crap unless they find Arlen's body which is probably fish food right now."

At that thought, Bernie winced. "Poor old Howland."

Moss chewed the kernels of popcorn stuck in his teeth. "Just think of him floating in the warm waters of the Caribbean. There are worse places to be."

They looked out the window at Johnny laughing at the kids chasing the puppy around the old fountain. "Anyway, Johnny's happy, that's the main thing. Happiness. You've got to get it while you can."

CHAPTER 15

On their way to the airport, Bernie and Trevor dropped off Howland and the puppy at Georgia Regional. "We don't allow pets," the receptionist told them.

"Don't worry. Chief Moss will be over to pick up the dog as soon as he gets through at city hall," they assured her.

By the time they got there, the party at city hall was in full swing, the meeting had been dispensed with, and so was Mayor Clark. When Moss arrived carrying Wilson with Kenya on his good arm the cheer that went up was deafening. By the time it was over, his face ached from smiling, and he could only nod in return as people welcomed him back. One by one, the revelers lined up to shake his free hand and make long speeches, Moss felt his family had grown to include the whole town.

Then his cell phone rang. "Chief Moss? This Bobo, remember me? I got shot Christmas Eve when they took your wife. Meet me in the men's bathroom. I got something to tell you."

Bobo was still all bandaged up. Seeing Moss, he smiled. "We look like there's a war on."

"Sometimes I think there is, only one of those sneaky

ones they used to call peace keeping operations."

Taking off his Vietnam veteran's cap, Bobo wiped the sweat from his forehead with a crisp, white handkerchief. "Sorry to take you away from your party," he said apologetically, "but something's been on my mind and being shot again makes me think I got to clear my conscience before I go through them heavenly gates."

"Amen to that, brother. What can I do for you, Bobo?"

"I know who killed John Howland and it's wasn't poor little Junior."

Suddenly feeling weak in the knees, Moss had to lean up against the wash basin. After a cursory glance under the stalls, he asked, "Who? Arqueta?"

"Naw, she just a little bitty thing. Like a bird she was. And Mister John Howland was a big son-of-a gun. Over six-two or three. No, it was her oldest boy, Julian. He was a big boy and strong. Athletic."

After twenty-something years as a cop, Moss thought he had heard and seen everything, but this was clean out of the blue. "He killed him? How do you know, Bobo?"

A sound from the far end of the men's room made both men look around, but the conversation had taken such a fascinating turn that they ignored it.

The old veteran folded his arms across his chest and leaned up against the sink. "See, I used to work at the mill back in the day when old Mister John used to grind corn. All hours for a dollar a week and a sack of corn meal for my family. That was before the Army did me a favor and drafted me for Vietnam. Five in the morning 'til sometimes eight in the evening. You see and hear a lot in those long hours. Arqueta would whip little Junior for the slightest thing and haul him upstairs and lock him in a closet. She was as mean a mama as I ever saw and I thought my own mama was mean. But she was an angel compared to Miss Arqueta. She would be sweet as pie to

Julian who was just as mean as she was and that's saying something."

"I hear he was quite a good baseball player."

Bobo nodded. "I'll give him that. But you'd think he was ol' Jackie Robinson or DiMaggio the way she treated him. Let him get away with everything—sassed his step-daddy, beat up Junior, even sassed his mother."

"How'd he treat you?"

Bobo laughed bitterly at the memory. "Like dogshit, not even human shit. He thought he was so big, ordering me around and here he was a kid just a couple of years older. One day I says to him, 'You want to take me on, lil' bro? Then do it, but quit telling me what to do, you hear.' I thought I was dead the way he looked at me."

"What'd he do?"

"Told his mama he saw me peeing in the corn vat. Arqueta told Mister John but he just laughed. 'That will give it a different taste, for sure."

"Sounds like an okay guy. So why do you think Julian knocked him off?"

"Because every time Mister John, he would get on to Julian about doing stuff around the mill and then Arqueta and him would get into it, saying her son was not a slave and he ought to go to Savannah to school so he could get a scholarship to a good university and on and on, day in and day out. So when Junior turned seven, Cousin Arlen came to give Junior his birthday present, a baseball bat and ball, Arqueta took it away and gave it to Julian. Then she beat Junior black-and-blue over some little unim-portant shit and locked him in the hall closet. I could hear the poor kin screaming, 'Let me out, Mama! Please, please let me out. I'm afraid of the dark!'

"When John protested, she screamed at him, some-thing about his family, and he slapped and pushed her aside, called her a whore, and said he was going in the house to let Junior out of the closet. I saw Julian's face. He was playing with his ball and bat—'scuse me, Junior's bat and ball—outside and laughing. When he saw Howland slap and push his mama around. I said to myself 'oh-oh, that boy's gonna do something to get back at his stepfather.' Not ten minutes later, Arqueta told me to go home, I said I wasn't finished, but she said, 'Yes, you are, boy' so I went. I remember she didn't pay me, and I didn't get no sack of cornmeal either 'cause I remember it was Saturday and my mama'd be waiting for the dollar and the bag of cornmeal. I was afraid to go home early so I stuck around behind some bushes, thinking I could steal me a bag of cornmeal to ease my way into my house, you know what I mean? My mama depended on that cornmeal to last us a week."

"So that's when I saw Julian go into the house carrying the bat over his shoulder. I was into the mill to get my sack of cornmeal. Like a flash, when I heard voices coming, I hid behind sacks of corn stacked up against the wall. Here came Arqueta and Julian dragging something heavy between them in a big gunny sack the farmers bring their corn in. They pried up some loose floor boards in the mill, all huffing and puffing, and pushed that sack down in the space under the floor. When it rains, and the lake floods with the streams that feeds into it, that space fills with water. I know 'cause they made me wade down there lots of times to make sure the wheel was clear of garbage people threw into the lake.

"When I went back in the morning, Arqueta said they didn't need me anymore, and gave me two dollars back wages. Two days after, I heard Julian was in Savannah. Arqueta ran the mill with a white guy helping her. Nobody ever seen John Howland again. I heard around town that he had gone off. People knew he wasn't happy with Arqueta. Who would be?"

Moss was silent, thinking how afraid John, Jr. had looked when he thought Julian was in the house. "Would you be willing to record that for me?"

Bobo didn't hesitate. "Yeah, I would."

"Good." Moss held up his cellphone. "Just in case, you said no. Tell me something, Bobo. Why haven't you told anybody about what you saw before me?"

"Now, you know the answer to that, Chief. Who's going to believe the great-grandson of a slave around here? Might just pin it on me, you dig?"

"I dig." As Bobo turned to leave the bathroom, Moss said, "One more thing, Bo. Did you ever hear Julian say 'Like hell for leather'?"

"Like hell for leather." The old soldier thought hard for a while, then he nodded. "I heard Mr. John say that a lot, but Miss Arqueta, she said it was cussing." Bobo chuckled. "Then Mr. Julian took it up. When he belted a ball, he used to say, 'Look at it go! Like hell for leather,' and Miss Arqueta would just laugh. He got away with everything, Julian did. Even murder."

CHAPTER 16

After picking up the puppy from a grateful receptionist, Moss spent the crotch of the afternoon binge-watching bowl games one after another, munching on Halee's special recipe popcorn. Zeb and Will played tackle with their miniature footballs, using the living room as their stadium until a dispute over who had recovered the ball got them evicted into the foyer.

This is the way it ought to be, Moss caught himself thinking between commercials. *Not fighting some night-stalking enemy lurking around behind every tree and god only knows there are enough trees around here to hide an army.* He voiced the thought aloud to Halee who had plopped in the armchair beside him to watch the game.

She took the thought with the matter-of-fact style of a coach analyzing a player's potential. "No, Dad, you get bored too easily if there weren't a challenge around. No, bad guys are your thing. Kenya says so."

The doorbell rang. "If it's those reporters, I'm not available," Moss called. But it was a friend of Halee's, a great length of a girl rightly called Amazonia whom Halee introduced simply as Zonia.

"Zonia said she wants to watch halftime at the Superbowl. We've recorded it just for you." Halee gave her friend a kiss before luring her out to the kitchen on the pretext of making more popcorn.

Zonia, silent as a giraffe and just as graceful, moved her six foot-something toward the kitchen, nodding at Moss as she went by him. He thought he had seen her somewhere before, probably on Halee's college basketball team. But that face…he shook his head to clear it.

Presently, he heard them go upstairs to Halee's room. "We're going to watch it in my room, Dad. So you can watch the game on TV," his daughter called.

Moss suddenly lost the taste for popcorn and, leaving Zeb and Will to watch cartoons in the living room, decided to step out the back door for some cool air.

He was thinking over Halee had just said about bad guys when a voice in the darkness said, "Evenin', Chief."

In a reflex reaction, Moss reached for his gun but he had left his belt and holster upstairs. A figure stepped out on the edge of the back porch light, shapeless as a splayed frog. It was Gator Joe, his dreads dripping in the mist, speaking in the third person way as if he were disembodied.

"Ol' Joe didn't mean to sneak up on you like that. Him only came to tell you something. See, Joe was in the swamp 'cross the road giggin' frogs last night and him seen the man who shot at you. Run right past ol' Joe, he did. Must've been in some kind of hurry not to see him down by the crick."

Moss took a couple of steps toward Joe until he could smell the gator hunter's unique organic scent of clothes never quite dried and pond scum. "Did you get a look at him, Joe?"

"Yeah, Joe did. Old like Joe. White-headed he was. Hunter. Knew his way around, like. Left this behind." The light glanced off a bullet casing which Joe held between thumb and forefinger.

Automatically, Moss reached in his pocket and pulled out a wad of bills, intending to give one to Joe. But the man took a step backward as if he'd pulled out a gun. "No, Joe got no use for money. God gave him frogs and gators and everything else free 'cept fishing license. You get one for ol' Joe?"

"You got it. Anything else?" Moss took the casing and Gator Joe faded into the night.

His voice came out of the shadows. "They's coming tonight. Up at the mill. That's why him's got to get up there before they scare Big Mama away. Thirteen footer. Make good meat. Make ol' Joe fat and rich."

It took Moss a few minutes to process Joe's patois. "Who's coming to the mill, Joe?" It was no use. Gator Joe was gone to get his thirteen foot Big Mama who would make him fat and rich.

"Who wouldn't?" Moss thought aloud as he dialed Cody Reed. He got the voice mail. Then he tried down the line—Owens, Prescott, Ears, and finally, Earlene. She said she was cooking collards, black-eyed peas, and ham—the traditional New Year's supper.

"It's just me and Mother. Why don't you come over and get some?"

"Sounds good," he said, "but I've got to go over to the mill tonight and need someone to back me up. Anyone available?"

"Only Herman and he's no good when there's trouble. I gather you're expecting trouble or else you wouldn't call for backup. The only other one is your daughter and that tall Lesbo friend of hers. But they're only part-timers."

"That's okay. I've just got to check something out." Promising to call if he needed backup, he hung up and went to get his gun belt. Ashlee was in the kitchen when he went back in the house.

She looked up from the broom and dustpan when she saw him. "Did the boys spill all this popcorn? It's all over the floor!"

"No, we did that." Halee and Amazonia thundered downstairs and came into the kitchen laughing.

Ashlee straightened at the sight of the two tall girls. She looked dwarfed beside them. "Then you clean it up."

"Where're you off to, Dad?" Halee saw him trying to slip out of the kitchen unnoticed.

"Oh, just thought I'd make the rounds, that's all."

"You ever stop to think Kenya might need you?" Ashlee appeared to have her back up like a wet cat. She was pouting about something, Moss could tell, but he didn't have time to sort it out now.

"I'm coming right back," he said.

Halee mimicked Ashlee's little girl voice. "Yeah, Dad, you ever think about her? And can we come with you when you're making rounds? There's nothing to do around here. We're bored, aren't we, Zonia. And besides, we need training."

"Yeah, house-training!" Ashlee zinged her back. "You can amuse yourselves by cleaning up the kitchen for starters. I'm not your maid."

What had been a thundercloud turned into a sudden storm. "Then stop acting like one, Minnie Mouse!"

"Oh, shut up, Halee!"

During the confrontation that followed, Moss faded into the background and out to the SUV. On the drive out to the mill, he kept an eye on his rearview mirror, just in case someone was following him. But the road remained empty behind him. Probably people were too smoked from last night to even think of going anywhere.

Before he got to the mill, he turned off his headlights on the stone bridge negotiating the rest of the way by moonlight. Moss suspected an ambush so he stopped just

on the other side of the bridge in the cover of some bushes He spent a long time just looking around before he got
out of his car. With gun in hand, he made his way by
flashlight to the house where John had told him about the
closet.

Testing the rotting floorboards as he went, Moss
creaked his way to the closet on the first floor. Opening
the door, he disturbed a nest of rats that raced squealing
over his feet. Gingerly, he felt around the papers they had
shredded to make their nest. No baseball bat.

The house was built early in the last century, he
guessed. People had armoires since the average person
didn't have many clothes. Closets came into vogue after
the Depression when people didn't have to move so often
and began to accumulate things. He looked at the stairs to
the second floor. They didn't look too promising, but he
had to try anyway.

With his pistol in his free hand, he mounted them, one
rotting step at a time. One stair gave way underfoot and
he had to leap to the next.

*What in the hell are you trying to do, win the Medal of
Honor posthumously?*

He made the second floor in two strides after that
close call, pausing to listen intently for any sign of
movement inside the house or out. The steady chorus of
crickets and peepers, toads and frogs stopped at the alien
sound but as he waited, they started up again.

Seeing a closet at the end of the hall, Moss stayed
along the wall, avoiding the center hallway where the
boards sagged dangerously. Reaching the closet, he
opened it and shone his flashlight around. What at first
seemed like a garden hose wrapped around some rubbish
turned out to be a black snake coiled beside a hardwood
baseball bat and mitt.

Moss resisted the urge to get the hell out of there but

the snake only looked cross at having its winter sleep disturbed. Then it moved sluggishly away into the deeper recesses of the closet, its belly full of mice.

At the thought of the jibes he would get from his deputies about his fear of snakes, Moss got it together enough to retrieve the bat and glove from the snake's nest. Although it was covered with mildew, he could see darker spots where the blood had spattered on it. His mind prevented the speculation on just where that blood had come from.

He was just making his way along the wall to the stairs when he saw through the gaping second floor window, car headlights turn off the county highway on to Howland's Mill Road. The headlights disappeared though the sound of the engine kept coming closer.

From the sound of the engine, Moss could tell it was a truck. He watched as the vehicle pulled in the clearing in front of the mill. Turning off his flashlight, he waited.

Two armed men got out and came toward the mill itself cautiously, as if they were expecting trouble. From his vantage point of the second floor of the house, Moss could see they were carrying automatic rifles. Finally, they exchanged nods as if all was clear and went in the mill building.

Moss could have easily stayed hidden until they left. They hadn't seen his car parked in the bushes beside the bridge and, if the episode on McDermott's landing strip was any indication, they would be gone in five minutes.

But this was his only chance to catch Arauja's operatives red-handed and he wasn't going to miss it. His cell phone vibrated in his pocket and he took a look at it. It was a text message from Cody Reed saying he was on his way.

Moss wasn't adept enough at texting to write a message in the dark so he called the deputy back. The voice mail picked up. In a raspy whisper, he left a message after the beep.

"Listen, Cody, there are two guys armed guys here already. With AK-Forty-Sevens, okay? Hang back unless you have back-up. Get their license plates and description, okay? Don't play hero. Your salary won't cover your funeral."

The old Kevlar vest which Kenya made him wear every time he went out now and his zeal to nail Arauja gave him the fearlessness of the foolhardy. Rats and mice scurried out of his way as Moss made his way gingerly down the rotting stairs and made his way by moonlight to the darkened mill.

Ducking inside, gun drawn, he paused by the door. He figured calling them out would just draw their fire so he waited for the two men to make a move. Suddenly, a flashback hit him and he was back in Iraq, fighting a house-to-house battle with an unseen enemy. Somewhere in the house, the whimperings of women and children took the place of cicadas and peepers. At a crouch, he moved deeper into the building, circling the place where part of the roof had collapsed and a shaft of moonlight pierced the floor. As he moved, Moss tripped over something—sacks of cornmeal piled and left to rot. But in his fear-strained mind, it was a body riddled with bullets. The body of a fallen soldier.

He started firing and yelling horrible things, things he had only thought to himself in his most rabid rages. Lost in the noise of a gun battle, a rusty overhead pulley started to move along a guano-filled track. Moss jerked his head around just in time to get smashed in the face by a cornmeal sack swinging with the force of a wrecking ball. It knocked him off his feet and he hit the floor, blood pouring from his nose. Before he could recover, someone hit him from behind and he blacked out.

The next thing he knew he was outside in the cold night air, facing up so he could see the merciless stars. He was perched on something high and round which put a painful arch in his back. Before he realized where he was, the old mill wheel began to move toward the black water of the pond below.

Realization slowly dawned on Moss as he neared the water that he was going to drown in silence so he began to yell, but something choked back the sound. There was something in the way, a dirty rag. He began to gag as he felt the freezing water on his feet and legs. He was nearly up to his waist when whoever his enemy was gave the wheel a final push and he was submerged in the icy pond.

He struggled to free himself, to kick his legs free from the ropes, but the bonds only tightened underwater. Suddenly, he felt a jolt and he went even deeper under the black water. Something wriggled past his chest. As his eyes adjusted to the murky light, it seemed as if the water was alive. Many oblong shapes—some of them as large as two or three feet long, were swimming away from his writhing body, disappearing into the blackness.

The word '*snakes*' appeared in his slowly freezing mind. *Copperheads!* The correction came as one large dark shape emerged from the muck, two red eyes glowing. It came directly toward him as Moss's lungs exploded his last desperate scream.

Gator!

His sluggish mind recorded the next part in a series of frames as his eyes slowly closed and opened. A powerful, brown arm shot forth, smacked something into the alligator's head that caused blood to spurt out and suffuse the murky water surrounding Moss. There followed such a thrashing and churning that Moss closed his eyes, giving in to the urge to enter into eternal sleep. Instead of blotting out the image of a man fighting a monster in its watery lair, the image appeared behind his closed eyes—a virtual reality show in which the terrible battle played out.

Then, miraculously, he was hauled backward, up, up to the moonlight and deposited on the muddy bank of the mill pond.

The next thing he heard were two female voices. Those would be angels, his water-logged mind concluded.

"He's gone! Here, get out of the way. Let me!"

"He can't be! Papa, you got to live! You just got to!"

Papa? Only his daughter Halee called him that.

Moss felt thumping on his chest, and then someone said, "There's something in his mouth! Get it out, get it out!"

Then someone else blew warm air into his mouth and pumped his chest again. He knew it was CPR and he must be in bad shape. He tried to push whoever it was away, but he was so limp, his arm just jerked and flopped like a hooked fish.

"That's it! It worked! He moved! Give him air, Cody."

"Somebody give me air." That was Cody Reed, sitting back on his heels. "Damn, that's the first time I ever tried that CPR on a real human. A black man, at that. Wheweeee!"

With his eyes still closed, Moss cracked a joke. "I'm not human yet. Kiss me again, Cody. Maybe I'll be white." He tried to struggle up on an elbow. "Did Joe get that gator?"

"That's my papa! Me and Amazonia got the bastards for you, though. So can we be real deputies since we saved your life?" That was Halee, rubbing his arm with her warm hands.

"Got who? The gator?" Moss squinted up at her as she came into focus. Somehow, she had the moon behind her, looking over her shoulder. He now realized he was lying on the bank of the mill pond among thistles and reeds trampled by the legions of rescuers.

Another girl's face joined Halee's peering down at him. It looked like Hazel, the woman he had shared a bathtub with so long ago, it seemed like ancient history. She surveyed him with the same proprietary look Hazel had back in the day. "Chief Moss, you've got snot coming out your nose. Blood and snot. It's kind of gross."

Thank God for daughters to rescue your dignity. Halee sounded less on the edge of hysteria now that he'd recovered enough to ask questions. "Zonia, honey, just get a tissue or something from my purse. Don't embarrass him."

Moss tried again. "Did Joe get his gator? One he calls Big Mama?"

"What gator? Dad, will you stop going on about gators?" Halee had that patient note in her voice she reserved for kids and dogs. "No, we got that snotty bastard I work for—correction, worked for. Reynolds Chapman, that's who we got, didn't we, Zonia? We tackled him just as he was running out of here and when Amazonia threatened to shoot him in the balls with her power bow, he showed us where you were. Claimed he was only coming to rescue you. Huh! As if!"

He looked up at the starry night above him, wincing at the thought of an arrow in the balls. "Where is he now?"

"I've got him in the car, thanks to your deputies here." That was the FBI agent Whitman's voice. "How many fingers do you see, Moss?"

"Why? Have you grown some more? You been living down here too long, Brian."

Halee attempted a laugh, but otherwise, his joke was met with silence. "I think you have a concussion," Whitman said. "The other two got away, but Reynolds will turn state's evidence, I'm sure. Then we'll nail them. He's singing like a canary now."

"I can't believe that city boy sandbagged me. He must've had help from those two armed men I saw."

"No doubt. Looks like he couldn't knock out a cat." Whitman disappeared into the haze again. "Let's move him inside, everybody. He'll catch his death out here."

"I've caught death and let it go." Moss lay back on the itchy grass and chuckled. "Ow," he said. "Laughing hurts."

Cody Reed's face came into view, then out again. "I've got some of floor boards from inside. Heave him aboard on the count of three."

Once back inside the mill which was now lit up with powerful flashlights hanging from the beams so they could see where they were stepping, they set Moss gently on the floor.

On the phone with his superior, Agent Whitman carried on a dual conversation. "Yeah, we've got him outside in the car. Just checking to see if the Chief's okay before we take Chapman up to Atlanta and charge him with attempted murder if nothing else sticks. Didn't find any drugs on him, but the Bureau thinks he's been Arauja's connection in the South because his dad is head of a real estate business directly linked to Spencer Talley's Global Finance and Trust. That's the umbrella company for all the shell corporations of which Howland Enterprises is just a blip on Arauja's radar screen. They think it was Reynolds who set up the attack on his uncle because Bernie was snooping around the Brazilian mafia. In fact, we strongly suspect he set the Christmas Eve fire at his uncle's place so Arauja's thugs could kidnap the chief's wife to keep him quiet. He had two guys with him tonight and, together, they almost drowned Chief Moss. Yes, sir, I'll write all that up in the morning. Good night, sir."

Moss rambled on from the floor, "Like father, like son, too used to the good life. That's what makes guys like Arauja so successful. They're like a virus. They find out where a person's weak spot is and zoom right in."

Halee was sitting beside him, covering him with her jacket. "Papa, now's not the time to philosophize. Just keep still, will you?"

"Okay," he said meekly. "My brain is full of chewing gum. Big Mama almost got me but Gator Joe saved me. I'll have to get him a fishing license."

"Dad, will you stop about gators? It freaks me out," Halee said. "Good, the ambulance just got here. Just lie still, Pops." Nevertheless, he kept trying to get up, but his body seemed to be made of rubber. "Don't move, I said. Just keep lying flat or I'll have to hold you down." Halee forced his shoulders back on his bed of pain.

"Ouch! Nothing like a strong woman." Moss closed his eyes against the pain. "So, Brian, just one thing."

The agent's face appeared beside him. "Only one?"

"Now, you know better than that. How did you know I was coming here tonight? Do you have my place bugged or what?"

Whitman laughed, kind of a phony laugh, Moss thought. "Now, you know you need a warrant for that, Chief."

"But police frequencies are fair game to anybody with a fuzz-buster, right?"

Amazonia held up a dripping plastic bag full of fine white granules. "This ain't no cornmeal I've ever seen. It was stashed in the mill wheel in old feed sacks. We found the hole in the wall where they stuck the sacks into the spokes in the wheel to be picked up by somebody and carried up to the city. It's street-grade coke."

His eyes squinted up at the tall girl. "You aren't any relation to Hazel, are you?"

Zonia's smiled blazed in her dark face. "She's my mother. You know Hazel?"

Halee stopped rubbing his limbs and looked at him quizzically. "Dad? Who's this Hazel?"

Moss thought he did a smart move by changing the subject. "Did anybody see Gator Joe around here to-night?"

That was followed by a chorus of "Who?" Halee rolled her eyes. "There he goes again with the gators."

He was saved by the EMTs coming in. They looked around cautiously. "Is it safe to come in with the stretcher?"

"Oh, don't be such pantywaists! Come on in, boys." Sheriff McKenzie forged ahead of the EMTs with Molly, the drug dog, who bounced all over Moss in her effort to reach the bag Amazonia was holding. McKenzie's cowboy boots clicked across the floor. "Moss, I always find you in a heap of trouble at the wrong time of night. Can't you ever stay home?"

The old floor boards creaked ominously threatening to plunge the lot of them into the murk below and everybody vanished again. The EMTs pulled him clear just as the floor where Moss was lying collapsed, disappearing with a distant splash.

CHAPTER 17

The lab test confirmed it was John Howland, Sr.'s blood on the bat. They got his blood type from Howland's medical records. His son was only six years old and couldn't possibly have wielded a hardwood bat. No doubt, some blood had gotten on the child when Arqueta threw the bat it in the closet and the little boy thought it was his blood, due to the severe beating his mother had given him.

That left Arqueta as the only other adult in the mill, but Arqueta was dead. So the next move was to question Wynnton Spencer, alias Arlen Howland, about the murder of his stepfather.

Moss was thinking about that even as the DA was talking.

"...anyway, that clears John Howland, Junior of his father's murder. He's been declared mentally unfit to stand trial, anyway. Kind of a moot point, I'd say, wouldn't you, Chief? I can call you chief again after all that chicken squabble over termination." Frank Blackmon leaned back in his squeaky swivel chair and looked out his office window at the mist that had settled over the Ocmulgee River. "Day like this makes you want to be at the beach, doesn't it?"

Moss made a negative sound in his throat. "Not me. I burn easy."

Blackmon laughed. "Oh, yeah, I forgot. How's the back?"

Moss winced at being reminded. He had tried to forego his pain medication that morning. It made him drowsy and he was afraid he'd fall asleep on the drive over to Blackmon's office. "If they have to stitch me up again, I'll look like my grandma's crazy quilt. Look, Frank, if Junior didn't kill his daddy, maybe Arqueta did and Julian only helped hide his body under the floor." He played Bobo Franklin's account of what happened, watching Blackmon's expression.

When it was over, Blackmon dismissed the whole story with a wave of his freckled hand. "She was quite a real piece of work from what I hear. Arqueta was like the Lucretia Borgia of the nursing home set. Tried to stab a doctor when she was a resident in a home here. Anyway, she's dead now, and it all happened so long ago, it really doesn't matter if she did or if she didn't, does it? I can't very well bring charges against a ghost, and you've done what you set out to do—clear Johnny Junior of murder. Now you can get him out of the funny farm and into a nursing home, and you will have more than done your civic duty, Moss. Believe me, if half my cases turned out as good, I'd be happy as a hog in a waller."

Suppressing the image of Blackmon as a hog sunk in a wallow, Moss stood up. "You're a busy man and I've taken enough of your time."

"I'm going to have to close out the investigation. That'll be one off my books, at least." Blackmon almost made the mistake of clapping him on the shoulder, but caught himself at the last minute. "Sorry, I forgot."

"What about Spencer Talley? Don't you want to bring him in for questioning, either?"

The DA avoided his eyes, pushing piles of papers around his desk as if they were chess pieces. "What good would that do? From what I hear, he's got lawyers up the wazoo. I got murders from yesterday I have to deal with, not one that somebody said took place fifty years ago. Get the case off your books, Moss, okay? It's taken up far too much time of yours and my valuable time, hear?"

Moss got the message loud and clear.

Walking toward his car, parked in front of the district attorney's office, Moss noticed a black sedan with tinted windows prowling through the lanes of pickup trucks and semis. Its shiny surface reeked of new Brazilian money. The car and Blackmon's words set off alarms in his mind. How did Blackmon, the district attorney for Bibb County know anything about Spencer Talley who lived in Savannah. Spencer Talley, the great, white hunter's thinly veiled threat that he had friends in high places came back to him now. "You said Julia Springs? That's near Macon, isn't it? In fact, tell you what. I go up there on business often so I'll pick you up sometime."

Bernie broke the story the next day. John Howland, Sr. being identified as the body found under the floor of the mill, killed by a blow to the head from an unknown assailant.

The weapon was identified as a baseball bat. Here Bernie's prose became flowery, extolling the virtues of the elder Howland, how he married a war widow with a child, how he ran the only mill in the area producing stone ground corn meal among other products as his father and grandfather before him had done, clear back to the Civil War.

He made only one mention of Arqueta Talley, his wife, the mother of his two sons, Julian, twelve, and John Jr., age six.

The story hit The Springs older generation like a

bomb. Late in the afternoon, the editor called Moss as he was watching re-runs of the Orange Bowl Parade with Wilson and Zeb. "Guess who called me? I'm telling you because you'll never guess from the nearly fifty calls I've gotten so far. James Harris, that's a name you should remember."

The boys groaned and looked pathetic as Moss turned the sound down on the TV. "I should? Why, is he on America's Most Wanted?"

"He not only used to be the leading pitcher for the Peaches, he coached the Georgia team for ten years." Bernie acted like James Harris should be a household word. The TV exploded with a cheer for a float carrying the Rose Bowl Court. "Sorry, didn't mean to interrupt your parade re-runs."

"I know a James Harris I arrested for DUI once. Okay, what's your point, Bernie?"

"Look, this is long distance, for gods' sake? This call is costing me a fortune, Moss. Turn down the TV and I'll tell you."

"Okay, just relax, Bernie. Hasn't the Bahama Mama ambiance done you any good at all?"

Even across the miles from the Caribbean, he could hear the editor impatiently sighing. "Will you please hurry up?"

He could tell Bernie never had kids. "Boys, go watch the one in the family room until I'm finished, okay?" They did so grudgingly, with backward looks that said he was being an old grouch.

"That's better. Here's the scoop. You saw my article on Howland, right? Well, Harris calls me to say that Julian was an up-and-coming young ball player he remembers from years back as attending summer baseball camp for three years in a row. He said he never such power in a twelve-year-old kid then or since. Said Julian Howland could hit one to the backfield wall every time. What d'you think of that, huh?"

Moss was stunned into silence for a while. "Can you verify that? I mean, there must be newspaper articles of high school games somewhere. Bobo said Julian went to live in Savannah with his biological dad's family, the Spencers. Maybe in the newspaper there."

"What are you holding out on me, Moss?" Bernie could sniff a scent of a clue from a mile away.

"Nothing. It can wait 'til you get back. I'm still chief of police, for what that's worth." He didn't want to go into the attack at the mill and Gator Joe saving his life. "Look, Bernie. I hate to burst your bubble but the DA said he's up to his eyeballs in murder cases and to let this one go."

There was a long silence, uncharacteristic of Bernie Segal. "I can see where you're coming from, Moss. Enough is enough, is that what you're saying? Don't mess with Texas, right?"

"Listen, Bernie. All I'm saying is better leave it to the feds. Spencer Talley already has a hit contract out on me, I'm sure of it. Someone shot at me New Year's just as I was getting off work. And when I was at the DA's office just a while ago, a black Mercedes cruised around the office with Brazilian Mafia written all over it. I could practically hear the samba music as it danced through traffic."

Bernie's voice had a weary note Moss had never heard before. It scared him because if the good people got scared, then who would be left to fight for the right? "You're right, If Spencer's connected with the Brazilian mafia, you'd better lay low for a while especially if he knows you're from Julia Springs. That's why I use Trevor's address in Atlanta. Always using the old gray matter as long as it's up there. I'll call you when I get the results back from my friend."

"Just be careful, Bernie, okay? Enjoy your vacation. Party it up big time, okay?"

"Take your own advice. Who got shot at the other night, huh?"

Moss demurred. "Could have been one of Clark's supporters or even a hunter that had too much to drink."

"Since when do drunk hunters drive through swamps without taking out a tree? See ya when I get back, Moss."

"Hey, Bernie, bring me back one of those hats they wear down there. You know, the straw ones."

"You think I'm made of money? Bye, Moss."

Moss called Copeland again. This time her phone said record your message after the tone. He called Agent Whitman and told him he was worried about Copeland. There was a long pause during which Moss had a sinking feeling. "Is she okay?"

"I'm afraid she hasn't checked in yet. And she hasn't been back to her apartment in several days. I'll let you know. But I do have a little good news. I located the girl Mimi's brother out in a detention center in San Diego."

"You work fast."

"I have friends in ICE. Anyway, the agency will get him a lawyer—that's the least we can do. In return, he'll have to tell us what he knows about Arauja's operations in Honduras.

"Which will put him on their short list for assassinations if he's already near the top already."

"Yeah, but we'll shuffle him around so they won't find him. Give him a phony name, fix some papers. By the way, Moss, we better do that for you, it looks like. The boys recovered a bullet casing stuck in the column of your front porch."

"It's got JJ written all over it, I bet."

"Yup. Or somebody who uses the same kind of bullets."

"Now, I'm beginning to believe in zombies. How could he be shot and drowned and still live?"

"Unless Agent Copeland was a plant working for Arauja."

Angela Copeland a double agent? "You mean it was all a fake? But I saw blood when JJ or whatever the hell his name is, fell into the pool."

"She might have nicked him, who knows? Anyway, we think she knocked off the girl you call Mimi."

"But so far, you haven't charged her with anything, right?"

"When the Bureau wants somebody for questioning, they know they're on the radar, Moss. I wouldn't be surprised if Copeland has skipped. Anyway, I'll find out when they're going to release the body and give you a call. By that time, I should know more."

Moss thanked Whitman for keeping him in the loop and rang off. He found Wilson standing in the doorway, looking at him with round eyes full of concern. "You mad-worried again, Daddy?"

"Come here, man." Wilson came over to where Moss was sitting. "What's that all over your face, man?" Getting out his hanky, he wiped the goo off his son's round cheeks. "Don't you know the girls won't kiss a guy that's not cool?"

"And your daddy knows all about being cool." Kenya glided over to sit beside him and together, they both cradled their son. "Isn't it time for another one? The clock is ticking."

"What clock is that? The time bomb or the alarm clock?"

Wilson looked at his mother, who just smiled and kissed him.

"Boom!" Wilson burst into a giggle which sent Zeb and the puppy flying from the dining room to land beside them on the sofa, anxious to join in the cuddle.

Moss pushed the puppy down off his lap. "I draw the line at one with fur and a tail."

"Not to worry. She doesn't have either. See?" From the pocket of her apron, Kenya drew out a sonogram and showed it to Moss.

Wilson frowned at the fetus and drew back. "Looks like a baby squirrel."

Zeb agreed. "Or an alien baby."

Moss just kissed his wife on top of her head. "Shame on your sneaky self, hiding her 'til we can't send her back."

Kenya looked at him in alarm. "You don't want that, do you? Send her back? 'Cause she ain't going anywhere. Not my baby girl."

"In that case, we ought to think of a name for her."

Sheldon, however, was less than pleased. "Not another girl. Isn't Halee enough though she's only technically a girl? She still has fits when I come into the bathroom when she's taking a shower."

"That's because you cover your eyes like a little girl." Halee mimicked a gesture of acute embarrassment. "You look like my old maid aunt, Mama's sister."

"Aunt Flossie Mae?" Moss said. "Is that dried up old string bean still around?"

Kenya looked from her husband to his daughter with growing resentment as Halee pretended offense. "I'll have you know Auntie Florence is a professor, Daddy. Even old maids can achieve their goals without a man."

"I didn't know they had professors of witchcraft. Wonder if your final is to fly around the classroom on a broom?" Waiting until the laughter died down, Moss said into the silence that followed, "What about Mimi?"

"Hey, we were talking about names for our baby girl, remember?"

They all looked at Kenya as if acknowledging she was still there. She realized, then that they all resented her for reminding them they only had a piece of Moss except Wilson who accepted that the fact he had to share his father with other people.

"How 'bout Flossie Mae?" That came from Sheldon who was just as surprised by the hoots of laughter as he was by Kenya's reaction. Getting up from the couch, she marched toward him with fire in her eyes, and he fled up the hall stairs as she swept across the foyer.

Later, Moss found her crying face-down on their bed. He just held her, knowing that anything he said would be the wrong thing. Instinct told him that much. Finally, she raised a mascara streaked face and looked at him. "What were you thinking about, Abe? What's this woman Mimi to you?"

"I just suggested Mimi's name because she saved my life. One life taken away and one life given, that's how it works, isn't it? I'm thinking I ought not to be this happy, but it's a blessing so I'm grateful as hell."

Kenya sniffed long and hard. "Really? Because just now, I felt like I was adding one more burden to your life."

Surprised by her bitter tone, he gathered his wife in his arms. "Honey, don't you see? We're the only family they know, and they all want to make sure they have a place in it. You must remember that feeling after your grandma passed like you didn't belong anywhere. That's how they feel—Halee, Sheldon, Ashlee, Zeb, all of 'em."

Kenya sat up and with a tissue from the bedside table, began wiping her face. "Then we'd better name her Mimi."

"Say what?" He would never get used to Kenya's mercurial shifts from one subject to another or from one mood to another.

"Our new baby girl, you forgot already? Mimi is a right pretty name for a girl, don't you think?" She looked at her husband with golden eyes still swimming in tears like a coastal sunset.

"'Long as she's got your face, we can call her Flossie Mae for all I care. I sure don't want her to look like no Flossie Mae or me either, though."

He stroked her hair and back until she fell asleep against his chest, exhausted by emotion. As she lay there in his arm, he thought how brave his wife was. All the while she had been kidnapped, she had guarded her secret knowing it would tear him to pieces if he knew she was pregnant. And it would have been extra leverage for his captors to torture him with if they had known.

'There are different kinds of bravery,' Quade Walker used to say. *'There's the duty kind that soldiers and cops have, the kind that women have, the kind that keeps the family together, and the kind it takes to get out of bed with hope every morning, hoping things'll get better. That's the bravest kind.'*

Moss didn't know why that came into his mind, but was glad he remembered it. Along with *'I've got your back,'* those words formed the most advice he had ever gotten from the taciturn policeman.

Later that morning, Agent Whitman called and said they were releasing Mimi's body from the medical examiner's office and would be shipping it home to Honduras to the little fishing village where she was from. She would have been twenty-six this June.

"Thanks, Brian. By the way, my friend Bernie Segal has some news for you. Want his number?"

"Way ahead of you there. Segal has already called me and I've already flown the samples up to the lab in Atlanta for a rush job to confirm his doctor friend's findings. But get this, if those aren't a match for Arlen Howland's fingerprints, then whose are they? They're still working on the DNA but fifty bucks says they're not on our national data base. The man could just be a proxy for the real Arlen Howland so he can represent Howland's business interests."

"My guess is he's Wynnton Spencer Howland and he's Arauja's man in Atlanta, one-in-the-same."

There was a lengthy silence and then Moss thought he heard a soft click. Then Whitman's voice came back on. "Who did you say you thought it was?"

Moss explained the whole Howland family tree, beginning with Julian's father, Julian Spencer, Sr. who was killed in the war. "Julian was years older than John so that would put him at about sixty-one or two now. Arlen was John's older cousin, then about fourteen."

"In that case, why pretend to be the old man with a face-lift and a comb-over at all? Why not just say he's Howland's business representative and be done?" Whitman shot back.

"How the hell should I know? All I know is he's the one running Howland's Enterprises as a front for Arauja's money laundering and drug trafficking operations. That's who sent the guys that worked me over in Savannah, and shot Bernie. And what's more, I can prove it."

Whitman sounded like he looking at his e-mail. "Oh, how's that?"

"The DA down in Savannah is keeping one of the guys on ice who robbed me until a grand jury indicts him for assault, armed robbery, and a bunch of other things. Name's Cory Williams but goes by CJ. If he accepts a plea bargain and turns state's evidence, we'll have both Howland and Arauja nailed."

Whitman was back. "That's a big 'if,' man. Bet this CJ'll take hard time rather that rat on the Brazilian or his life won't worth a wooden nickel when he gets out."

"All I'm saying is he may drop us a hint in exchange for a lighter sentence. If he's a pimp involved in a human trafficking ring, he might do business with Arauja."

"Okay, but let me handle that. I'll send our undercover guy down as his cell mate. He'll be the fake Arauja contact offering to spring him."

Moss snorted. "I just hope there's not a real Arauja contact in the slammer. Otherwise CJ will be toast."

Upstairs on the landing, Sheldon was listening to the conversation, about to burst with pride. He had protected his mother wholly without the help of the great man himself. He checked to make sure his mother's credit card was in his jeans pocket. He had overheard her saying to Ashlee she wouldn't be traveling anywhere for a while. Morning sickness, you know.

To a teenage boy the very thought of barfing up your breakfast was gross, much less your breath which made your kids flinch when you went to kiss them goodbye in the morning.

No, if it was anything like when his mom was carrying Wilson, it was much better that the sexy Chantal West wasn't seen by mortal eyes in the daylight. Still, as the future manager of her company, he thought he would leave a few brochures around for her CD's and where interested parties could get in touch with her agent. Business with pleasure that's was what it was all about.

He was still on the landing when Moss got another phone call. It was Angela Copeland. He was so sure Angela Copeland was calling to see if Olivia could come stay with Kenya, he made up his mind on the spot to run away to Atlanta and stay with Aunt Toya.

Moss was on his guard. "So how's business these days?"

She got the message. "I don't have time to talk about business. I'm taking a risk just calling you. But I wanted to see the right thing done by Mimi. After all, I got her into this, and I got her killed."

He noticed the distinction between "I got her killed" instead of "I killed her." He said, "Wrong, Angela. Arauja got her killed."

"Listen, Moss. I'm from Honduras, same village as Mimi, but I was kind of drafted into Arauja's sex racket. Pressure on my family to pay kickback for protection or else their plantain stand would be out of business. When Mimi's father got in trouble with the Brazilians, I told her where they had taken him. I remember I said 'you'd better dress like a boy because if they catch you and find out you're a girl…well, you know what happens.'"

"Yeah. I heard the rest from her. Brave girl. So whose side you playing on, Angela? You with the Brazilian team or the Americans?"

"Both. You don't ever leave Arauja. He'll hunt you down and squash you like a cockroach. So I figure I can give him to the FBI a little at a time, starting with Arlen Howland. The one in Atlanta, only he's not Arlen, you know that already. He works for one of Arauja's fronts, the company Howland sold to Arauja. The real Arlen is dead, take my word for it. I know but I won't say how. It's just that Arauja never leaves loose ends that could bite him in the ass."

Moss couldn't resist asking, "Am I one of his loose ends?"

She didn't answer. Bait-and-switch, he thought. "Look, I've got to get off the phone. Can you send me some money for Mimi's funeral? I've got some but I'm going to fly back to Honduras and that's going to take a lot."

"Would a thousand do?"

"That would be grand. Thanks, Moss. You're a good man." Sound of a wet kiss came over the phone.

"Oh, yeah, and they found her brother."

"Who?"

"Mimi's brother."

"Oh, good. Where was he?"

"Out in California like you said. They're working on getting him asylum."

"Good, good, Okay, I have to go now. Bye-bye!"

'Indians took captives from enemy tribes as slaves, and on pain of death, one such slave was given the task of keeping a wolf away from bodies being prepared for ritual burial To make matters worse, he had to listen to the screams of the slave from the night being skinned alive for letting the wolf carry off one of the bodies. That night, the slave fell asleep and woke up to find the wolf dragging one of the corpses into the forest. In desperation, the slave tossed his spear into the darkness and spent the rest of the night praying to his god.' Incongruously, Walker played the punchline out slowly in Moss's head. *'In the morning, he heard whooping and shouting and thought, oh, lord, I'm toast.'*

"Get to the point, Walker, was he toast?"

Finally, Walker, with a drawl as slow as cold honey, had gotten to the punchline. *'They had found the corpse that the wolf had dragged away and nearby was the body of the wolf with the slave's spear stuck in him. A shot in the dark just might hit its target. But you know wolves run in packs. They're sneaky bastards.'*

CHAPTER 18

oss hurt all over. He wasn't ashamed to admit it. Not surprisingly, his shoulder wound had opened again, bleeding through the bandages on to the pillow. At eight o'clock, Moss was back in the ER.

The weary young surgical resident said the muscle tissue had begun to knit back but the outer stitches were torn loose.

Looking at Moss's chart, he said, "I thought I recognized you. You were in here only four or five days ago."

"Exactly twenty-six hours ago."

The door opened and a nurse said something in urgent tones. The doctor sighed. "Tell them I'm on my way." Scribbling something on a prescription pad, he said, "You cops keep us busy."

"Tell me about it. It's a war out there."

"I'll give you a prescription for the pain, but you probably have a whole medicine cabinet at home full anyway."

"Thanks, Doc, but Jack Daniels is my only pain killer."

"Take care, Chief. And don't try any Judo moves any time soon, okay? Stay the hell the way from the ER or next time I'm going to put you in a body cast."

Now Moss sat alone in the living room, thinking about Angela's phone call. Mimi died from sepsis, not strychnine, Angela told him. No doubt her wound was infected. No doubt. He thought about what he'd seen in Afghanistan, how soldiers from both sides along with civilians had died, their blood mingled together. Somewhere there was someone to mourn their passing. If they were lucky, he thought. But Whitman had said Angela had killed her.

Sheldon looked at his stepfather's face again, as still as any Nubian Pharaoh in repose, and thought how much death and tragedy he had seen. He could overlook Moss sending money to another woman for a while. Men had to stick together. Placing his hand tentatively on Moss's huge one lying on the armrest, he left it there at the risk of looking gay. After all, it was his dad, Sheldon told himself. And he needed some comfort right now. Games could wait. There were more important things in life.

Sheldon quickly removed his hand. "You okay, Dad?"

"Yeah. I'm okay now that I'm home. You?"

With a nod, Sheldon shrugged. "Yeah, I guess." He hoped Moss wouldn't see the crumpled newspaper he had pushed under the sofa with his foot. "Dad, why can't we name the new baby Angela? I think that's better than Mimi." Trying to look casual, Sheldon picked at his face and found soft down on his chin. "Hey, look, I've got a beard!" Moss burst into a loud guffaw. "Calm down, it's not that funny,"

When he caught his breath, Moss apologized. "I'm sorry, man, it was just the way you said it. We'll see if your mom likes it, the name, not the beard. Maybe we name her both? Whaddya think? Mimi Angela Moss or Angela Mimi Moss. Sounds kinda classy, huh?"

His mind was telling him this was a reaction to shock, pain medication, or Jack Daniels on the rocks. Or maybe all three. But Sheldon, with the newfound maturity on his chin, pared his answer down to man-speak. "Sure, Dad, whatever."

Moss checked in with Earlene. As usual, her nasal twang brought him back to reality. "How're you doing, Chief? Good to hear from you," she said without taking a breath. "I heard you had a rough night last night, huh?"

And so will everybody else for ten miles around. "I guess Cody told you about that. So what's new?"

"Well, we located old Mrs. Wilkes' ghost. Nobody speaks his lingo, but he's apparently a Mexican illegal who came with a farm crew and wants to stay here but is afraid immigration will send him back. That's what Cody Reed said anyhow. And the Simmons lost a cow down in the quarry so we had to get a helicopter to get him out. That was the big news of the day. Everybody turned out to watch the cow-lift. People taking selfies with the poor cow in a sling. Rory Simmons says his insurance is going to cover the helicopter fee if that's what you were going to ask."

"So where is this Mexican guy?"

"In our lock-up. He certainly appreciates being out of that basement of hers and the three squares he gets now. Bet he was living on the cheese in her mouse traps, poor thing. I brought some homemade brownies yesterday evening and they were all gone when I left. Oh, by the way, your daughter applied for the part-time deputy spot. Says she still wants to keep her manager's job at the station until she makes up her mind which one she likes better. She gets along with the guys real good."

"Guys?"

Earlene realized her slip too late. "Oh, well, you know Pres and Tommy say they were just obeying orders when they fired their guns above the crowd and let's face it, they were."

"So you let them come back to work after I suspended them, right?"

One thing about Earlene, she could back-pedal faster as she could go forward.

"Well. Chief, Cody said he needed some time off and I didn't reinstate their salaries so they're working for nothing, you gotta face it."

"Earlene, what I gotta face is you contradicting my orders."

"Well, but you wasn't here and there was the Mexican man and the cow and things kinda got out of hand, you know what I mean? Oh, yeah, and one of those big, tall Arizonian guards, or whatever you call them. Lesbians, I guess. Anyway, she came in to fill out an application for deputy. Said she was a friend of your daughter's. Miss Lois gave her a good reference and Miss Isis, too. And it says here she has two years of college majoring in criminal justice."

"Those the only two that applied for the deputy position? The two girls?"

Earlene trotted out one of her endless platitudes. "Times they is a-changing, Chief. Oops! Gotta go! There's the dispatcher's board."

"Hold on, where's Ears? I mean, Marv."

"He's taking a personal day. Gotta get some sleep, he said."

"I'll be there in ten minutes, Earlene. And get me somebody who speaks Spanish. A missionary or something."

They were waiting for him when he drove up, a plain-looking girl and a man who looked like her father—thin, gray, and wearing a clerical collar.

He introduced himself as Reverend Spears and his daughter, Tabitha. They were Baptist missionaries who had spent the past ten years in South America, and they had already found out a lot about Mrs. Wilkes mysterious lodger.

"For a start," said Rev. Spears, "he is not Mexican, he's from Honduras. His name is Miguel Vega."

"Vega?" It came out wrong, more of a reprimand than a word he recognized. The young man in the cell, who was nodding and smiling at what he perceived to be an adequate translation, suddenly changed to a look of panic. He looked from the clergyman to Moss to the girl in desperation, erupting in a stream of Spanish.

"Slow down, man. What's he saying?"

Everything about Tabitha was quiet, even her voice. Moss could imagine birds roosting on her outstretched arms like statues of Saint Francis. "He asks do you know someone named Angela?"

Trying not to give anything away, Moss nodded. This could be an attempt to pass as off as Mimi's brother. Migrants bought fake passports all the time and traded them off like baseball cards. "How does he know her?"

With shaking hands, the migrant pulled from his pants and yellowed, crumpled piece of paper folded in small squares to fit god only knew where. Unfolding it, he presented it to Julia. "I," he said, putting his hand on his chest.

"It's his birth certificate. It says Miguel Fernando Vega, born October 10, 1997. In San Antonia Hospital, San Pedro Sula, Honduras."

"So he's still a minor. Seventeen years old. No telling where he's been."

There was a further interchange of Spanish, then Tabitha said, "He gave somebody else his passport in exchange for food and water. It was all he had to bargain with, he says. Except his body. Oh, yes, Chief Moss, the ones with no money and no family to take them in usually wind in prostitution, they are so desperate."

"So how does he know Angela?"

The young man's face lit up at the name and he burst into a rapid explanation, none of which Moss could understand a word of. Tabitha nodded as if she were keeping time to the rhythm of his words. "They are from the same village outside San Pedro and she was a friend of his sister, Marisa. Mimi, they called her."

Moss was glad he'd been a cop for twenty-five years because the words hit him like a punch in the gut, but nothing registered on his face. Giving no hint of recognition was what had made him a relentless interrogator. Stone Face, they called him back in Memphis, at least, to his face. "So how did he get here?"

"I can answer that." Rev. Spears had been listening quietly, but now took over. "He signed on with a migrant crew in Arizona. They came to Georgia picking tomatoes and peaches and, when they left, he stayed behind, using up what money he had made which wasn't much. He tried to get a job with a crew of sub-contractors from Guatemala putting tin roofs on buildings, but when the contractors didn't pay them, they went back to Guatemala, leaving him high and dry again. He was virtually starving when Mrs. Wilkes mentioned there was someone living in her house and we found him."

"You? But I thought—" He looked over at Earlene who was on the phone, giving a blow by blow of what was going on to her mother. "So if you're willing to sponsor him, I can release Miguel in your custody, Reverend. I promised his sister I'd try to get him a lawyer to file for asylum. I believe there's a loophole in the law that allows juveniles to seek asylum. I'm sure he's in real danger if he goes back to Honduras. Ask him what happened to his father and see what he says."

The boy's hopeful smile faded when the clergyman posed the question to him. Looking directly at Moss, his eyes filled with tears as he hesitantly told the story of his father, a poor fisherman, making some extra money by taking drugs around the Caribbean. One day, he didn't return home to San Pedro and Marisa, his older sister set out to find him. Someone from the village, another fisherman, had seen his boat in another port and asked where Vega was. The new owner of the boat just shrugged and said he had purchased from a friend of a friend. When Marisa didn't return, Miguel got pressured to join a gang of thugs. He left his mother and little sisters and began the journey to the States. It took him two years."

"That means he was fifteen." Just about Sheldon's age, given five months or so.

"At that age, boys are expected to contribute money to the family. And girls are expected to marry. Miguel isn't an exception. He sends his entire wages home, at least, he did." Spears looked at his hands. "It's hard to get them to change, given their poverty."

Miguel sensed the clergyman's despair and put a hand on his arm. Spears listened as the boy set out what seemed to be a five years plan. "He says he must go to school in order to better himself, but he must also find a job. His mother and sisters depend on him."

How could Moss explain that he wouldn't be safe anywhere that Arauja had an operation, especially right here in Julia Springs. "Ask him if he's ever heard of a man called Arauja, Reverend."

As Spears translated, Moss zeroed in on the boy's face, reading hunger, poverty, and tragedy in those sad eyes that had seen too much for a fifteen year old. Yet Miguel wasn't so hardened not to have sensed Spear's despair at bringing the message of salvation to a culture so steeped in blood and corruption. He thought of Sheldon saying indulgently, "Sure, Dad. Whatever."

Now, at the mention of Arauja's name, Miguel went

through another transformation, eyes flashing with anger and macho posturing which left no doubt as to what he intended to do if he ever caught up the Brazilian.

"I gather he's knows him," Moss said.

Pastor Spears gave Moss a look that made him feel like a stranger who had stumbled on an even stranger world. "Of course. Everybody does. Arauja is the biggest sex slave trader, drug lord, and just plain crook in the Caribbean and believe me, down there he has a lot of competition."

The clergyman's words were so incongruous with his staid persona as to appear the Rev. Spears was into ventriloquism. "And Miguel is saying Arauja killed his father."

'*It took him five days to die.*' Mimi's words flashed through his mind. '*After that, they threw his body to the crocodiles.*' Finding his voice was hard around the lump in his throat. "How does he know?"

Spears folded, looking at his hands again. Without having to consult with the boy, Tabitha spoke up. Looking him straight in the eye, she didn't flinch. "Because they would send various body parts by courier to his family—fingers, an ear, and finally, his privates. His mother collapsed and lost the will to live. Miguel and his family scraped a little money together, hoping that would buy them time until they could raise some more. But it wasn't enough." Tabitha was on automatic now, not looking at anyone, but gazing into space as seeing a vision of a better world. "One last package came. Mrs. Vega opened it. It contained her husband's severed head."

"Diablo," Miguel said and burst into tears which poured through his brown, calloused fingers and down his red knuckles. "Diablo." He didn't need the added burden of knowing his sister had died as well. That could wait.

Moss cleared his throat. "If you take the boy, I'll see to it he gets a good lawyer. But I want to talk to him later about…things, okay? And don't let on he's here, Pastor, okay? You never know who might be looking for him, and I don't mean ICE."

After they left, Moss sat at his desk a long time without turning on the light, so long that Earlene became concerned. "You okay in there, Chief?"

"Yeah, I'm okay, Earlene. Hey, and thank you, hear?"

"For what? What'd I do?"

"For just putting up with me, I guess."

Earlene put down her knitting and came to his office door. "Let me tell you something thing, Chief Moss. You're the best damn-tootin' police chief I've ever worked for, except Quade Walker, bless him. The rest of 'em I wouldn't give spit for—a bunch of panty-waist good for nothings, friends of Ashton Clark's. Or his relatives, God help 'em. And don't you go thinking otherwise, okay?"

That wasn't what he was thinking, but he thanked Earlene anyway. He was thinking about what Miguel had suffered in his young life, and like Pastor Spears, he was helpless to stop people like Arauja.

Another thing that stayed in the very back of his mind, but now came forward, unbidden, was the way Kenya had described her captor as "a nice man."

"He was actually charming—for a gangster. He said he wanted to make my stay with his family as comfortable as possible, found out what I liked to eat, let me go to the gym—everything. Even asked me to sing to him and his wife."

"You didn't, did you?" They were lying in bed the night she had told him about the baby, the house was quiet, and she was fooling with the bandage around his chest, playing her long fingernails over it.

She laughed, a sound he had ached to hear. "You better believe I did! Honey, I sang my little heart out. What's the frown for?"

"Because I would have told him to piss off, that's what. Honey, he shot two people—one of who was Kedzia, and kidnapped you."

She kept running his fingernails over his chest. "Hey, baby, you gotta do what you gotta do, right?"

He realized that was how little Kenya Jones had gotten through life until she morphed into Chantal West, the creation of her manager-lover. Angela Copeland had been telling him the same thing, not in so many words, but in her looks, every man's fantasy of a sexy woman. Only trouble was that pose made them vulnerable, able to be exploited, and then tossed aside by men with half their abilities.

"Right, baby?" she asked.

He realized he hadn't answered Kenya's question and she was propped up on one elbow, looking at him with a worried frown. His answer had been an automatic, "Sure, sure, honey."

"No, you're not sure, Abe. It was only a few songs, "The Girl From Ipanima," some James Taylor, Cole Porter tunes, you know what I'm saying? Hey, I got to practice and what else was I supposed to do? Get rusty?"

That got a chuckle from him. "Well, we can't have that happen, can we? You getting all rusty, now. Gonna be like that character in the Oz book I used to read.

"I know, like The Tin Woodsman." Kenya relaxed and snuggled back against him.

"Gonna have to get out the oil can every time you stove up."

"Oh, hush." In spite of their various conditions, they made love that night.

Now, sitting in his office in the early dark of January,

he wondered what Kenya would have done if she had received a package with his head in it like Mrs. Vega had. Then he put away the image and went home to his growing family.

The evening wasn't over yet. They were just sitting down to supper when the phone rang. Not his cell phone, but the house phone. When he asked the caller's name, he found himself talking to the dial tone. Probably the Bradley kid wanting to prove his case, Moss thought. They were all startled by the doorbell and went in lockdown mode—Kenya and Ashlee ran into the kitchen holding Zeb and Will in their arms, Moss drew his gun with Halee right behind him with a chair raised over her head. It was Trevor, Bernie Segal's partner. Not the same dapper dude that left their house for the airport just two days ago, but a disheveled, sad wraith of a man who looked like he had been through hell and come back. He stood in the mist and rain in front of his Bentley and Moss, cautiously opening the door, saw tears running down his face.

"Bernie's dead," he said. "He bought this for you." With a half-hearted gesture, Trevor indicated a box on the porch. Then he turned and walked to the driver's side of the car Bernie called The Grand Duke.

"Wait! Trevor, wait!" Speechless for once, Moss recovered his voice.

"I don't want to talk now, Grover." He got behind the wheel of the Bentley. As he was shutting the driver's door, Moss who was running down the steps heard him say "Not now or ever." Spitting gravel, the Bentley roared away.

The doctors had ordered bed rest while they read the X-rays. They thought he had a pinched nerve, they said. Whatever it was hurt like hell and Moss had spent most of the day knocked out on painkillers. The docs had given him an antibiotic shot and a prescription for pills but whatever was in the pond was there before antibiotics were invented. He had managed to piece together what had happened to Bernie down in the Bahamas. By calling everybody he knew and everybody he didn't, it looked like a simple case of robbery and assault turned fatal. They had even caught the two young thugs and beaten the confession out of them. It appears that Bernie called somebody while strolling on the beach the night he was killed. The thugs mugged him just a stone's throw from the terrace where a steel-drum band drowned the sound of Bernie's moans as he lay dying on the sand. The inquest determined he died from a head wound. His skull was crushed, they said. Moss pictured Trevor identifying the body of his lover and friend. It couldn't have been easy.

In the evening, Sheldon was sitting on the floor, working on Piglet with Moss lying on the sofa, pumped full of pain-killers when the doorbell rang the first bars of Amazing Grace.

"What the hell—"

"Mom's idea." Sheldon sighed with the ennui of fourteen-a-half. "To give thanks for our safe return or some lame idea like that."

"Sounds like a funeral."

"Yeah, Piglet's going to need one if I can't fix him."

"A doorbell?"

"No, Dad, a funeral."

As if on cue, the doorbell rang again.

"Is anybody going to get that? I'm washing my hair." Halee's voice came from the upstairs bathroom

Jealous of Halee's new status as superhero of the month, Sheldon didn't miss an opportunity to snark. "Like she has any to wash."

"Now…"

"I know, I know, Dad. She's your superhero for saving you from getting dunked. Sounds like a blast to me, riding a big wheel down in the water."

"Shel-don!" Halee's voice echoed through the house as if she was calling a foul.

"Okay, okay, keep your hair on. I'm going."

As Sheldon got up, Piglet came to life, swinging around drunkenly and following him as he went toward the foyer. "Wait, master," came out too high up the scale to be human, but distinctly Piglet all the same. "Don't answer the door alone."

"Whoa!" Moss had to get up on one elbow to see this transformation, but the pinched nerve in his back sent him lying flat again. "Piglet's been born again."

Sheldon ran back and fell on his knees, hugging Piglet and laughing. It was a good sound, Moss thought. Kind of like the first snowflakes of winter with Halee as the blizzard that followed. Her hair wrapped in a towel and wearing a short white robe, she stormed across the foyer in bare brown feet.

"I might have known he'd be playing with that thing. Why am I the only one to answer the door in this whole place?"

"Just do it, Halee. We have a resurrection going on here."

There was short conversation at the door, then Halee ran back upstairs. "Dad! Trevor's here!"

Bernie's lover began with an apology. "I'm so sorry to barge in like this." He combed his graying blond hair back with nervous fingers. "But I'm leaving town and I just wanted to apologize for last night when…I said some awful things"

"There's no need. I totally understand." Moss stood there in foyer, weaving on his feet. "Want to come in where it's warm? Have a drink?" he asked hopefully.

To his credit, Trevor had all the instincts of a gentle-man. "No, no, I can't stay. I just wanted to tell you what happened that night. I saw Bernie talking to some woman at the bar when he went to order drinks. The service is awful down there. They do things on their own sweet time. Anyway, during dinner, his cell phone rang. He said, 'I have to take this call.' and took off, even though I had specifically told him to turn the damn thing off when we went down for dinner."

"Did he say who he was talking to when he came back from the bar? The woman, I mean."

"No and I didn't ask him either. I don't mind telling you, Grover, I was getting so fed up with Bernie, I was thinking about breaking up with him. He was really ob-sessed with this man Arlen Howland who he said was an imposter or something like that. Anyway, he got so crazy, I got angry with him and threatened to leave. That's why I didn't ask who the woman was, although she was cer-tainly attractive in a kind of cheap way, Bernie said. I thought he was attempting to make me jealous."

"She was hot? Like real hot?" Angela Copeland with her orange sheath and beautiful legs in those high-heeled silver sandals came to mind.

"I guess so." It was plain that Trevor didn't care a rap about how women looked. "Anyway, he never came back. I have to admit I was a bit jealous."

Jealous enough to kill Bernie? The fleeting thought crossed Moss's drugged mind. "Did anybody recover Bernie's phone?"

Trevor shook his head. "No, the police said the thugs must have taken it. Look, Grover, I've got to get going. Buckhead's a beast what with traffic at Five Points and all. I won't be back. Got a home up there. My business is there, and I'll just put the whole thing behind me. You take care now. Bernie thought the world of you." He choked on the words. "I do, too." He was out the door before Moss could tell him goodbye.

He was sitting back down when Halee handed him the cellphone. "It's Prescott."

As soon as he said "Pres, how're things?" Stu Prescott began a long stream of narrative in his native dialect that Moss handed the phone back to Halee. "Here, I think he's drunk."

Halee took the phone and shouted, "Pres! Zip it, okay?" Then with a grin, she handed the phone to Moss again. "Go ahead, Dad."

What Pres was saying amid all the god almighty damns was he and Tommy Lee chased a man in dreads running from the mill late last night. "The sheriff was there. He can tell you how me and Tommy chased the guy all around the mill pond. But then, damned if he didn't dive right into the water with the copperheads, old mattresses, and all. And guess who it turned out to be under all that shit?" Without waiting for Moss to guess, Pres said, "Gator Joe."

"I figured, Pres. Did he get the thirteen-footer he was after?"

"Yeah, yeah, he did. When he came up, he had that gator by the tail." Prescott paused. "How'd you know about that, Chief?"

"Because he was using me as bait." Through gritted teeth he said, "I'll be in the office tomorrow, Pres. Come see me then, okay?"

There was a note of hope in the deputy's voice. "You better rest like the doc says. We got everything under control, Chief."

"I know and don't worry. I'll see what I can do to get your jobs back."

"We were just following orders, I swear, Chief."

"I know. I should have been there and that wouldn't

even have happened. But you know, family comes first."

"Same here. But these folks here, they are my family, Chief." Pres wobbled off and then sounded like he had suddenly lost his voice.

"I know, Pres. I hear you. I'll make your case in front of the city council. What's left of it."

Following Prescott's call, he was just about out of it but he wanted to phone Reverend Spears to see if the man calling himself Miguel Vega was still there.

CHAPTER 19

When Spears answered, there was a choir in the background singing "The Old Rugged Cross" to piano accompaniment which struggled to keep up with them.

When he asked if Miguel was there, Reverend Spear gave a dry laugh. "He disappeared like smoke after I faxed Immigration his fingerprints, and they didn't match the ones for Miguel Vega. I know they all swap IDs, but he was so knowledgeable…"

"That's because he's one of Arauja's men. I know he's only a kid, but kids grow up fast down there. You're lucky if you reach thirty."

"I feel like such a fool, being taken in like that. I, who thought I was a proxy for God. The vanity of man."

"Just keep on doing what you're doing, Reverend. You and Tabitha. You never know, you just might be the light of hope for somebody else."

Moss spent the night on the sofa, making three painful trips to bathroom across the hall. In the morning at five, Moss took a shower and got some clean sweats out of the dryer. He made coffee and went to the station. It was locked and dark because the jail was empty. Moss was answering the hotline between trips to the bathroom when he heard someone in the main room. Thinking it was Earlene or Ears, he didn't bother checking because the hotline was flashing again.

Answering it, he heard the sound of someone trying to talk but only managing to squeak.

Then a deep, menacing male voice took over. "You better let him go or you'll get her back in pieces." Then they hung up.

He called the number back that was on the tracer. It was a public phone. Moss called the phone company to see where they had public phones. Apparently, the call came from the Hartsfield-Jackson airport.

"Earlene? Ears?" Not getting an answer, he came out of his office. There was a box on the station counter wrapped in brown paper. He called 911 and told there was a suspicious package. They sent the bomb disposal unit from Macon and opened it. It contained a bloody finger at the end of which was a long painted fingernail. On it was written in permanent black marker La Toya. There was a note that read, "This is the first installment. We will give her back if you let him go and back off."

The security camera in the office showed a thin figure in a black hoody wearing jeans entering and placing the box on the counter. Back on the street, he disappeared around the corner of the building into the park.

Figuring she could be the next victim, he called Ashlee. To his vast relief, she answered and started talking. "Grover, I'm on my way down to The Springs. Halee called me and said Kenya wanted me to come down. Any idea why?"

So she hadn't heard. He couldn't risk scaring her so he tried to sound casual. "Oh, just nerves, I guess. Giving up her career to have a baby. You know what that means to her. After the first one and all."

Figuring he'd said enough, Moss couldn't wait to get

off the phone. "Well, nice talking to you, Ash. See you when you get here."

It sounded like Ashlee exploded at the other end. "Moss? Have you heard from Toya?"

Stumbling around over his words, he finally got it out. "No, no. She wouldn't be calling me, her worst enemy, now would she?"

When she didn't answer right away, he said, "Ashlee Pearl, honey?" There was the sound of soft sobbing. "What's wrong?"

The answer was a wail so profound, in such despair that it encompassed all the grief of womanhood. "It's Toya. They've got her, Grover. They're going to kill her."

Not wanting to tell he knew already, he swallowed hard, hoping his voice held steady. "How do you know? And who is they?"

"You know who they are." Another wail, this one ending in soft sobs. "About an hour ago, she called me, she was screaming, and then some guy, it sounded like Cory, cut her off and got on the phone. He...he..." He waited as Ashlee struggled to get hold of herself. "He said..." Her voice wandered off into a soft mew.

"Never mind. I can guess what he said. You drive safe, stay on Seventy-Five 'cause they have highway patrol, and I'll see you at home, okay?"

Through a fog of tears, she said okay and rang off.

All this misery is because of me, because I just wouldn't let things go on like they were going, he thought. I had to be the hero, the good cop putting a stop to the parasites thinking they could get away with any damned thing because they could. Bad people are always going to be there. If I'd have let them alone, this wouldn't be happening.

He stayed in the outer office until seven when Earlene

came in, with Brian Whitman right behind her. "Chief! I thought the doctor ordered bed rest." Earlene put down her knitting bag which bulged with the additional weight of her lunch, coffee thermos, and purse. "I see you're hell-bent on ignoring good advice."

"Now, Earlene, I would be missing out on all the action down here, ain't that right? Come on in, Brian. Want some coffee? I could sure use a cup. Looks like this is going to be another long day."

"So I heard. Black, two sugars, thanks."

"Oh, yeah, I heard you had to call the bomb squad," Earlene yelled from the other room. "I can see the place is still standing so it must not have been a bomb. Mother said it's just some kids playing a joke. Be awful if she was wrong, wouldn't it?"

"That's what drives me nuts about social media. They get the information twisted every time." Moss poured two cups from the coffee pot he kept going all day, put two sugar packets in one and handed it to Brian.

Earlene came in with a plate of cookies. "Mother's double fudge specials, But don't eat them all. Ears will want his share."

Brian sipped his coffee gingerly. "Did the bomb squad take the package with them to the lab?"

"No, I got it the fridge. Want to see it?"

Whitman nodded. "Yeah, yeah, I would."

Earlene dropped the plate so the cookies jumped off on to Moss's desk where they wandered over the papers. "Oh, sweet ever-lovin' Jesus, I just put my lunch in there!"

The FBI man smiled. "I thought that would scare her out of here."

To Earlene's vast relief, Moss took the box of the fridge and brought it to his office, closing the door. Whitman took out his digital camera and took pictures of the finger. "That's definitely Arauja's trademark—cutting off people's appendages to apply pressure on the families. Any word on what they want?"

"CJ and to back off Arauja's man in Atlanta. Julian Spencer."

"Of Howland Enterprises?" Brian was sharp, a little too sharp, as if he had all the details of the case at his fingertips.

Moss told him about the phone call he had at the time someone left the box in the front office, and his conversation with Ashlee.

Brian pressed a button on his phone. "What kind of a car is she driving? She coming down Seventy-Five?"

Moss nodded. "Red Mercedes SL Three-Fifty. License plate PRL nineteen-ninety."

The agent whistled. "Can't miss that one. She must do all right."

"Spends everything she makes." Moss sipped his coffee, the fourth of the day and it was only noon. "Like Kenya. That must be why they picked her to call first."

Whitman repeated everything into the phone and rang off. "We've got a surveillance plane in the area looking for someone else. They'll keep an eye on her."

"Thanks, Brian. They wouldn't happen to be on the lookout for Angela Copeland, would they?" He told the agent about Angela's call last night. "You know what? I think JJ told her my number because my home number is unlisted."

"So that means she's still working for Arauja." Whitman acted like all this was news to him. "Why didn't you call me?"

"I figured you already knew. Besides that I was knocked out on those pain killers the doc gave me. Plus a little Scotch."

"Better watch it, friend. Those things can get addictive

real fast especially with back trouble. They got to me when I hurt my back during an operation that required us to jump a six foot fence. My pole-vaulting days are over, I guess."

"Mine, too. For good. Too many hard hits when I was playing for Alabama." Putting on disposable gloves again, he wrapped up the box again its brown paper. "Better keep this in the freezer until the lab gets it. That is, if Earlene will move all the leftovers she leaves in there. I've got a messenger coming directly."

"Have they got a negotiator on it?"

"This all happened so fast, I haven't had time to call them yet."

"Our best negotiator has a good track record of sixty percent saves. I'll call and see if they can borrow her."

"What are the chances she's still alive. Toya, I mean."

Whitman made a face. "If that is Toya's digit in that box, probably not good. Only testing her fingerprints will prove that. Has she ever been arrested?"

Moss snorted. "That girl's spent more time locked up that she has on the street. And she is on the street some, believe me. Her son's father is her pimp."

Whitman shook his head. "And she has two sisters that have made successes of their lives. What happened?"

"The same old, same old. He started as her boyfriend and supplier. She got hooked on drugs, he was her pimp. Hooked her up with Arauja's prostitution ring. Toya got so stoned, she left Zeb in a beauty shop when he was six months old. Kenya rescued him from going into foster care. We've raised him ever since."

"Could be a bargaining point, though."

"Never. A kid is not a bargaining point."

"To get the dad to rat on Arauja."

Moss got up and topped off his cold coffee. "If I know CJ, he'd rather be tattooed all over with pink flamingoes than ever rat on Arauja. That name even holds sway in prison so why are the rest of us trying to put him away?"

Whitman cocked an ironic brow. "They said the same thing about Al Capone and look where he ended up. What's the matter, Moss? I know the Brazilian has given you a hard time but look at it this way. A small town police chief is doing what powerful international agencies failed to do. That says a lot for the power of a good cop versus all the bad ones. A good cop never gives up until the perp is caught versus the bad ones that knuckle under."

"You've been watching too many cop movies, man. When a man's family is threatened, that's different. And like it or not, Toya is my sister-in-law. My wife's little sister. Kenya's already lost her best friend to drugs. I don't want her to lose Toya, too."

Putting down his coffee cup, Whitman leaned forward. "What if you step out of the negotiations, seeing as the victim is related to you and I take over as a proxy for the family. Would you agree?"

"Yeah, I would. That way, she can't blame me if—"

"Exactly. You give me permission to wiretap this phone and the one at your house? Only temporarily, of course."

"Yeah, I do." Why did he feel like he was giving his life over to the man? *Get a grip on, Moss. You're doing this to save your wife's sister, for God's sake. Zeb's mother, regardless of what she is or has done. You've messed up too.*

The tense moment was interrupted by the messenger. Moss handed him the cold box. "Keep it refrigerated, will you?"

"Sign right here, sir. Mind telling me what's in it, just so I know?"

"Believe me, you don't want to know."

The messenger nodded. "Right. Here's the number. They'll call you when it arrives. Have a good one."

When he got home that night, Moss could tell by the frosty look Kenya gave him that Ashlee had told her about Toya.

"Get a beer from the fridge and then come to the living room. I want to speak to you alone, Grover." He knew she only called him that when she was mad at him so he played dumb.

"Can I eat first? I only had a bowl of chili for lunch. Doc said—"

Her eyes flashed warning signals. "I don't care what they said, just come in the living room, I said."

His back hurt and pain made him mean. "You're talking to me like one of your band buddies when they make a mistake. I know you don't care about my back, but it's my back and I care! I'm going to get a beer. Then I'll come into the living room, okay?"

Moss took his time in the kitchen. When he finally got to the living room, Halee was there covering up Kenya with a shawl. But seeing Moss, his wife sat up and slapped away Halee's hands. "Oh, don't make a fuss! I'm okay. I always black out when I'm pregnant."

His daughter threw him a worried look. "She fainted."

"You have to rest, baby—" Moss began.

"Don't you baby me! Like I can rest when you're getting everybody killed and kidnapped, even my poor little sister Toya!" Kenya gestured in his direction. "And you, all beat up and crippled."

He took a chair and eased back, feeling every vertebra complain. "It's my job, remember? And poor little Toya was being pimped out by CJ who works for Arauja so she got herself into this mess."

She pouted. "I don't care, they sure don't pay enough to get you and everybody else killed. Why did you have to go and stir up this hornet's nest for, anyway? Why couldn't you leave it alone?"

He indulged her and sipped his beer. "Oh, uh-huh! This is beginning to get old."

Sheldon appeared at the doorway. "But, Mom—"

"Don't butt in, little man! I'll deal with you later! Get upstairs to your room, hear me?" Kenya was in full ranting diva mode now, on her feet, advancing on Sheldon.

In spite of the oncoming storm, Sheldon stood his ground. "What'd I do, anyway? You don't appreciate anything I do."

Moss couldn't resist stepping in. "Don't talk back to your mother. Just get upstairs like she asked you to."

Kenya addressed with that cold note in her husky voice that put up a wall between them. "I can control my own son, thank you, Grover."

He made no effort to climb the barrier that was growing between them. "Right! I forgot. Like he ever minded you, Kenya. Who makes him mind when you're away, huh?"

"When I'm away making the money that keeps this house running and everybody eating, you mean. Like your salary goes anywhere."

They were on first name basis now, a sure sign the fight was going to escalate. "So it all boils down to money. Why don't I just give up my job and be like that 'nice' man, Arauja, who kidnapped you and who now has Toya!!"

This was her opportunity to be funny. But Kenya was really dug in now. Her authority—no, her very contribution to the family—was being threatened by male dominance, and she wasn't going to let it pass. Especially when she thought he was seeing another woman and giving her the money that Kenya herself had earned. That was the way to disaster.

What began as simple jealousy turned into a power struggle. Moss felt his own position demeaned by her superior earning power and her flaunting of it. With Halee and Sheldon looking on, he had to stand up for what was right and it certainly wasn't a question of who earned the most. No, it was a question of doing the right thing, no matter what it cost. Why couldn't the woman see that? He had risked everything to go get her back from the kidnappers and to bring them to justice. But it had turned out to be a far bigger task than he had figured on. Like fighting an octopus or a sea monster. So what if he had help from Mimi and Angela? It wasn't a romantic alliance at all, although he had to admit, Angela was a temptation.

It all went south from there. Moss ended up by spending the night on the living room sofa for which he was secretly grateful. The king-sized bed would have been murder on his back and, besides, it held a potential challenge to his manhood. Being a reasonable man, he visualized Kenya apologizing in the morning and making love to him which he knew he couldn't resist.

"Are all pregnant women as bitchy as that?" Halee came back down after making sure Kenya got safely into bed. "If that's how they act, I sure don't want to be one."

"I guess." His painkiller pill was beginning to work. "She wasn't this bad with Wilson as I recall. Just wanted ice cream and pickles together."

"Yuk."

He decided he could even afford a laugh. "Like you used to say, double yuk."

Halee folded her six-foot-something frame up on the floor beside the couch. "Dad, Prescott just called. You didn't hear it because you and Kenya were too busy shouting. He said somebody wanted your home phone. I said okay. Hope that was all right."

"It's in the local phone book. They say what it's about?"

Just then the house phone rang. He signaled Halee not to answer it for a minute to let the wiretap kick in then picked it up himself. A man's voice asked, "Chief Moss? Go to the strip mall out on the highway. Alone. We'll contact you there." And Moss was talking to a dead receiver.

He got out of his chair slowly. "Help me up, will you? Gotta meet some guy out on the strip mall."

"Not without me," Halee said, pulling him to his feet. "I'm your backup."

"No, he said alone. It's about Toya. I recognize the man's voice." Moss strapped on his gun belt, barking orders. "Contact Whitman. Tell him to get his white butt over there, okay."

"Okay."

On the way to the strip mall, the thought occurred to him that reply was far too agreeable for Halee. Sure enough, there was a car following him as he threaded his way across the countryside to the brightly-lit highway that bypassed Julia Springs like the orbit of a comet. There was only a convenience store and gas station combo open. The rest of the stores had closed at five except an adult video place that advertised All The Fun You Have Without Leaving Your Couch. There was a public phone, an anachronism in a world where just about everybody had a mobile phone. He took up a position by it, hoping to scare off anybody who wanted to make a call. He got curious looks from customers who streamed in and out of the store, paying for gas, getting coffee and stocking up on cigarettes. Like he was hustling something, he thought.

The phone rang and he was on it. "Moss?"

"Speaking."

"Are you alone?"

"Maybe. Maybe not."

"Don't play games. You got the package?"

"Yeah, I got it." He wanted to call the caller every name in the book and then some. But he held his tongue, thinking about Kenya.

"Tomorrow night bring fifty K in a plastic shopping bag and leave it behind the dumpster in the alley here. We've got eyes on you so if you bring cops, your sister-in-law will die slowly, one piece at a time, understand?"

"Got it. What kind guarantees are you offering?"

"None."

CHAPTER 20

That night Moss made a calculated decision. He moved into a motel out on the highway. Of his nearest and dearest, only Halee understood. The moment he lay down with a groan she called.

"Dad, Kenya thinks it's because you want to carry on with that woman who you were seeing in Savannah. The one you gave the money to."

"Like I don't wonder what she's up to every time she's away on a gig. Or practicing all night with those boys in her backup? Let her stew a little bit, Halee. That what I say. Let her stew. I get tired of sleeping on the sofa, and it sure doesn't do my back a heap of good."

"Now, Dad, those boys in her backup are either gay or fifty years old or gay *and* old so don't get your shorts in a twist, okay?"

"Halee, it's late, hear? I took a pain-killer and washed it down with Jack Daniels so I'm turning out the lights."

There was that amused, tolerate-old-folks tone in his daughter's voice. "Sorry, sorry, Dad. People will talk, you know. This is a berg, a sneeze on the map, and you got a public profile."

"Not to change the subject but has Ashlee got there yet?"

"She arrived about an hour ago. If you don't mind my saying, scared white. Said an airplane tracked her all the way here. Is she getting paranoid or what?"

"No, she's not. Just tell her hey for me and have a glass of wine."

"Sounds good. Shall I keep you company?"

"No. stay there in case…just in case."

There was a long pause. In it he could hear the wheels turning. Then "Dad? You're not playing decoy are you? Like you did last night. Like your whole attitude is Bring it on, boys. Is that it? What you're doing, playing David to Arauja's Goliath? Only David didn't get hurt, remember?"

"Have a good night, Halee. I love you, hear?"

"Dad, don't you dare hang up—"

He rang off. Settling down on the bed, he sipped Jack over chunks of ice, the hamster slowly going around on its wheel in his brain. Where could he get fifty thousand dollars by tomorrow night? He could borrow against his pension but that would take too long. The answer came sooner than he expected. To get that much cash, he'd have to drain their joint savings account.

The knock on the door made him slop Jack Daniels all over the bed. Getting his service pistol out and slipping out of bed, he used the door for a shield and then jerked it open. A figure in a hoodie stumbled into the room. With his pistol to the back of the intruder's head and an arm around his throat, Moss growled, "Tell me why I shouldn't blow what little brains you've got out right now."

"Because there's somebody right behind me that's got something you want," came Angela Copeland's voice from the hood. "Better play nice, Moss." Using two fingers, he pulled the hood back. Copeland's hair shiny copper hair cascaded out, revealing her lovely, but terrified profile. "Give me the one you call Miguel Vega and he'll let me and your sister-in-law go."

"Tell him fat chance. Anyway, Miguel or whatever is picking peas in Florida."

Between the door hinges, Moss caught a glimpse of a dark figure lurking in the shadow of the trees. Just then a familiar black SUV pulled into the parking lot, illuminating the whole area. Copeland's backup faded into the trees but 1000 watt spotlights on the SUV's roof tracked him down. Moss jerked the woman into his room and slamming the door, prayed it was bulletproof.

"Get down," he yelled just as a volley of gunfire blazed from the SUV outside. A squeal of tires and then another round of automatic weapon gunfire shattered the window of his room, embedding in the mirror over the sink in the dressing room, cracking it into a maze. He found himself on top of Copeland.

"Let me up! It's my only chance. Let me go, Moss. I've got to get away."

He got up so painfully slowly, she could have shot him a half dozen times. Instead Angela Copeland helped him up, grabbing his free arm.

"Jesus, what have they done to you, Moss, *mi amor*?"

She eased him on to the bed where he groaned, lying down again. They could have been a glitzy, mature Juliet and a well-padded but wounded Romeo. This woman, so polished on the outside and so needy inside, was Kenya in so many ways.

"How did you get hooked up with Arauja? I thought you were going straight."

"Arauja's *pistoleros* caught me on the way to the airport. They said if I didn't cooperate, they would kill slowly all my family back home in Honduras. You heard Mimi's story about her father. I'd rather die myself that let that happen. What could I do? Women will survive, no matter what. We are like cockroaches, laying eggs everywhere. Some will hatch, others won't."

"You're about as safe out there as a snowball in hell, Angela. I'll call Brian Whitman. He'll escort you to Atlanta himself."

Sitting on the edge of the bed, she laughed scornfully. "Whitman? What a joke! He's in Arauja's pocket, too. They all are—judges, sheriffs, magistrates, politicians. You Americans are like greedy children. Enough is never enough. Got to have more and more money."

"You know what you're saying, right? Brian Whitman is on the take from Arauja." Moss looked up at Angela's face bending over him. It was unreadable like a book without words.

"He hangs around you all the time, no? Like flies on donkey *caca*. It's so he can tell Arauja everything you do. The States, it's as bad as Honduras, *verdad*!" Angela tossed her hair back, twisted it into bright rope, then pulled the hood back to hide her face. "I'm going now, *mi amor*." She leaned down and kissed him, a long, lingering kiss. "Too bad I can't lay some eggs from you. They'd all be strong, black warriors like you. Goodbye, Grover Moss. Remember your *cucaracha*." Taking off her shoes, Angela then slipped out the hall door.

Hearing a car door slam in the parking lot, Moss tried to get up again. He was half sitting with his pistol pointed at the door when someone knocked politely. "Mr. Moss, are you all right?" He recognized the voice of the motel night clerk.

"Dad? Answer us!" That was Halee, pounding on the door. With a groan, he got to his feet and unlocked the door.

If Angela was right about Whitman, Moss had to get some proof on the agent first before turning him in. *Leave it to me to trust the wrong person*, he thought. Angela was an unknown quantity and a woman with a considerable track record, Brian Whitman was with an agency that vetted everybody up the ying-yang and then some. He had all the right credentials, but so did JJ and Moss was dead wrong about him.

He said as much to Halee who was helping him get his shaving gear and clean shirts packed into his over-night case. There was a disappointed expression on her face he remembered from her childhood when she had anticipated some gift at Christmas and it wasn't under the tree.

"You mean that woman who was just here? I can still smell her perfume. She must take a bath in the stuff. Dad, I know Kenya is a mess right now. No telling what those animals have done to Toya but it's her sister, dammit. You don't have to be cheating on her with that…that hoochie-mama."

He was hurting too much to set her straight. "It isn't what it looks like, Halee. Nothing is, baby. Now take me up to Macon like a good deputy should."

Slightly mollified, Halee drove him to a motel in Macon and got an adjoining room. Although it was close to midnight, he called Murphy, somebody he knew in GBI and told him about Whitman. To his surprise, Murph said, "Where you been, Moss? That's old news, man. We're just tailing Whitman to see if we can bring in the big fish himself. We've already got enough on the Brazilian to put him away for a long time but we want to put him away for life. But first we got to catch the son-of-a-bitch. By the way we got your package. It looks like a match for your sister-in-law, but they'll know definitely in the morning. Sorry to give you bad news."

"Let me get this straight. You guys knew Whitman was crooked but you were using me as bait so Jaws would come after me?"

"No offense, man, but when they shot up your church

and kidnapped your wife, would you want us to sit on our hands? Even when they took her across state lines and the FBI took over, our agents were there. Give us some credit, man. We even had an agent watching your son when they kidnapped you. Even carried his suitcase downstairs for him. We were even right behind Sheldon when he T-boned that limo. You got some kind of Double-Oh-Seven there, man. Like Bond Junior or something."

"Thanks, Murph, but I don't mind telling you I don't appreciate being used for target practice and you wouldn't either."

"I hear you, brother. But when the powers that be order something like that, it means you've made waves where you should have ripples, know what I'm saying?"

"Hell, don't I know? See you in the morning." Moss's voice reflected his anger.

Murph stifled a yawn. "I got news. It is morning."

Moss hung up and took a pain pill, falling asleep with his gun under the pillow beside him, being careful not roll over.

Halee woke him up. "Dad, Dad, wake up. Something's happened at the house. It's bad, Daddy. Somebody put an envelope on the porch. There's photos of Toya and she looks beat up and dead."

Magnolia Alley was lit up like a New York skyscraper. Ashlee was waiting in the doorway as they drove up. As he got out of the car, she clung to his arm. "Heard you had some trouble last night. Motel called at eight to see how you were. Said there was a drive-by. You okay, Grover?"

"Okay, thanks, Ash." He stepped inside looking around as if seeing it for the first time. He still wasn't used to the grandeur of the place. It was like a movie set, one-dimensional with nothing behind it except more decorated rooms. "Where're the boys?"

Still in her robe and barefoot, Ashlee looked pale and tired as if she had spent a rough night. "School bus picks them up at seven-thirty. Kenya's in her room."

"Figures. It's going on nine. She's never up before eleven."

Ashlee yawned and rubbed her eyes. "Be easy on her, Grover. This Toya thing…" She shook her head. "I don't know. Has us all tied in knots."

"Speaking of Toya, somebody left some pictures Halee told me."

"They were on the porch early this morning. I thought it was the morning paper. I tell you that was a shock. They're in the living room on the coffee table. You want some coffee? I made some fresh."

"Sure, I'd love a cup. Why don't I just come sit at the kitchen table? That saves you running back and forth. I'll get the pictures first."

He was moving more painfully this morning after going into duck-and-cover mode the night before. Easing into a straight-backed kitchen chair did wonders for his back, he discovered. Halee joined him and they went through the photos together while Ashlee busied herself with the coffee things.

When Halee asked Ashlee if she wanted to join them, she said, "I've seen the damned things. Toya's dead and she should be, leading that kind of life. Only thing is, it could have been me in those horrible pictures. Makes me sick just thinking about it. If Kenya hadn't invited me down here…" Her thin shoulders started to shake. Then Ashlee nee Baby Pearl sat down on the kitchen floor, sobbing and retching at the same time.

In two giant steps, Halee had Ashlee in her arms, rocking her and stroking her hair. "Go on, sweet sister, have a good cry. Let it all hang out. Whatever she was, she was still your flesh and blood."

"I don't think she's dead." Moss stared at one photograph and then at another one. Then looking back at the first one again, he repeated, "She isn't dead. Looks kind of like a bad trip to me."

"Say what, Dad?" The kitchen was silent except for the coffee gurgling away on the countertop and Ashlee's occasional hiccups as she wiped up the mess on the floor.

"Look here," He showed one photo of Toya stretched out on her back, eyes wide open, staring upward at the ceiling. Ashlee covered her eyes. "Dead people's eyes usually roll up in their heads. She's just stoned out of her skull. See, in this one she's curled up on her side, eyes closed. 'Course the missing finger looks bad, like she hasn't seen a doctor. And in this one, her mouth is open, but her eyes are closed." His phone buzzed on his belt. Taking it out, he glanced at the caller ID. It said Unknown Caller. He growled, "Moss."

A jocular, accented voice on the other end said, "Is this the famous detective Grover Moss?"

Moss said it was. "This is Julio Arauja speaking. How are you? You are walking most painfully."

"Yeah, thanks to your goons. You'll be glad to know we got both of them in the slammer. What do you want, Arauja? If it's a trade, no go."

"No, it's what you want, Mr. Moss. You are looking at her this minute, I assume."

"Hurry up, Arauja. I haven't got all day."

"I want to make a gift to your lovely wife, Miss Chantal. A gift of her sister."

"You mean her body, don't you?"

"No, no. As you can see she's quite alive, although I must say my boys got a little…what you say?…carried away when they were interviewing her. I am not a heartless brute, no matter what you think. I appreciate what you did for my daughter. Your wife, that is. By offering her your hospitality. She is a lovely woman, you wife. I hope that you appreciate her."

"Get to the point, Arauja. My phone is melting just listening to your bullshit. What about the fifty grand?"

"The what?" Arauja's voice changed to a hard American accent.

"So the deal's off or your boys just want a deal on the side, is that right?"

Either Arauja was feigning innocence or Moss was right. Some of the Atlanta cartel were cutting their own deal. "I'm calling ship to shore so this is very expensive call I'm making," Arauja said. "You will find your sister-in-law behind the supermarket on Cascade Road, lying in the dumpsters there."

"And your hoods will be waiting there to pick me off as soon as I step out of the car. If this is a set-up again, Arauja, I swear..."

"But can you take the chance it is not? Oh, Mr. Moss. You disappoint me. Your lovely wife is far more gracious. You could at least thank me."

"Go rot in hell, Arauja."

"Probably." Again the jovial laugh.

"Since you're in a gift-giving mood, would you mind telling me who your man in Atlanta is, the head of your Spencer-Howland dummy corporation? Is it Julian Spencer? Or somebody posing as him?"

Again Arauja's voice switched accents. "That's for me to know and you to find out, Mr. Moss."

"Spencer? Is that Julian Spencer?"

Whoever it was hung up.

Moss turned off the phone before he pitched it against the wall. The girls ducked and the dog shot from under the table and hid in the pantry.

He had to use Halee's phone to call his friend Murph in GBI. Relating what Arauja had told him, Moss was surprised to hear Murph say, "Yeah, we heard him. I sent the team to see if he was bluffing. Hang tight, there's the team leader calling." Moss pictured Murph with two phones on either side of his head like some cyborg alien. "We've got her, Moss. She's alive. They're getting an ambulance right now to take her to Grady ER. I'll meet you there."

"Thanks, Murph. I owe you one Brazilian bastard. I'll talk to you later about tapping my phone." But he was secretly pleased. Murph would be able to tell where the call was coming from. Off-shore or locally. Something about the way Arauja's accent switched countries aroused his suspicion, like someone pretending to be him.

The answer was police-speak. "Hey, it paid off, didn't it? See you. Moss."

"Get dressed, Ash. Halee, get the car. We're going up to Atlanta."

Halee sprinted toward the door, but Ashlee froze, her tissue in mid-air. "What shall I tell Kenya?"

Moss was buttoning up his shirt painfully. "Tell her she can come too, but no telling what we're going to find when we get there. Or if it's really Toya they found."

Neither Kenya nor Ashlee went up to Atlanta to identify their sister. Ashlee came downstairs with a worried look on her face. "She isn't feeling well, Grove. She thinks she may have to go to the doctor. I'm going to take her and be here when the boys come home."

"Tell her to take care of herself and call me if you need me, hear? It'll be okay, Ashlee. And get Isis to come over and watch the boys."

"Kenya already called her. She's on her way over."

"Good, good. It's all good." He wasn't good at comforting women, figuring they always regarded him as part of the problem. "Well, got to rumble. Now, call me if...if..."

His sister-in-law smiled thinly. "I will. Like everybody else in town that has a problem."

"That reminds me. If Earlene calls, tell her I'll be back this afternoon. Halee's going to drive me both ways. Don't tell Earlene why I'm going to Atlanta. It'll be all over town in five minutes."

"I won't." Ashlee sighed. "But they'll find out anyway. Jungle drums."

On the second floor landing, Sheldon breathed a sigh of relief. Ashlee hadn't ratted on him for staying home from school. He knew how Kenya would take the news of Toya's death. His biological mother had died in the same way, beaten to death by drug dealers. Kenya and Holly Simpson had been best friends and even gone on the road with the same gospel group. Both girls had affairs with older men which left them pregnant, but Holly had gotten hooked on drugs. She had ended up the same way as Auntie Toya, thrown out like the garbage in a dumpster. So Kenya had raised him as if he were her own child because she had lost her baby. Now she was in danger of losing another one.

Sheldon wiped his nose on the sleeve of his sweatshirt. No use crying about it now, he told himself. Life is what it is. But he lingered outside Kenya's bedroom door, drawn by her pain and the love he felt for her. He had to protect her from anything that would interfere with her having the baby sister he had always wanted. Even though he had to share her love now, she was the sun that lit his world. Arauja was the cloud hanging overhead threatening to dim her light. More than anything he had ever wanted, Sheldon wanted to rid the world of anything that came between his mother and her happiness. He, Sheldon, was going to be her superhero. Daddy Moss had his chance but he blew it. Now the Hutu warrior would take over.

It turned out to be Toya behind the dumpster. She was in a coma from an overdose, missing a ring finger, suffering from exposure, but otherwise alive. The ICU doctor couldn't say for how long though. "She's malnourished, and I don't know what she's taken."

"Been given," Halee corrected. "She was kidnapped and held for ransom."

The doctor who was just out of medical school and doing his residency thought he had seen it all. "Ma'am, there are needle tracks all over her arms. This woman has been a drug addict for at least ten years. Also she's HIV positive."

Halee bristled. "You act like she's not worth saving."

Moss gave her a hard look. "Deputy, will you wait outside please?"

Halee made a noise as if she were going to spit and then stalked out. "Sorry about that," Moss said. "Affirmative action and all. They get really touchy about things."

The doctor looked around to see if anyone would overhear him. "Boy, I'll say."

Their rapport established, Moss looked back at his sister-in-law, her thin body stretched out on the stark white bed as if she were floating on ice. "I've seen way too many like her in my time. Do you think she'll pull through?"

Doing his best not to shrug the question off, the doctor looked at the woman on the bed. "Depends."

"On what?"

"We're doing everything we can, but I honestly don't know. I can have the sickest, most damaged patient who nobody cares about side by side with one who has everything going for them. Family, friends, kids. And something inside the poor, sickest dude pulls him through where the one that had everything going for him dies. Is it karma or fate, I just don't know."

"I know exactly what you mean, Doc. Listen, give me a call in case anything changes, would you? I left my information at the desk outside."

Nailing Halee with a hard look wasn't easy, but he did it, barking orders at her. "Get the car, Deputy."

"Dad, I—"

"Deputy Moss, let's get one thing straight, okay?"

"Okay. Sir," she added. "I know I was out of line."

"Number one, keep your feelings in check. You represent the law. Your own personal take on what's wrong with the universe's got no place in the business of doing your job. The law's your shield, your badge of honor. But it doesn't give you the right to be rude to people. Ever. Especially people who are just doing their jobs, okay?"

"Okay, Chief. I'm truly sorry. Really." His daughter had tears in her eyes. "Will she be okay?"

Turning her into an automaton was hopeless. It took years of seeing people throw their lives away or other people's lives away to do that. "Maybe. Now get the car. I got to get back."

He tried Ashlee's number for the tenth time. Voice mail said she wasn't taking any more calls. Her message box was full. She finally picked up, but her voice was wooden, cleansed of emotion. Like a person who has reached emotional overload. "I'm glad Toya's alive, but that still means as long as Arauja's gang is around, they'll get her."

"That's one way to look at it. 'Course if she pulls through, the judge is going to send her to rehab anyway. Where are you? I hear an echo."

"At the VA hospital in Macon. Kenya's having a miscarriage. I'm with the doctor now."

Moss received the news like another rabbit punch to the gut. "Oh," was all he said without knowing what he said.

"Better do better than that, Chief, when you get here. Room one-thirty-two. I've got to go. See you later, okay?" Ashlee clicked off.

In Atlanta, Faun woke at five, ran six miles, came back to her loft apartment above the Chattahoochee, showered, and was eating her power bar when the phone rang. It was Rey Chapman, and he had just been released on bail, thanks to Uncle Bernie who had lectured him all the way back to The Springs. As soon as he got back to his apartment in Atlanta, he called Faun.

"First, don't believe what you hear until I've had a chance to explain."

"I haven't heard anything. Why? Are you dating Mary Beth Etheridge again?"

"No. Look, Faun, could we meet somewhere? I think it would be better if I told you in person."

She hesitated a long time. "I have to be at the lab in half an hour."

"I thought they—you had to shut down."

"This is the last few days. It's kind of like a death."

"I'm really sorry. How about lunch? We can grieve together."

"You don't give up easily, do you?"

"Not when I have my whole life at stake."

Taking a deep breath, Faun said, "Hey, I know what you mean there, buddy. Noon at O'Tooles. I'll be the one with the bag over my head."

Faun was fidgeting in a booth at O'Toole's precisely at noon when her phone rang. It was Reynolds Chapman. "Where are you, Rey? I'm short on time."

"Right around the corner in the public parking lot. You sound annoyed."

"Very perceptive. Point is, why aren't you here or am I missing something?" She played with the glass of sweet tea in front of her.

"Because there's someone tailing me, and I don't want you to get mixed up in this mess."

In spite of being annoyed, Faun made an attempt to be funny. "Which mess is that out of the many I'm already in?"

The sound of his exasperated sigh came over the phone, and she pictured a wrinkled brow on the handsome face she fell in love with.

"I know and I really wanted to be there for you. To help you ride it out, you know what I mean?"

"Look, Rey, I don't mean to pry or anything, but are you in trouble with the police or something? You say there's somebody following you? What's that about?"

"It's about the fact that I got busted last night." Again the sigh blowing in her ear.

"What for? I told you were driving too fast." The waiter set her veggie burger and sweet potatoes fries down on the table. "Thanks, and could you bring me another tea, this time don't forget the lemon?"

"My bad, I'll bring it right away."

She thanked him with a smile she didn't feel.

"Cocaine possession."

"Is that all? I thought for a minute it was murdering an old girlfriend or some awful thing like that."

"That, too. Not an old girlfriend, but Chief Moss, although they have the wrong guy on that one."

"What?" She practically screamed it. Conversation stopped around her, heads turned.

Her waiter came flying over to the table, a plate of lemon slices in his shaking hand. "Sorry, sorry. Here's your lemon. Is there anything else I can get you? Tranquilizer, maybe?"

She made a go-away gesture, her ear glued to the phone as if her life depended on it. At least, her love life depended on it.

Chapman went on. "Don't worry, he's okay. I was at the mill at the wrong time, that's all. I think they got CJ and Miguel and the rest of the guys that tried to drown him. Look, the point I'm trying to make is—"

"CJ? He works for Arauja. Don't tell me you were part of that whole thing all along. Why, you rat! And I slept with you, thinking you were Prince Charming! I hope whoever's following you is one of his thugs and beats the living shit out of you so you never touch cocaine again!" She threw the phone over to the empty seat across the booth from her and hid her face in her hands.

From the tables around her there came applause, at first a few hands clapping, and then the whole section around her gave her a standing ovation.

A woman near her came over and gave her a hug. "Don't worry, honey. We've all had losers like that. That just means you're gonna know the difference when the right one comes along."

CHAPTER 21

When they got to the hospital, Kenya was asleep. "She's had a rough few hours. Lot of blood, though none of it lost from her arterial system. Just giving her a glucose drip to pep her up. Pretty scary all the same." The nurse smiled up at him. "Just take it slow and she'll come around. You'll see."

He entered the room, feeling too big for it like he would knock something over if he made a sudden move. Kenya's face was a dark oval against the pillow, her hair rippled out from her exquisitely sculpted cheeks bones. Beside him, Ashlee looked like she would break in half any minute while Halee lingered out by the nurses' station talking to somebody on the phone.

Finally, Kenya stirred, moaned, and opened her topaz eyes, lighting up her face. Focusing on Moss, she frowned. "About time you came. Hand me the water, somebody. I'm thirsty."

Before he could react, Ashlee jumped up and handed her a glass of water.

"Feeling better? Nurse said everything's fine."

"Yeah, real fine after losing a baby. It hurts like hellfire if you want to know." Kenya cradled the empty glass and glared at him. "What're you looking at, Grooover?"

The way she mocked his name he knew there was more coming. "Haven't you got anything better to do than just look at a woman who's lost a baby? Like get somebody else killed?"

"I just meant…"

With a look that desperately told him to leave, Ashlee tried to block her sister's attack with words. "I guess that comes from not having kids of my own. I don't want any either. I'll just be an old auntie to the boys." She made an empty gesture with her hands. "Like Flossie Mae and have a career. Nice and neat."

In an effort to put an end to sister torture, Moss said abruptly, "Toya's alive. She's in Grady in a coma. Pretty beat up, though. Doctor gives her a fifty-fifty chance."

"Fifty-fifty?" Kenya cut him with a cold look. "Always the cheery one, aren't you, Groover?" She made a joke of his name again, always a wind-up for the pitch. "It's all your fault, you know. Me losing my baby girl and Toya, too. And Bernie. And what makes even shittier is, you were giving that woman my money the whole time, weren't you? Well, you damn well better pay it back, every penny or I'll throw your ass in jail, you hear me, dumb ass? Or did you think I wouldn't notice fifty thousand missing from my bank account, huh, Grooover? You're about as groovey as white bread, aren't you?"

He had seen the many faces of Kenya before so it wasn't much of a surprise. But he had never seen the mean look on her face before now. There was actual hatred in her topaz eyes. She looked like a tiger about to attack. He made a good target just standing there.

"That money was so they wouldn't kill Toya—" he started to say, but she cut him off.

Mimicking his cool tone, she said, "I don't believe anything you say so don't you dare open your mouth about Toya. My little sister wouldn't be chopped in little pieces if you hadn't kept on and kept on digging and snooping like a big ol' hound dog until you got a lot of nice people shot up or killed and me kidnapped!" Kenya was up on one elbow, in full rant mode. "I hate the sight of you! Get out! Get out, hear me? I never want to see you again! And you better give that money back or I'll get the law on you!"

"Now, Yaya, you don't mean that," Ashlee began.

"Damn right I do! I want you out of my house before I get home! Get your stuff and get out, you hear?" This was directed at Moss like machinegun fire.

Moss turned to go, and Kenya threw the water glass at his back. Instead it crashed and broke against the dresser, its contents dripping down the side.

The nurse came to see what all the noise was about. "I think you'd better rest now, Mrs—" She stopped short, seeing the mess on the floor.

But the tiger was in full attack mode. "Oh, get him out of here! Get out, you hear? Leave me alone! Call the police if he ever comes back here!"

"Don't worry, I'm out of here. I'll tell the desk about the mess," Moss said as he went out the door. He resisted turning around to look at the tiger crouching in the bed.

Looking relieved, Ashlee joined him. "Me, too."

A shout from the bed followed him. "Wait, you bastard! I'm not through with you yet!"

Moss stepped back in the room to shout, "Oh, yes, you are! I got the message loud and clear. Nurse, I'll call the K-nine unit, the one they use for rabid dogs."

"I heard that, you sonofabitch. Come back here!"

The nurse followed them out in the hall. "It's just the loss talking, that's all. They always look for someone to blame. It's hard to blame your body for something it's done. Believe me, she'll see the light and be sorry about all this."

"I appreciate the concern, but you don't know my wife. She's never sorry."

Ashlee tried to hug him but he was rigid in defeat.

"I'll be at the motel," he said. "Halee knows where it is."

When Moss got back to the office, Earlene was talking on the phone with her mother, and knitting without dropping a stitch.

"Hey, Chief, how're you? Yeah, go on, Ma. What'd she say then? No kidding! No lie! She did? What'd you do then? No, you didn't!"

"Great multi-tasking, Earlene," he muttered, passing through to his office.

"Say what, Chief?"

"Nothing. Don't let me disturb you."

She didn't. "Yeah, yeah, go on, Ma. You're kidding! Well, I never."

For the first time in a long time, he was grateful for the peace and quiet. Putting his briefcase down in the one extra chair, Moss sighed a big man's sigh as he sat behind his desk in his squeaky old chair. All was well in Julia Springs. Until the phone rang.

It was Prescott. "Another body's turned up at Howland's Mill, Chief."

"I'll be right over, Pres."

"No need to disturb yourself, Chief. I've called the coroner and he said to call McKenzie since you're laid up and all."

"Pres, I'm not in a wheelchair yet. I'll be right out."

"Chief, it's only ol' Gator Joe. Somebody put a couple of bullets in him. Maybe a hunter mistook him for a gator or a deer. Happens all the time. It's okay, though. Your daughter's here. And that real tall girl that was here last night. Whatshername? Arizonia or something."

Only one thing stuck in his mind. The way Prescott

had said "only Gator Joe." Like he was a frog or a fish. Only Gator Joe who saved his life.

He must be getting slow, Moss thought. He should have seen that coming.

And then he wiped his eyes.

The great distributor of information came into his office with a paper plate of key lime pie. "Your daughter said not to worry you about it so I won't tell you what she said." Setting the pie down on his desk, she went on. "Here, this is for you. Mrs. Wilkes sent this over. Said it's Miguel's favorite."

Looking at the gooey green mixture, his stomach rolled. It was the color of Gator Joe's eyes, the mold that seemed to cling to his hair and clothes. The sickening sweet smell blocked his nostrils, gagging him. "I can't. Anti-biotics are tearing up my stomach. Put it in the fridge, and I bet it will be gone by this evening."

Earlene put both hands on her boney hips, a signal that a lecture was coming. "Chief, round here if somebody sends you pie, you eat the gosh-darned pie or throw it in the garbage and say 'thank you, I loved it,' not ask them why they didn't give it to somebody else."

"Sorry, Earlene."

"I should think you would be, her a widow woman and all. It's not like she could afford to bake a key lime every day of the week, what with the price of eggs and sugar and all. Beside, Miguel's not here, Tabitha said. Said he had some peas to pick or tomatoes or something down in Florida."

Moss had long ago learned that arguing with a woman when she was on a roll about manners was futile so he took a forkful of the mess on the plate, faking delight. "Mmmm, that's good! So you going to tell me what Halee said?"

Earlene had a satisfied expression on her face. She had

won, and she knew it. "You know already. About Gator Joe being found at the Mill and all."

Moss choked and exploded pie all over his desk.

CHAPTER 22

He was back in Memphis, living with his mother when the phone rang. Same old faded wallpaper, same old smell of fried food permeating the furniture, same old mother. Moss winced as he listened to her babbling on, sharing every detail of his life with complete strangers, to him. How he applied for his old job back and been offered a desk sergeant's job at half his former pay grade.

"He'd better take it," his mother was saying over the phone to someone who called to inquire about him, "'cause that woman's not going to give him nothing. And you know what nothing from nothing is. He's going to get back on his feet only he misses that baby and the kids. Talks about them all the time."

He couldn't stand it anymore and went to the neighborhood bar for a drink. He nursed the bourbon and branch until they played Chantal West's retake on Stormy Weather. Then he took his time walking back to his mom's apartment in the rain. Meanwhile, he went over his failures in his life for the thousandth time. How he failed to protect Kenya first and foremost. Or Mimi or Bernie or Gator Joe after he had put them all in jeopardy by continuing to track down the cancer that was Arauja.

He tried to tell himself he wasn't responsible for all the criminal acts in the world, that it was his job to protect the public from harm and, if individuals got hurt or killed in the process, like the military said, that was collateral damage. But it didn't work that way. When you couldn't protect the people you loved, you felt like you'd failed them.

Failed them. Failed them. Every footstep he took seemed to spell it out.

He passed a newsstand and ducked inside for cigarettes—in his despair, he had taken smoking up again. The *Atlanta Constitution* newspaper snagged his eye and he paid for that, too, just in case his mother hadn't gone to bed yet. He could hide behind it like his father used to do, shielding him from a barrage of words.

Rolling it up and tucking it under his arm to protect it from the rain, he stepped outside into the downpour. It seemed to be raining everywhere he went these days, he thought. *Maybe I'm just a big black cloud, hovering overhead, clouding out the sun.*

When he got to his mother's place, she was in the kitchen on the phone as usual. When she saw him, she said, "Here he is now."

"Mom, I can bore whoever it is myself, okay? Why don't you see what's on TV?"

"Halee, he's getting to be a cranky old man just like his father and his paw-paw. Thinks I'm senile." His mama fixed him with her steel rimmed gaze of pity disguised as proprietary good-will. "For your information, Abraham, it's your daughter Halee. She called to see how you are, and I know you'd just say 'Fine, baby, I'm fine' and leave at that so I'm filling her in on a few details, okay?"

"Just let me speak to her when you're finished with the details. Don't hang up now, hear?"

"Oh, here, just take the phone, grouch." She thrust it at him, shuffling off to the living room where he visualized her lingering in the doorway.

Halee was laughing when he got on the phone. "Same old Gran. You better come back here before she has the preacher come around to scare the devil out of you."

"He's already been here, done that. I think I scared the devil out of him. How are you, baby? How's Wilson?" It was hard to disguise the ache in his voice but he figured he was doing a good job.

"He's right here, waiting to talk to you through all that."

"You talking about the details? Poor little man. Put him on."

"Wait, before I do, Dad, there's something I want to tell you. McKenzie's retiring and he wants you to run for sheriff of Stewart County. That means you'd have to move back here. You're still a resident, so why not?"

"Why not? Halee, where have you been the last four months, girl?"

"Same place you have, Dad. The salary is sixty-five K with full medical and pension benefits, and you get a sign-up bonus as well. Here's Will, now."

There was the sound of a bottle clanking the phone. "What? You still sucking on that bottle like a little bitty baby, huh, man?"

He heard Will's chesty baby laugh on the other end. "Daddy, come home, an' I won't do it no more."

"Promise?" Moss was suddenly fighting back tears. Again.

In the last six months, he had cried more than in his whole lifetime.

"Prowmus."

There was sounds of a struggle over possession of the phone, then Sheldon said, "And I promise not to wreck your car anymore. If you buy me one of my own. My birthday's coming up, you know."

Hoping the agony didn't show, he countered, "How do I know you don't have your fingers crossed, tech man?"

"He does," said a robotic voice in the background, "Master, you have your fingers crossed. That's not sportsmanlike."

"Shut up, Piglet!!" Sheldon hissed.

It was Halee again. "You better come home, Dad. We need law and order around here. Dad? Have you seen the TV recently?"

He started to say he didn't get a chance because his mother watched the game shows until all hours, even the re-runs when he glanced down at the damp newspaper he had placed on the kitchen table. It had slowly unfurled revealing its headline.

SMALL TOWN COP SNAGS BIGTIME DRUG LORD. Byline Reynolds Chapman, freelance reporter.

It was all there, reading like a cheap thriller, bound to be picked up by every TV news and talk show in the country. How he, Grover Moss of the Julia Springs Police Department, had followed his kidnapped wife to Cayman's Key, been held captive, escaped, put the finger on the fake Arlen Howland, been shot at, and nearly drowned.

"Dad, you still there?"

"I'm here, baby. Thank God I'm still here." Tears were running down his cheeks and Moss didn't bother to wipe them away. "Pick me up at the Macon airport tomorrow afternoon. There's only one direct flight from Memphis. And don't tell Kenya I'm coming."

"Don't worry. It's only Ashlee and me and the boys. Her majesty's on the road again."

⟐⟐⟐

Halee and Ashlee were in the Macon airport when they called everybody who was waiting for passengers on Fight 117 from Memphis into a side room and told the assembled people the plane had exploded over the Mississippi on take-off. There were no survivors.

⟐⟐⟐

On his terrace above Ipanema Beach looking down on the beautiful bodies glistening in the sand, Julio Arauja received the news on the speaker phone and smiled.

"Moss is out of the way," said his informant. "He won't bother you anymore."

Jeweled fingers slid down his open shirt collar and long fingernails sent chills up his spine as they trailed lightly down to his belly. Her perfumed breasts pressed against the back of his head. "*Mi amor*, what is it?"

"The *negrito* is dead, *Angela.* Are you sad?"

Angela Copeland thought just for a split second. "No, although I would have liked to sleep with him just once."

"Only once?"

"Only once. Because then I would kill him, like the black widow spider I am."

About the Author

Even as a child, Trisha O'Keefe was impressed by the inherent power of alternative medicines. Indigenous healing practices are an ongoing theme in her novels. As a native Southerner, O'Keefe claims to have "a lot of red dirt" flowing in her veins. Growing up, she spent summers on her uncle's farm in South Georgia, "mainly getting into trouble." That trend has continued throughout her life. After traveling abroad for fourteen years, running into revolutions or governmental coups nearly everywhere she went—even Britain was in the midst of a labor strike when she moved there—she returned to the States. She is the daughter of Jimmy Jones, a well-known journalist for the *Atlanta Constitution* under Editor Ralph Magill. One of her earliest memories was the sound of a typewriter rattling away in the middle of the night. You would think that would have cured her from ever putting two words together, let alone a book. Still, at age six, she co-wrote *Spot, The Dog* with her sister, followed a long time later by *Hanahatchee, Poseidon's Eye*, and *Lovesong of the Chinaberry Man*. Two more novels, *The Magi's Well,* and *The Mama Tree* were published in 2016, followed by *Flight to Trezarium* in 2017. "I guess some things you can't cure," O'Keefe says. "You just have to go where they take you."